FREE SPIRITS

Blanche Pagliardini

CHAPTER 1

March 2013

Maddalena and the abbot, wrapped in white towels, were sitting gently sweating it out in the sauna. Outside it was a fine early March day. The sun shone, patches of colour—blues and reds, yellows and whites—had begun to spread over the hillsides around the lake as the first spring flowers sprung up again between pale grey limestone boulders. A gentle breeze blew. There was still snow on the far off peaks of the southern French Alps.

'Do you think Brother Ange-Dominique's mother is going to survive?' said Maddalena. 'Are *we* going to survive?'

'Sounded pretty serious,' replied the abbot, answering the first question. 'He should be there by now. He was sailing from Toulon to Ajaccio.' His monk had left early the previous day for Corsica following a call from his family to say his mother was gravely ill. In answer to Maddalena's second question, he said, 'I suppose we'd better go back to the monastery and see what's happening in Rome. All this work, our work—it could be about to go up in smoke,' he said with a rueful smile. 'Don't cry, Maddalena. It may not happen.'

'I'm not crying, it's just perspiration in my eyes,' she lied. She could not think of anything comforting to say so she said, 'Are you going into the lake?'

'Certainly not. I shall take a shower next door. Are you going to take the plunge?'

'Yes.'

They left the sauna. The abbot headed for one of the two changing rooms. Maddalena went outside and walked over to the small lake. She took off her towel, laid it on the bench by the silver birches, hesitated an instant at the water's edge, then jumped into a pocket of the lake that formed a small naturally deep and perfect plunge pool. The water, fed by the melt waters higher up, was freezing. Her whole body started buzzing as the blood raced around her system. Invigorated, she climbed out of the lake, covered up again with her towel and sat relaxing on the bench. The abbot joined her, bringing out a couple of large glasses of cold low strength beer.

When their body temperatures had returned to normal and they had stopped perspiring, they dressed and walked slowly back up to the monastery and into the abbot's office to watch on his computer the events in Rome. The abbot knew that his other monks, apart from the Ancients, would be either watching or listening to events, too. There was one name—just one name—that they did not want to hear announced as the new pope. If that cardinal was elected it would almost certainly mean the end of their community and its work.

The abbot made them a couple of espressos. Then they sat down to look at the images of St Peter's Square, the basilica, the Vatican, Rome in general and, along with the rest of the world —or at least those that were interested in papal matters—they waited for white smoke to curl out of the Sistine Chapel chimney.

The priest was not with them. He was meeting their most important visitor to date in Marseille the following day. They would then drive up to the monastery. 'When does he arrive?' said Maddalena.

'Mid-morning, I think,' said the abbot. 'They were going to meet in the city— down by the Vieux-Port, under the Ombrière —more discreet than meeting him at the airport—safer. He's taking a huge risk.'

Suddenly Maddalena and the abbot, whose eyes had been fixed to the screen as they talked, heard what sounded like a couple of small explosions. Smoke started curling up into the blue Roman skies. They peered in astonishment at the screen. It was not black smoke again. It was not white smoke either. It was grey smoke, and it was not coming from the Sistine chimney.

CHAPTER 2

Maddalena had met the priest one October evening at the opera. They had both decided, separately and at the last minute, to go and see "Norma" and found themselves together at the ticket office half an hour before the performance started.

He saw a woman whose southern Mediterranean complexion was even more tanned after the long hot summer, a woman with smiling dark brown eyes and curly almost black hair loosely held up from her neck by a large flame-red hair clip. She was wearing a colourful mid-calf length cotton dress and a flame-red shawl. He thought she must be in her late forties or early fifties—he wasn't very good at judging ages.

She saw a man younger than herself, fortyish she reckoned, wearing a beige linen jacket, lighter beige cotton chinos and an olive green T-shirt overprinted in white with the words "I think" above a rather complicated line diagram. Light brown hair flopped across his forehead and down over his jacket collar; out of a pleasant open tanned face gold-flecked hazel eyes sparkled with a disturbing intensity. She instinctively took a step backwards. For an instant she felt as if he could see right into her very soul, that she would follow this man to the ends of the earth—then the intensity in his gaze waned but the gentle warmth remained.

'Do you think there'll be any tickets left?' he asked.

'Oh yes, there may be some numbered seats left up in the gods, but I always buy an unnumbered one—the cheapest and there are always some available,' she said. 'I often come at the last minute like this.'

'This is my first visit,' he said. 'I don't suppose we'll have a very good view.'

'Well, no, but you will if you don't mind standing. You can stand on the circular bench almost directly opposite the stage. And sit down facing the wall when you get tired, and just listen to the music.'

Maddalena, who was ahead of the priest in the small queue, said to the cashier, 'Bonsoir Monsieur, un billet au paradis en placement libre, s'il vous plait,' and handed over her ten euros. The priest, who had also planned to ask for a seat in the gods but a more expensive numbered one, said, 'And the same for me, please.'

It seemed at the time perfectly natural to Maddalena to wait while the man bought his ticket. She could have walked off, but she didn't. She waited the minute or so it took for the priest to buy his ticket and together they walked out of the ticket office and back in through the main door into the crowded foyer. He headed for the queue by the lift, she walked right past it towards the stairs, he followed her and together they climbed up to the sixth floor.

Maddalena showed him where they could stand if they wanted a good view, and where they could sit if they didn't. The usher was not sure if all the numbered seats were taken—if was the fifth and final performance—but confirmed that if they were not, the couple could move for a better view.

The priest was quite happy to stand on the bench with a view right opposite the stage. However, by the time the recorded message in French, English and Italian reminded them to turn off their mobile phones and the lights dimmed, they slipped into a couple of unoccupied numbered seats nearby.

Maddalena just had time to whisper, 'Is this your first visit to the opera, or your first visit to this opera house?'

'My first to this opera house. I live here but I travel a lot so —' He was interrupted by the applause announcing the arrival of the conductor. Then, leaning on the balcony rail, they settled down to an enchanting evening of bel canto in Roman Gaul. The soprano sang the opera's hit tune "Casta Diva" divinely, the first act drew to a close, the lights came on.

'I am enjoying this,' said the priest with a smile. 'Shall we stretch our legs?' They left their seats to stroll around the semicircular passage behind the seating.

'Maddalena Rizza,' said Maddalena with a smile, holding out her hand. The man shook her hand and introduced himself. Did he hold it a fraction too long, or was that just her imagination? As he held her gaze, again she was startled by the burning intensity, just for a couple of seconds, of his hazel eyes. As they strolled around the corridor, the man talked enthusiastically about the opera. 'He was born in Catania, you know, Vincenzo Bellini—on the east coast of Sicily. He composed the music when he was just 30—and died three years later. The librettist was the great Felice Romani. He was born in Genoa and collaborated closely with Bellini. It was first performed at La Scala in Milan. I've got a recording of Callas singing it there—she really made it her own, the role of Norma, didn't she?' As he spoke, the priest smiled to himself as he recalled another rendition he had heard of La Callas singing the role.

Maddalena, with an occasional silent nod, listened happily to the man chatting beside her. He was good company. They made their way back to their seats by which time he had told her just about everything there was to know about "Norma" and Vincenzo Bellini. 'He died near Paris and was buried in the Père Lachaise cemetery, near Chopin and Cherubini. He was there for over forty years. Then they moved him to Catania cathedral.'

As they settled back down in their seats he was still talking. 'I went there once, to Catania. Mount Etna was active at the time and at night you could see the red lava flowing down the mountain side. It was quite fantastic.' *The colour of your shawl,* he thought, looking at Maddalena. 'I went to the fish market behind the cathedral, the San Benedetto monastery and the MACS —that stands for Museum of Contemporary Art in Sicily. They have little kiosks selling delicious citrus drinks with sparkling water, there are always people gathered round drinking a cio-scu, at the kiosk, really refreshing in the heat, although I was there in February for the Feast of Saint Agatha—the three day agatini, they call it there.' As he said all this, Maddalena, while listening to him, had been watching the members of the orchestra returning to the pit.

The lights dimmed. He said in a whisper, 'You're Italian, aren't you? The way you roll your 'r's when you talk.'

'Yes, I am,' she said.

'Where are you from?' he asked.

The audience applauded the return of the conductor. Just before the orchestra started up Maddalena turned to the man with a wide grin and said, 'I was born in a little fishing village on the east coast of Sicily. Just south of Catania.' The priest's jaw dropped but before he could remonstrate with the woman the orchestra started playing and the second act began.

The opera ended and after numerous curtain calls the two of them climbed with the crowds down the six flights of stairs and out into the night. It was a mild evening but he put on his linen jacket, she covered her shoulders with her scarlet shawl, and having ascertained that they lived more or less in the same direction they set off to walk home along the seafront. The gibbous moon, hanging over the bay like one of those large ivory paper-thin globes used to shade a ceiling light bulb, cast a silvery path of twinkling light on the water.

As they walked, they talked. 'You should have told me you were born near Catania instead of letting me chatter on about things you must have known all your life,' he said.

Maddalena laughed. 'Sorry, I suppose I should have but I was enjoying listening to you—you sounded so enthusiastic. That T-shirt of yours...'

He looked down at his chest. 'Charles Darwin's Tree of Life illustration, he jotted it down in one of his sketch books twenty years or so before he published *On the Origin of Species*. Good, isn't it?'

'You said earlier that you travelled a lot. What do you do?"

'I'm a priest.'

7

Maddalena stopped in her tracks. 'Ah,' she said, recalling the Feast of Saint Agatha. 'You don't look like one.'

He laughed. 'Well, you will see that I do if you ever pop into the church where I live when I'm not travelling, on a day I'm celebrating mass.'

'Where do you travel to?'

'Oh, various places—but tell me about you. What do *you* do, Maddalena?'

She told him that she was a translator. They chatted on, passing other folk out for late night strolls until the priest stopped walking. 'I live down there,' he said, fishing in his jacket pocket. 'Thank you for your company. A lovely evening. I've really enjoyed it.' He pulled out a pencil and piece of paper, which he tore in two.

Maddalena, suddenly seized with inexplicable panic at the imminent departure of the priest, said, 'I—maybe—perhaps we could meet up again, when you have time, when you're not travelling, that is, if you would like to . . .' Her voice trailed off.

He handed her the scrap of paper. 'Here's my number. May I have yours?' She wrote down hers. The priest said, 'I leave tomorrow. For a few weeks. I'll call you when I get back.'

'Grazie. I'd like that.'

They shook hands, smiling at each other. 'Thank you for a lovely evening, Maddalena. I'm so glad we have met. Ciao!' *So am I,* thought Maddalena as she watched him cross the road leaving her and the sea behind him.

Neither of them knew it then, of course—or maybe they did —but that moonlit evening with Norma's enchanting air still echoing in their heads was the beginning of a friendship that would last a lifetime.

Maddalena continued walking home thinking about her meeting with the priest. She felt embarrassed now about asking if they could meet again. After all, he was a priest. But she had enjoyed his company. And he, so it seemed, had enjoyed hers. After all, she reasoned, he had been looking for paper and pencil to write down his telephone number before she had spoken about meeting again. That made her feel much better.

The following morning she had work to do but she knew she was not in the right frame of mind to work well so she walked back to the sea. At a beach café she ordered an espresso and fished out a rolled up news magazine from her bag. She started reading but had trouble concentrating and had to keep starting the article again. She gazed out over the bay, at the bobbing brightly coloured sail boats from the yacht club. The beach was still quite busy with holiday makers enjoying the October sunshine.

Again, she picked up her magazine. Again, she put it down as her mind wandered back to her meeting with the priest. She paid for her coffee and walked home. The work was still waiting to be done. But she knew herself too well. She was not in the mood—it would be bad work that she would probably have to redo so it would be best to wait until tomorrow. She would take the day off.

She left her apartment again and walked to the butcher's for a piece of bavette—not the most tender part of the cow but cheap and tasty—and at the greengrocer's scooped up into a paper bag a handful of dark green peppery rocket leaves and selected a couple of dark purple figs. Back home, she put on the radio, tuned it to France Musique, and poured herself a glass of cool Brittany cider. What an extraordinary evening, she thought, as she heated up her little frying pan, rubbed her meat with some olive oil and threw it into the pan. It sizzled. She loved that sound. A couple of minutes, then she took it out, reheated the pan, popped the slice of bavette back in flipped over, sea-salted the seared top side, covered the pan with a lid and turned off the heat. Would he ring? Should she ring?

She rinsed the rocket leaves, dried them in kitchen paper and put a handful into a small bowl. The rest she popped into a plastic bag, sprinkled them with a few drops of water to keep them crisp and put them in the drawer at the bottom of the fridge for the following day. He had mentioned the church where he lived. She knew where it was. Perhaps she would walk over to it, she thought, as she picked up a half lemon and squeezed some juice over the leaves. She added some walnut oil, fine grey sea salt, a couple of grinds of black pepper and tossed it quickly with a spoon and fork.

I like him, I think I have made a new friend, she thought, as she quickly ran the figs under cold water, wiped them dry with kitchen towel, and cut herself a chunk of rye bread from a small loaf bought the day before.

She laid the table and got out from the fridge the glass jar of Dijon mustard. She had bought it the previous week to accompany a comforting choucroute garnie. They had had a couple of days of high winds and torrential rain—rare in these parts, but it did happen—so she had decided to treat herself to one of her favourite dishes from a little shop selling only Alsace specialities.

Everything was on the table including an opened bottle of costières-de-Nîmes. With her finger, Maddalena prodded her rested steak, decided it should be rare or thereabouts, put it onto a plate, transferred the rocket leaves to the same plate and tipped over the meat juices from the frying pan. She then sat down to eat her lunch listening to Liszt—wondering where in the world he was flying to, the priest

CHAPTER 3

Later, much later, Maddalena realised that she had never really lost her faith. She had just stopped going to church. There had never been a moment when she had denied the existence of God. It was simply that over the years he and she had parted company. She thought they had stopped talking to each other. Until she realised that he was still talking to her but she was simply not listening to him.

Her baptism and the other major events in the life of a young Roman Catholic had all taken place in the same small church in her dusty Sicilian village, north of Syracuse, overlooking the Ionian Sea. She had accumulated an impressive number of rosaries which she kept in a small green and gold hand-painted wooden box—rosaries given to her by aunts, godmothers, and the small white mother of pearl rosary that had belonged to her mother.

She had memories of praying the rosary as a child in Sicilian, the language of her childhood. '*Ave Maria, cchina di grazia,'u Signuri è ccu tia . . .*', kneeling by her bed, fingering the beads as she ran them through her small hands – '*Tu si benedeta fra li mugghièri e benedeto è 'u frutu d'u to ventri, Gesù.*' She remembered the Angelus pealing out over the sun-baked village streets; she remembered swimming in the sea at dusk watching the fire-red flow of molten lava moving inexorably down the upper slopes of active Etna to the north.

She remembered the groves of mandarins and clementines in the volcano's foothills, glimpses of bright orange against glossy dark green leaves, the white blossom of the almond trees in

February in the Valle dei Templi further south. She remembered displays of large tuna and swordfish, smaller spanking fresh locally caught fish, laid out on ice in the tiny village fishmonger. And old fishermen, deep wrinkles etched into dark brown faces, mending their nets and calling out to the smiling carefree child, 'Salve, Lena!' as she wandered past talking to her piece of seaweed or an interestingly shaped piece of driftwood that had caught her child's imagination while wandering along the beach.

When she was five, her mother died of cancer. Corrado Rizza, her father, was grief-stricken. All his life he had loved her mother, he loved her when she moved away to the mainland, he loved her for all the years that followed, he loved and married her when she returned to the little fishing port. Everyone in the village could see that when the woman he had loved died his will to live died with her.

A year after his wife's death, Corrado Rizza went out fishing early one morning. He crossed himself, as all the fishermen did, as he steered his little boat through the increasingly choppy water past the statue of the Virgin Mary hidden in its grotto, visible only from the sea, a sea that on this particular day had kept the other fishermen ashore at their nets. They found the wreckage of his boat and, a few days later, his body was washed up along the coast. If you ever visit the village, you will find him buried alongside his beloved wife in the old sailors' cemetery.

Over the decades various members of Maddalena's extended family had moved away from the island—to mainland Italy and further afield. A year after her father's death Maddalena, too, left the village of her birth. Accompanied by her favourite aunt, her mother's youngest sister, she travelled by train up the Italian peninsula and eventually crossed the border into France.

Once she had settled Maddalena with kind and loving relatives on the southern French coast, her aunt, having carried out her sister's wishes, returned to Sicily. Maddalena's parents had always agreed that at some point their daughter, while retaining strong links, of course, with her island home, would leave

Sicily like her mother had done, and experience life elsewhere. Then Corrado Rizza had gone out to sea on a day when the other fishermen had stayed at their nets and had not returned.

The evening her aunt arrived back home to her village she opened her bedside drawer and took out a sealed envelope addressed to Maddalena. Corrado Rizza had given this envelope to his sister-in-law a few days before he drowned. He had told her that it was only to be given to his daughter when she, the aunt, was dead.

Accidental death by drowning, they had said. It is true that occasionally village elders may have spoken quietly to each other as little Lena walked by talking to her twig. But village events were private affairs. They did not concern outsiders.

In her new home with her cousins Maddalena showed a proficiency for this new language of French. She grew up loved and cared for by her relatives; later, she travelled around Europe, found work using her languages, had passionate not always prudent love affairs, and no longer went to mass. She did not trouble the Catholic Church when she married, and so did not trouble it when she eventually divorced. She decided—in honour of her parents—to revert to her maiden name. Later, when she made her first confession in decades—to the priest—she realised that she had in some form or another probably succeeded in breaking most of the Ten Commandments.

She thought about moving to Canada to be nearer her daughter who now lived in Vancouver but Maddalena was a European. She could not imagine herself happy on the North American continent, and in any case her daughter travelled regularly to Europe, and her son currently lived in Brussels. She could not envisage settling permanently back in Sicily, but she wanted to be near the sea again. So in due course she returned to the town where she had lived for the longest consecutive period of her life—to the luminosity and ochre facades, to jasmine-perfumed boulevards and small squares of spring-scented linden trees, and fragrant fig trees overlooking the Mediterranean, backed by the winter snow-capped Southern French Alps—and bought a small apartment.

Occasionally she popped into one of the Baroque churches, often hidden away in a small square or narrow lane. She would kneel or sit for a few minutes, looking around, taking in the large paintings in the side chapels, the altar, watching the other people. There were always other people—old olive-skinned women who reminded her a little of her home village and looked as if they were part of the ecclesiastical fixtures and fittings; bare-armed Bermuda short-wearing tourists, walking around looking, talking quietly, usually, to each other, taking photographs; women carrying leather-strap wicker shopping baskets from which protruded tall scented basil plants, dark green leaves of leeks, long crispy baguettes, women who knelt down, closed their eyes, hands joined, and left a few minutes later to go home to prepare lunch. Once Maddalena had entered a church just before mass was due to start and had smiled to see that a woman had made practical use of the open-fronted dark walnut confessional by a side chapel to store her shopping trolley.

She did not pray then. She did not pray now, a failing often discussed later with the priest. She used these quiet moments to reflect on her life. With time, memories of her parents and childhood became more distant, although if she concentrated she could summon up images, flashes, souvenirs of her early life under the blazing Sicilian sun.

And now she had met the priest who, a few weeks after their first meeting at the opera, sent her a text.

They met down by the port early one evening in November for a glass of wine—a cool pale pink Provence rosé—and carried on meeting, now and then, in various venues—under a parasol at a beach café, under a plane tree in the market square, under an old gnarled olive tree up near the cemetery overlooking the bay where, in the height of the summer heat there was usually a gentle marine breeze—over the months and years to come.

They talked about music, about books, about art, never about him. He never saw her in church when he was celebrating mass. He never asked why. He would disappear again for a few weeks, sometimes longer. And she missed him. He collected stamps She would receive a scribbled postcard on the understanding that she steamed off the stamp and gave it to him upon his return. He never talked about his work. She did not pry. Something ecumenical, she assumed. Perhaps, she thought, one day he would feel able to talk to her about it. In the meantime, she did not pursue it.

Over the years she received cards from faraway places—often arriving back in France some time after he had. They bore exotic stamps from Egypt and Lebanon, Sri Lanka, India and Indonesia, China and Vietnam. Once she received a card bearing a Muscat postmark. Can't be that many Christians in Oman, she mused, as she steamed the camel off the envelope.

CHAPTER 4

Over the decades Maddalena had occasionally attended mass —old habits die hard—on high days and holidays in whatever country she had been living in. A Christmas midnight mass here, a Palm Sunday one there. And so it came to pass that one April she decided to attend Easter Sunday mass. The priest was away so she walked to a church near her apartment. It was a sunny spring morning, the air scented with orange blossom. The cloudless sky was a deep blue, the sea sparkled invitingly. This could be the first swim of the year, she thought, as she walked into the church. She read the small notice pinned to a door: "It is possible that upon entering this church you will hear God's call. On the other hand, it is most unlikely that he'll contact you by telephone." She turned off her mobile.

It looked like standing room only until she spied a spare seat halfway down the aisle on the left hand side. She wondered what the clergy thought about it all—celebrating mass day after day, week after week, to a small number of the faithful and then on a handful of Sundays in the year the place was heaving. She had her answer when in his homily the celebrant commented with a gentle, wistful smile how lovely it was to see the church so full at this mass of the Resurrection—the high point of the liturgical year.

She mumbled and stumbled her way through the Confiteor and the Gloria, certain phrases returning effortlessly, others less so. The Credo was a disaster. She did much better on the much shorter Sanctus, hadn't forgotten the Pater Noster and was word-perfect on the Agnus Dei. The celebration reached its culmination, the raison d'être of the mass, the receiving of the Eucharist. The celebrant held up a large round white host, 'Behold the Lamb of God, behold Him who takes away the sins of the world.' Maddalena listened to her neighbours replying in unison, 'Seigneur, je ne suis pas digne de te recevoir . . .' Lord, I am not worthy to receive you, but only say the word and I shall be healed. Her lips remained closed.

As people stood up and moved along their rows it seemed to Maddalena that every soul in church was joining the two queues in the central aisle to receive the Eucharist. She remained seated. She listened to the muffled sound of footsteps shuffling slowly, slowly down the aisle to the two white and gold-robed priests. Again and again she heard them repeat the words, 'Le corps du Christ,' as they raised the small round white host. Again and again she heard each communicant reply 'Amen' as they received the host. 'Le corps du Christ.' 'Amen.' 'The body of Christ.' 'Amen'. The continuous shuffling of feet, getting closer and closer to the altar, the repeated words. She could still relive the scene now, years later.

Hot tears welled up in Maddalena's eyes, and started to run silently down her cheeks. She let them flow. Nobody seemed to notice. She felt a dull ache which seemed to come from somewhere deep inside her chest. The moment passed, mass ended, she left the church. That was in the spring.

On a sunny autumn day later that year, Maddalena decided to take the boat to one of the islands. There was a monastery on this island where monks had lived for centuries. She had read about this island but had never visited it. There were plenty of passengers with picnics on the boat—young families, couples, teenagers and tourists, two young veiled Muslim women—who were going to spend the day on the island. A handful of passengers had small suitcases and were going to stay at the monastery on retreat.

Less than half an hour later she was strolling along paths bordered by Aleppo pines and forests of green holm oak, past four men playing pétanque on a stretch of the sun-baked reddish earthen path, breathing in the sweet scent of honeysuckle. She turned into a long alley, walked past olive trees and vineyards harvested of their grapes now but still bearing wide vine leaves in their autumnal livery of russet, gold and red. A gentle breeze caressed her face. A bell chimed.

When she reached the monastery, she walked along the geranium-bordered path to the abbey church, opened the door and stepped inside. The church was plain, simple, no flowers apart from a vase in front of the statue of the Virgin to the left of the altar, no candles, or religious paintings, no organ. Stained glass windows in muted shades of grey, white, pale pink. Straight ahead, behind the altar, a large lit crucifix on the wall, white-cowled Cistercian monks either side of the choir in wooden stalls. Mass had just begun. Maddalena took a seat by one of the pillars, watching, listening.

The celebrant raised a large round ivory-coloured host for the consecration. Out of the long thin speaker affixed to the pillar came a continuous snapping sound as he broke up the host into small pieces. Snap. Snap. Snap. Tears filled her eyes and slowly trickled down her cheeks. Snap. Snap. Snap. She felt a pain, dense, continuous, all-pervasive. It was as if her heart was being broken, again and again and again.

She had forgotten her similar experience at the Easter Sunday mass. Now, as she ate her picnic sitting on the rocks looking at the sea shimmering in the sunshine, she remembered. And started to wonder what it all meant. Perhaps she would mention it to the priest.

She didn't mention it to the priest. It wasn't until after the third time—the following spring, a year after the Easter Sunday mass—that she told him. After the third time, she realised something was really not right.

A girlfriend wanted to visit Thoronet Abbey. Although the Cistercian monks were long gone you could visit the abbey and concerts were held there during the year. The two women set off one fine spring morning aware that there had been torrential rain—what Météo France called a "Mediterranean episode"—

the previous day but unaware—because neither of them had listened to the radio until they were in the car and on their way—that people were advised not to make unnecessary journeys because of severe flooding in the area they were headed for.

The sun shone. They had been looking forward to the day out so they decided to continue their journey. From the motorway they could see that rivers had burst their banks. They drove through the village of Thoronet. When they reached the abbey they parked and walked up to the entrance to read the notice informing them that the abbey was closed due to flooding. They peered through the bars of the gates. There was a fair amount of muddy water swishing around in the courtyard.

Maddalena had noticed a sign for another monastery, a few hundred metres away, so the friends walked along the path through the woods and arrived at a small modern church. There did not appear to be a way in. They walked around the side of the building and found a spiral staircase which led them up into a first floor gallery with a handful of pews. They sat down. Below them on either side were stalls, two or three of which were occupied by silent white-cowled and hooded figures. Straight ahead, on the altar, Maddalena could see a pale round host displayed in a simple gold monstrance. They had arrived during the Adoration, she thought, when the host, the body of Christ, is displayed on the altar for a certain period of time.

Suddenly the silence was broken by, surprisingly, a female voice reciting a verse from the Psalms. Then silence again. A minute or so later another voice recited another verse from another psalm. Then silence. And so it continued.

As soon as she entered the upper gallery Maddalena's whole body was slowly but inexorably pervaded by the same heavy, dull, almost painful ache that she had now experienced twice before. Again, tears welled up and tumbled down her cheeks. But this time, unlike the other two occasions, there seemed to be no ebb and flow, the powerful sensation, on the contrary, seemed to increase in intensity. It did not subside until the two women left the gallery and walked back down the spiral staircase. Her friend, who had seen the tears, wisely made no comment.

Maddalena now realised that these three experiences were linked to the Eucharist. The first two had occurred, briefly, during mass, at defined moments—feet shuffling down an aisle to receive the host, the snapping sound of the host magnified through a loud speaker in the island monastery.

But this time seemed different. Her experience—would you call it mystical, she wondered, feeling rather uncomfortable with the word—her experience in this little church in the woods had started the moment she entered the building and had only ceased when she left it.

The answer was provided by a brief notice displayed at the front of the church, unnoticed by the two women on their arrival. The Blessed Sacrament was exposed continually in the church, twenty-four hours a day, seven days a week, fifty-two weeks a year.

Maddalena knew the priest had just returned from his travels so as soon as she arrived home she rang him. They normally communicated by text messages. He rarely answered his mobile and this was no exception. She left a message. She had not really prepared what she was going to say. She tried hard not to cry but could not stop the tremor in her voice. 'It's me. Something's happened. I need to speak to you...'

He called back within half an hour. 'What's happened?'

'I don't know but I must take communion, I have to take communion, and I can't because I know I have to go to confession and it must be over thirty years since I've been to confession but I have to be able to take communion,' she babbled in a shaky voice the priest had never heard before.

'Five o'clock tomorrow? At the church.'

When they met the following day he led her to the sacristy. Maddalena and the priest sat either side of an old oak table. He smiled, she tried to. Maddalena took a deep breath and started, hesitantly, to describe her experiences. The tears fell. The priest didn't take his eyes off her. There was nothing lovelier, he thought, than a beautiful woman crying. 'I don't understand what's happening or why it's happening I just know that I have to be able to receive communion,' she started. 'It's ridiculous really, I could go to communion at any old church and nobody would stop me. Nobody's going to jump up and yell out "Don't give that woman the Eucharist—she hasn't been to confession for thirty years!" But *I* know that I'm not in a state of grace to receive communion and I know that I have to receive absolution for, for . . . I don't understand why this is happening.' She fished in her bag for tissues, wiped her eyes, blew her nose. The priest remained silent, watching her. Then he said, 'It's funny how He creeps up on you like that, isn't it?'

They made the sign of the cross. They said the Lord's Prayer. 'I'm not sure I can remember the Ten Commandments but I'm pretty sure I've broken most of them at some point or other,' she said.

She took a deep breath and in a quiet voice, head bowed, skipped speedily over what she considered run-of-the-mill stuff. And ended with what she knew, from the Catholic Church's point of view, were more weighty matters.

'The thing is, I feel bad because I can say I'm sorry for those things now. I knew they weren't right. But I did them anyway . . .' Her voice trailed off.

'You've come here to bare your soul in front of God. What is past, is past. We're wiping the slate clean, tabula rasa,' said the priest with a gentle smile. 'We're wiping the slate clean.' As he pronounced the words of absolution she felt a weight she had never really realised was there being lifted from her soul. She wiped away a couple of tears, gave a deep sigh and sat looking at the priest. 'Grazie, grazie. When are you next saying mass? I'd like to receive the Eucharist from you.'

'Oh, don't wait. I'm off again tomorrow. Don't wait.'

Maddalena didn't wait. The following day she attended mass in the same church she had gone to on that Easter Sunday a year ago and for the first time in decades walked down the aisle to receive the Eucharist.

CHAPTER 5

The first visible sign of Maddalena's return to the Church manifested itself in a desire to express in words the nice thoughts she had about other people. She had always been, she thought, a reasonably kind and thoughtful person. She smiled and greeted bus drivers, offered her seat to pregnant women, the elderly, people on crutches. Now she felt herself filled with a sense of serenity she had never known. Her whole being radiated joy. People she knew when they met her in the street commented on how lovely she looked, how much younger she looked, how happy she looked. And she wanted everybody to be as happy as she was.

She had always loved bright colours. She stopped a tall African woman wearing a long cotton dress and matching head turban in gorgeous shades of emerald green, scarlet and gold to say how lovely she looked. The recipient of the compliment thanked her with a wide smile. She had always loved street music. When she passed an accordionist who could play (well) at least two other tunes apart from La Vie en Rose and Una Paloma Blanca, she made a point of stopping to say how happy it made her and to thank him for his music. The accordionist would smile and nod his thanks, even if she gave him no money.

One afternoon along the sea front she saw an elderly gentleman with a gold-topped cane walking towards her, tall and tanned, his longish white hair tied back in a ponytail, wearing immaculate white slacks and T shirt with an unbuttoned sky blue linen jacket. As they were about to pass each other Maddalena complimented him on the colour of his jacket. He stopped, slowly looked her up and down, and said, 'Allez vous faire foutre.'

A woman sitting on a nearby bench, who had overheard the exchange and seen the surprised and hurt look on Maddalena's face, stood up, laughing, and said, 'Oh, don't worry, Madame,' and added to cheer her up, 'your skirt is very pretty. Lovely colours.' She paused. 'But I think you're wearing it inside out,' she continued, pointing down to the label sewn onto the seam. 'Mind you, that brings good luck, my grandmother used to say.' Good luck or no, this setback upset Maddalena and for the rest of the day she kept her complimentary thoughts to herself. By the following day she had recovered her joie de vivre.

The priest saw the difference in Maddalena. She positively radiated joy. He enjoyed her company even more than before. Very occasionally they lunched or dined together. They were sharing a seafood platter down by the port when she told him about her encounter with the elderly man. He threw his head back and roared with laughter.

As the priest refilled their glasses from the carafe of muscadet, Maddalena told him that she had been cat- and plant-sitting for a friend who was away on business for a couple of weeks and who lived some way from the town centre. Most days she took the bus to his apartment, usually having to stand all the way for the thirty minute journey. On the way back, however, as the terminus was nearby, the bus was almost empty when she got on so she had a seat.

She encountered no pregnant women and no people on crutches for whom she would have gladly given up her seat. Sadly, however, there always appeared to be an inordinate number of women all perfectly able and healthy as far as she could see but undoubtedly considerably older than her. She got fed up giving up her seat to them.

'So I decided to take a different bus back to town. It means walking an extra ten minutes to a different bus stop but it's never full so I always have a seat.'

'That's good,' said the priest, squeezing lemon onto an oyster.

He had always been captivated by the workings of the female mind.

'No, it's not.'

'Ah.'

'I have to wait ages because the service is not nearly as frequent,' she said winkling out a whelk with the little pin. 'And it doesn't go where I want to go.'

A curious strangled gurgling sound emanated from the priest as he simultaneously choked back laughter and choked on his oyster. Maddalena, who was not looking at him because she had started to dissect her brown crab, continued, 'So do you know what I did?'

The priest managed a tremulous, 'No. What did you do?'

Maddalena counted the empty oyster shells on her plate— she was less keen on oysters than the priest who was less keen on the whelks and winkles—and said, 'The rest are yours. I went back to taking the original bus into town.'

'And resigned yourself to standing.'

'Aha! No!' Maddalena raised her claw crackers in the air to emphasise the point she was about to make. 'I decided that I would only give up my seat to older women who didn't colour their hair.' The priest looked up from shelling his langoustines. The look of astonishment on his face could not have been greater if the Holy Trinity had just walked into the restaurant and asked for a table for one.

Maddalena spooned some thick yellow mayonnaise onto the side of her plate. 'I don't feel the need to offer them a seat on the basis that they colour their hair to appear younger. So they can stand.'

'Ta logique,' said the priest, 'est irréprochable.'

For the first time during this particular conversation Maddalena, who had never possessed a particularly logical mind, raised her head to look at the priest. A huge smile spread across her face. 'Thank you. That's the first time anybody has ever said that to me.'

As she methodically scraped out the brown meat from the

shell, she said, 'This crab is absolutely delicious, the meat is so sweet. That reminds me, I'm thinking of going to a monastery.'

The priest, who always tried to follow Maddalena's trains of thought, with varying degrees of success, was unclear on the connection between the crab and going to a monastery— hermit crabs, perhaps, was that the link, he wondered?

'Permanently? Or just on retreat?'

Maddalena ignored his comment. 'Have you been to one?'

The priest busied himself extracting large juicy pieces of white meat from his crab claws. He could not lie so he said, 'I have a friend at one but they're not really my thing, monaster- ies.' And hoped she would not pursue it.

She didn't. 'I thought I'd go back to the island one, where I . . .' She stopped. It was odd, she still felt emotional when she thought about her experience in the abbey church. 'I'll go for a few days. Go the offices. Take some work with me. See how it goes.'

'I look forward to hearing all about it,' said the priest. 'Take your alarm clock. They get up early, the monks.'

Maddalena said, 'You know, I still don't understand what hap- pened. Why after all these years did this happen to me? I was living a perfectly happy life, I don't recall feeling that there was anything missing in my life. Although—' She hesitated. 'Now I think about it, I've always had the sort of feeling that I was waiting for something to happen. I didn't know what. I married a man I loved, I have children I love, work I love. And yet now I think about it, there was always this sense of, I don't know how to describe it, I've never talked to anybody about it, this sense of marking time, waiting, not unhappily, but waiting for some- thing to happen.'

'The Spirit blows where it will,' said the priest.

'She,' said Maddalena. 'The spirit blows where *she* will. The Holy Spirit is female.'

The priest looked up from his crab claw.

'She should be included in the weather forecast,' said Madda- lena. '"And here's the weather forecast for today. The mistral

25

and tramontane will be blowing in the Bouches-du-Rhône with gusts of up to seventy kilometres per hour, and the Holy Spirit will be gently wending her way along the coast from Marseille to Menton.'"

When they had finally finished their platter and had wiped their hands on hot cloths brought over by the waiter, Maddalena fished out an envelope from her bag with the stamps she had saved but forgotten to give him for several months. She had been under no illusion right from the beginning of their friendship that the cards he posted were actually meant for her, not least because they usually contained only a couple of scribbled lines, sometimes not even that. One envelope had contained a virgin sheet of folded paper. The envelopes however bore an inordinate number of stamps which she imagined vastly exceeded the required postage.

She emptied the envelope onto the table, sifted through them separating out a handful. She put all the others back in the envelope. She ordered an espresso; the priest ordered a mint tea. She picked up each stamp from her little pile. Two stamps each depicting an Afghan Emperor with the words "National Unity" printed down the left hand side. A Struggle against Narcotic Drug Day stamp depicting what she assumed was the seed head of an opium poppy, crossed out by what appeared to be two eaves of corn, against an outline map of Afghanistan.

'More camels,' she said looking at a stamp depicting four different coloured dromedaries. 'And horses, Arabian horses, it says.' She showed him the six stamps printed in Arabic with the English translation.

'This is an interesting one, isn't it?' she said, looking him straight in the eye. The stamp was an attractive minimalist design in pink and grey. At the bottom beneath the Arabic writing and printed in capitals was the English translation—National Society For Human Rights. This group of stamps all bore in the top right hand corner the same emblem—the crossed blades of two curved gold-handled swords with a palm tree in the space above and between the blades. The stamps were postmarked

Saudi Arabia.

The priest held her gaze, smiled, returned the stamps to the envelope, and asked for the bill which as usual they split between them.

A few weeks later Maddalena took the boat again to spend a week at the island monastery. She loved it. Her alarm buzzed quietly a few seconds before the church bell clanged out reveille at 03:55, she walked in the moonlight to the abbey church for Vigils, went back to bed, got up again for Lauds at 07:30.

The office of Terce was celebrated by the monks around nine o'clock in the work place. Later, she made her way to the abbey church for mass, the shorter offices of Sext and None, either side of a silently-eaten lunch, again for Vespers and, after supper, at day's end, Compline.

By day three she no longer returned to bed but walked round the island between Vigils and Lauds. She spent her days walking, reading, working on translations, not talking to anybody, thinking, the tranquillity disturbed only by occasional squawks of pheasants, the soothingly eternal sound of the sea—and the bells. She really, really loved it.

Rather oddly, she thought, she felt no desire to return to the female monastery with its perpetual Adoration of the Eucharist. And she never did get round to visiting the abbey of Thoronet. Instead, she headed for the lavender fields around another purist example of the Cistercian builder monks, les moines bâtisseurs, the mighty medieval and Provencal monastery of Sénanque.

Having acquired the abbey habit, she set off two or three times a year to spend a quiet time of reflection in other monasteries, mainly in France, some in Italy. Ancient buildings, simple tasty food eaten in silence in refectories listening to religious readings or Mozart or Bach, walks in beautiful unspoiled countryside, a time to read, a time to think—and always the bells ringing out to call her to the Liturgy of the Hours.

She heard a small scops owl hoot as she made her way beneath the Milky Way to Vigils; a wild boar and her two babies trotted out of the woods and crossed her path on an afternoon walk; one year, when she had decided not to spend Christmas in Sicily, she watched in the early morning hours of Christmas day a blue-white shooting star streak across the sky. It disappeared behind an abbey church where the Christ child lay in his crib in a side altar Nativity scene sculpted out of olive wood.

Between Vigils and Lauds, after a breakfast of strong black coffee, baguette and jam or marmalade—sometimes home-made from bitter oranges from a monastery garden—she watched the orange-red sun rise and marvelled, yet again, at this daily proof of the speed that our little planet orbited the sun.

She laughed out loud when she read a leaflet pinned up on a monastery notice board advertising a talk entitled "What purpose do monks serve?" *If there were no monks, we wouldn't have any of this*, she thought, as she gazed around her at a twelfth century limestone monastery. No monks? No ancient cloisters to walk through, no cloister gardens to read in, no divine offices to attend. No monks? No silent sanctuaries to meditate, reflect, to leave behind, if only for a few days, the hurly-burly of daily life. That was the purpose of monks. She didn't go to the talk.

She watched monks carefully remove delicately embroidered coverings from their zithers to accompany the psalms they chanted at the offices; in other monasteries monks sang a cappella; in either case Maddalena joined in, singing in a lower tonality than she normally would to blend in with the male voices.

In one monastery the only other person at Vigils was wearing a black windcheater with "Légion Etrangère" printed in white on the back. Later he told Maddalena that he was a Foreign Legion chaplain. It was heavy stuff. He came every month to the monastery for a couple of days of respite.

At Vespers, she was entranced by an evening ray of sunshine slanting through stained glass and illuminating wisps of incense smoke rising up from a small gold dish placed on altar steps. She was delighted that usually she could receive both the body and blood of Christ although she wondered why it was always white wine—often a slightly medium-sweet one—rather than a more appropriate blood red one.

In the Drôme, strolling in an olive grove, she paused to turn and look behind her and saw towering up above the green hedgerows three giant monolithic statues of the Holy Family. One October morning after an espresso – the machine was positioned on a table just outside the refectory—she walked through woods decked out in their autumn hues of yellows and reds and gold deep in a Piedmont valley. A couple of shots rang out through the crisp autumn air; at lunchtime the young monk in charge of meals that week produced a very tasty rabbit dish. She wondered at the time if the two events were connected.

And when she returned from one of her monastic sojourns, the next time she saw the priest she would, in great detail and with infectious enthusiasm, describe her visit.

'At most of them we receive both the body and blood of Christ, I like that,' she said one day over a cold beer on the beach. 'Although why is it white wine instead of red, which would be more appropriate, wouldn't it?'

The priest opened his mouth to say something, changed his mind, took a swig of his beer, and then said, 'I imagine it must be something to do with the difficulty of removing red wine stains from the white linen cloths we use during the mass. Laundry issues.'

Not for the first time, Maddalena had the strong impression that he had been about to say something else, but had yet again decided to keep his own counsel. She let it go. Whatever it was he would tell her when he was ready. Wouldn't he?

CHAPTER 6

Maddalena decided she would like to do some voluntary work. A colleague living in London had told her about his work with the Samaritans. She looked for an equivalent in France and found SOS Amitié. She got through the rigorous selection process for listeners, passed muster with the psychologist, hadn't changed her mind by the end of the year's formation, and started listening. Non-judgemental, non-directive, no advising, empathy, congruence, provide a space for callers to deposit their fears, anxieties, concerns, anger, suffering. Don't get involved in the back story.

***

Monday 17:27

'Bonjour, SOS Amitié, je vous écoute.'

'Well, at long last, do you know how long I've been waiting to get through to somebody? I've been trying to get you for hours, always that wretched recorded message, why doesn't anybody answer? This could be an emergency. I could be about to commit suicide and nobody answers!'

'Well you've reached somebody now, Madame, I'm here, I'm listening.'

'Yes, *now* you're here but I've been ringing different posts all afternoon, Rennes, Strasbourg, Montpellier, ring, ring, ring, then that wretched recording, I'd like to complain to whoever's in charge, it's appalling.'

'I'm sorry you had to wait, Madame, we have a lot of calls and we're always short of volunteers, but I'm here, I'm listening, perhaps you'd like to . . .'

'What I'd like to do is to complain to the head of SOS Amité, all afternoon I've been trying to get hold of you, all afternoon . . .'

'You mentioned suicide . . .'

'Who mentioned suicide? I'm not feeling suicidal, I just want someone to answer the bloody phone. I'm going to write a letter of complaint.'

'You can contact the association via the web site if you want to compl—'

'Oh yes! Send an email which will go straight in the bin? What's the point of that?'

'Perhaps you'd like to tell me why you—'

'NO I WOULD NOT YOU SILLY BITCH!' The line goes dead.

***

Tuesday 02:40

'SOS Amitié, bonsoir, je vous écoute.'

Silence, except for the almost imperceptible sound of someone breathing. Male? Female?

'I'm here, take your time.'

Silence. A minute goes by.

'It's hard, isn't it, to know where to start sometimes. No rush.'

Another minute goes by. In the background a cat meows.

'I . . .' A female voice. Old? Young? Hard to tell.

Silence.

'I can hear your cat, what's his name?'

'It's a she. Blandine, she's fourteen, tortoiseshell, she's all I've got now.' An old voice, a tired voice, hesitant, monotone.

'They're wonderful company, cats.'

'Yes, I don't know what I'd do without her. I really don't know what I'd do without her. Sometimes I just don't think it's worth carrying on.'

'You said she's all you've got now.'

'Yes.'

'Your family—'

Silence. 'They don't come to see me. They have their lives. Busy. Always busy. Too busy. I haven't seen my daughter for six months. She only lives sixty miles away.'

'I understand that you must feel lonely.'

'She's just had her second child. I haven't even seen him.'

'I'm sure she'll get over when she can to introduce you.'

'She's sent me photos.'

'Oh, that's lovely.'

'Yes, he's gorgeous.' Silence. 'Sometimes I don't speak to anybody for days on end.'

'You said, "They don't come—"'

'My son lives eight hundred miles away.'

'That makes it harder for him to get over to see you.'

'Yes.' Silence. 'But he rings me every week. Since my husband died, he rings me every week.'

'You must enjoy that. It's so hard to come to terms with the loss of someone you loved.'

'Love? LOVE? He was a miserable bugger. Glad to see the back of him. But, you're right, I do miss him, I suppose, in a funny sort of way.'

'So you've got some lovely photos of your new grandson. Your son calls you each week. You've got Blandine.'

'Yes. And I've got you. SOS Amitié. Sometimes I just need to talk to someone. Thank you for being there. I think I'll be able to sleep now. Goodnight.'

***

Wednesday 00:10

'Bonsoir, SOS Amitié, je vous écoute.'

'It's been a dreadful day absolutely dreadful it started this morning first thing this morning when I went downstairs to get the mail and that horrible, horrible concierge looks like the back end of a bus told me not to leave my bicycle where I'd left it I don't normally leave it there but when I got back yesterday evening I was in a hurry I can't remember why now but I was in a hurry so I left it propped up against the door and meant to go back down later to put it away but something happened I can't remember what so I oh yes my friend Monique rang that's it my friend Monique rang and she went on and on and on she's got problems with her husband who drinks like a fish if I was her I'd throw him out he comes back night after night three sheets to the wind I mean he doesn't hit her or anything like that he's just drunk and the money he spends I don't know how she manages do you mind if I smoke? so she went on and on and on and by the time she'd finished I'd completely forgotten about my bike and then my favourite TV programme was about to start and by the time that was finished and I'd made myself a verbena tisane before going to bed well I'd completely forgotten about the bicycle so this morning that witch of a concierge said, "You can't go leaving your bicycle here, Madame," I mean to say it's the first time I've left it there apart from once before a couple of months ago that was because I was intending to go out again on it and when I got home something happened I can't remember what perhaps the telephone rang probably Monique again going on and on and on about that drunk she's married to and so I didn't go out again and forgot about the bike so yesterday was only the second time I'd forgotten to put it away and her talking to me like that this morning has ruined my day just ruined my day but I feel so much better now thank you so much for your help goodbye.'

***

Thursday 07:32

'Bonjour, SOS Amitié, je vous écoute.'

'Bonjour, Madame.' A quiet male voice, hesitant, no background noise. Silence. 'It's very hard being on your own. I can't bear the solitude.' Silence. 'My partner has left me. Seven years together and she's gone off with a mate of mine.'

'Separations are painful, it takes time to get through emotionally difficult times like that, doesn't it?'

'I'm lonely, I can't bear the loneliness. When I go out, everybody seems to be with somebody and I'm all alone. And I come back to an empty apartment night after night. It's really hard being on my own.'

'I can understand how difficult it must be for you after seven years.'

'It's so nice to hear a friendly female voice. I'm lying on my bed and I'm about to start mastur—'

'Bonne continuation, Monsieur, au revoir.'

***

Friday 21:46

'Bonsoir, SOS Amitié, je vous écoute.'

'I'm schizophrenic. I've been ill for twenty years. I have a treatment. It's not working so well now.'

'I'm glad you've called, Monsieur.'

'It helps me to talk. My psychiatrist is on holiday. He tells me to ring you when things are bad. I ring you a lot.'

'You say your treatment is not working so well.'

'He's changed it, I'm taking new medication. He's told me that gradually Pierre will disappear. But I don't want him to go away.'

'Pierre?'

'Yes, he came when I was fifteen. He arrived a year after my mother died. I'm thirty-five. He's been with me for twenty years. I don't want him to disappear. I don't know what I'll do without him.' The voice trembles, cracks.

'He's been with you a long time. I can understand your concern.'

'He talks to me. He's my friend. And now he's going to disappear.' Whispering sounds. 'He's talking to me now. He tells me things. People think I can see into the future, but it's Pierre who tells me things. People come and ask me what's going to happen and Pierre tells me. I don't know what I will do without him.'

'He arrived a year after your mother died, you say.'

'Yes, she sent him. To be my friend.'

'And he's been a good friend to you. Twenty years is a long time. Your psychiatrist wants to help you get better. I imagine he thinks this new treatment will help you. Perhaps Pierre has to go so you can get better.'

'I think I'll die if Pierre disappears.'

'He hasn't gone yet.'

'No, but he's with me less often. Sometimes he's not here for a couple of days. Before he was with me all the time.' A yawn.

'You sound tired. You can ring again later.'

'Yes. I think I'll sleep now. Goodbye. Thank you.'

***

Saturday 15:54

'Bonjour, SOS Amitié, je vous écoute.' Silence.

'Hello, SOS Amitié.' A male voice, deep and rich. Birdsong, cicadas singing. 'This is the first time I've called you. I'm not sure what to say now.'

'It sounds like you're outside.' Silence.

'Yes, I'm in the kitchen garden.'

'Busy time of year.' Silence.

'Yes. I've got courgettes, tomatoes, beans, lettuces. In the orchard there are plum trees—the quetsch and mirabelles will be ready soon.'

'Sounds like you've enough home-grown produce to feed a small army.' Silence.

'Not exactly an army.' Birdsong and singing cicadas. 'I have chosen a way of life—it was a free choice—that has given me many years of contentment, serenity, peace. I have no regrets. Except that . . .' Silence.

'No regrets—it's marvellous to be able to say that. I suppose we sometimes do wonder what would have been it we had made different life choices.'

The cicadas are stunned into silence as a distant bell chimes out the hour.

'Yes. I have not married, I have no children, I live in a happy, united community. I would change nothing. And yet . . . and yet sometimes I feel an almost painful emptiness in my life. Just hearing a female voice, your voice, has lightened my soul. It's very odd. I didn't quite know what to expect when I dialled your number. I've dialled it many times and hung up when someone answered. But today, I don't know why, something about your voice, maybe. Today I didn't hang up. And we are having a conversation. It's very odd indeed. I feel . . . I feel rather light-headed.'

'Well, now you know the number please call again. If it helps.'
Silence.

'Will it be you who answers?'

"It could be, but it's very unlikely. Calls are dispatched to the first free listening post regardless of which town you call. So you can ring Montpellier and be answered by a listener in Brest.'
'Oh, I see. Well, I must go now. Thank you for being there. It's been quite a revelation.' And the owner of the deep, rich voice ended the call.

***

Sunday 04:23

'SOS Amitié, bonsoir, je vous écoute. ' Silence. Nothing, no breathing, no noise, nothing. 'Bonsoir, I'm here. I'm listening.' Silence. One minute, two.

'There's no point in going on.' A woman's voice, slow, flat drained of all emotion.

'Things are that bad in your life. We can talk about that, if you like.'

'There's no point. There's nothing you or anybody can do or say. My life isn't worth living. It's never been worth living. There's no point in going on. I've made my decision.'

'To end your life?'

'Yes.'

'I can call the emergency services. They will come and help

you. You will need to give me your name, telephone number and address. I can call them now from another phone.'

'No. I don't need anybody to come. I just called because I wanted to hear another human voice before I die.' The voice is even slower now.

'Is there really nothing in your life worth living for? Your family . . ."

'There's only my mother. I've written her a letter. I posted it this morning. She'll get it tomorrow morning. It'll be over by then.' Silence. Then, 'I've taken pills. I'm a nurse. I know what to take and how much.'

'I'm so sorry you feel that this is the only way out. You really can't see any other solution? You know there are professional people who may be able to help you.'

'Nobody can help me. My life has always been shit, it's never been worth living. I just wanted to hear another human voice . . .' The words are drowsily drawn out, the voice slower still.

'I shall stay on the line as long as you want. I won't hang up.'

Silence. The line goes dead.

***

Monday 23:58

'SOS Amitié, bonsoir, je vous écoute.'

'Madame, I am VERY unhappy.' A female voice, loud, aggressive.

'Oh dear, I'm sorry to hear that.'

'No, you're not. How can you be sorry when you don't know what has happened? I am VERY unhappy.'

'Perhaps you'd like to talk about what has made you unhappy.'

'Why on earth do you think I've telephoned SOS Amitié if it wasn't to talk about why I'm VERY unhappy?' Silence. 'Hello, HELLO, are you still there?'

'Yes, Madame, I'm still here.'

'I am very, VERY unhappy. I am also VERY, VERY angry. They are all against me and I'm going to write to the President. Do you know his address?'

'Not offhand but I imagine if you address your letter to him at the Elysée Palace, Paris, it should get there.'

'And the postcode?'

'I'm afraid I don't know it. Perhaps you can find it on the Internet.'

'Internet, INTERNET! I don't have INTERNET. What is the President's postcode? It won't get there without the postcode.'

'Perhaps you could tell me why you are so unhappy. And angry.'

'What's it got to do with you?'

'I rather thought that was why you'd telephoned SOS Amitié'

Long silence.

'I am VERY unhappy and VERY angry because I have VERY big problems, VERY big problems indeed. But they won't get away with it. Oh no, I won't let them get away with it.'

'And these very big problems make you very angry.'

'Are you sure you don't have the President's postcode? Why don't you have it? Can't *you* look it up on the Internet?'

'Perhaps you have a friend who could help you with your problems.'

"A friend? A FRIEND? If I had any FRIENDS I wouldn't be calling SOS Amitié, would I?' The line goes dead.

***

Wednesday 16:10

'SOS Amitié, bonjour.'

A male voice, thick, slurred, slow. 'I've started drinking again. Four weeks in a detox clinic, I thought I'd cracked it this time, I really thought I had, got back last Friday, no alcohol in the house . . .' The voice cracks, the man sobs, recovers. 'I've managed all weekend, went out with my brother and some friends, I managed, soft drinks . . . then today . . .' He starts sobbing again and lets out a long almost animal like moan. 'I've lost everything – my wife, my kids, my job. There's no point, no point in going on, best to end it all, life's not worth living, it really isn't.'

'You said you thought you'd cracked it this time. So you've managed to stop before?'

'Yes. I was so scared of losing my job I managed to stop, didn't drink for six months, seven months. Then I was made redundant. Started drinking again.' Sobs, a deep sigh, then the slurred voice continues. 'My wife said if I didn't go into rehab she'd leave me. I stopped drinking for over a year. Then she left anyway, took the kids and left.'

'So you know you can do it. You know you have the will power to stop.'

Silence. 'Yes, but ...' The man breaks down again.

Silence.

'You stopped drinking for over a year. You know you can do it. One day you will succeed.'

The man talks on, seems calmer, more coherent. Time to bring the call to a close before he starts sobbing again. Be positive. You have people around you who care about you, you know where we are, don't forget you have managed to stop drinking before, you can do it again.

'Thank you, thank you. I can't tell you how much better I feel having talked to you. Au revoir, Madame, et merci.'

***

There were far, far more callers than there were listeners so over time Maddalena did hear voices she recognised. She was exasperated by callers who rang repeatedly always recounting the same tale but dutifully listened hoping to hear something new in the discourse; she gave short shrift to the horrible man who hurled racial abuse down the telephone; and to the ghastly woman whose sole reason for calling appeared to be to insult all the listeners in the association.

She was perfectly happy to talk—for a limited period of time, they could be very garrulous—to solitary little old ladies in retirement homes; she recognised callers like the man with the cicadas and bells ringing in the background who was just happy to talk for fifteen minutes or so; she always gave time to those diagnosed with schizophrenia and other psychiatric disorders who rang when things were very bad.

Then there were the callers she was listening to for the first time. Perhaps they called in regularly—they were often told to ring by their doctors, psychologists, psychiatrists, emergency services—but the association had fifty listening posts throughout France and for her, Maddalena, it was the first time she had heard their story.

The desperate man who was spending astronomical sums on telephone astrology; a young man from one of the French overseas territories convinced he was cursed because girls always refused to dance with him; what seemed like countless numbers suffering from bipolar disorder. Depression, loneliness, anxiety attacks, suicidal tendencies, loneliness, anger, revenge, despair, loneliness, bigotry, sexual abuse, bereavement, loneliness, long-term illness, unemployment, violence . . . the list went on and on and on.

The longer she carried out her voluntary work as a listener, the more she realised how important it was for people to be able to talk to someone. They did not expect solutions from her. They just wanted an attentive listening ear. They just wanted someone to talk to.

CHAPTER 7

Sometimes Maddalena didn't see the priest for a couple of months or more. He was travelling doing whatever he did (she made it a matter of principal not to ask, he would tell her in due course, when he was ready. Wouldn't he?) When he returned she was away visiting the family in Sicily, meeting up with her daughter or son, or both, visiting friends. By the time she got back, he was off again.

The postcards arrived saying very little, she received the occasional text message saying even less. There was so much she wanted to tell him so in order not to forget she noted things down on a sheet of paper. When she did see him she usually forgot to bring it with her and had to do it from memory.

'This praying business,' she said, late one afternoon down by the harbour.

The priest let out an almost—but not quite, but Maddalena didn't notice anyway— sigh, picked up his glass, a pale gris de gris vin de sable from the Camargue, took a slow sip, followed with his gaze a small pointu, one of those little fishing boats with a pointed bow, gaily painted in blue and white, and waited.

'I can't do it and I don't really see the point.'

The priest helped himself to a couple of small almost-black olives. He popped the stones onto the saucer and thought what a lovely colour Maddalena was. He had noticed over the time he had known her that when her summer tan faded, her natural Mezzogiorno complexion was not the deep dark mahogany hue —rather unattractive he had thought at the time—of the folk he remembered seeing when he was in Sicily. Her skin was a little lighter and more golden in colour.

'I don't pray for myself,' Maddalena continued. 'I've never been happier, I don't need anything. And I don't see the point of praying for anybody else. I don't mean I'm not affected by what happens to others, illness, poverty, terrible tragedies around the world. Of course, I am, I just don't see what God's got to do with it. If someone dear to me is diagnosed as terminally ill with, I don't know, cancer, say. I don't mean I'm not going to be devastated but it's happened because our scientists haven't yet found a cure for cancer. It's not really anything to do with God, is it? And if thousands die in an earthquake in Japan it's to do with plate tectonics, not God. That's how I see it, anyway.'

The priest waited to see whether Maddalena had finished. She hadn't.

'Now, I talk to him. That I *do* do, I thank him for my life, I thank him for my return to the faith. When I'm in the sea floating on my back looking up at the clouds, the sky, watching the gulls fly over and listening to that, you know, that shushing sound the water below makes as its dragged back through the pebbles on the sea bed, when I'm doing that I thank him for all the beauty that surrounds us.' She omitted to mention that she was naked at the time, having discovered many years earlier a tiny isolated rather inaccessible but worth the effort to get there naturist beach.

The priest said, 'Well, that's a kind of prayer, I think, isn't it? And when you attend the divine offices that you love so much, that's a prayer, too. Just walking round a church, admiring the stained glass windows, the architecture, thinking of the men who carved out those pillars, sculpted the capitals on top of the columns. I don't think praying necessarily means *asking* God for anything. Reading thought-provoking books, not just so you can say you've read them or so you can disagree with them, but for the pleasure, for the love of truth'

Maddalena remained silent and motionless, looking, too, at the little fishing boats bobbing about in the bay. 'I have a problem with the Credo, too. The beginning's OK. I believe in God.'

'That's a good start.'

'I don't believe Jesus was conceived by the Holy Spirit, or in a virgin birth, and I'm not sure I believe whole-heartedly the bit about the Catholic Church—it's rather a flawed institution I think.'

'It must be confusing for your neighbours in church.'

'What do you mean?'

'When you all recite the Credo, presumably you get to the end well before everybody else.'

Maddalena laughed. She fingered the cover of a book the priest had brought for her to read. It was called "Joie de Vivre, Joie de Croire" by the Père François Varillon. She glanced at the back cover—"conferences on the major points of the Christian faith'" and further on, "This spiritual master, traditional and audacious, possesses better than anyone else the art of dusting off Christianity..."

'It goes back to the early 1980s. They don't write books like that anymore. I think you'll find it interesting,' he said.

'Thank you. And the rosary. When I was little, I remember listening to the old women in our village church, dressed in black, wearing headscarves. They really raced through the rosary at a rate that seemed to me inversely proportional to the achingly slow speed at which they walked to get there. I can't see the point.'

The priest knew what she meant. He, too, had watched the moving lips of elderly black-clad white-haired women with dark olive-skinned wrinkle-etched faces reciting the Ave Maria ten times in a row at the speed of light, while slipping rosary beads through gnarled arthritic fingers. But although he, too, had his doubts about the validity of this top gear Marian devotion, he had to confess that as an onlooker he found it rather soothing to listen to the background sound of low mumbling voices—Spanish, Portuguese, Italian, French—united in prayer.

'I have to say I do really struggle with the virgin birth,' she continued.

The priest, not for the first time, rather wished that Maddalena had been indoors when the Holy Spirit had wafted along the Mediterranean coast. It had been a long flight home. He was still suffering from jet lag. He really, really did not want to get involved in discussing dogmas of the Catholic Church. He sensed that this was going to be a two-carafe conversation. He caught the waiter's eye and indicated they wanted the same again.

Maddalena had what he usually found a rather perplexing habit of moving seamlessly from one topic of conversation to another one which, on the surface at least, appeared completely unconnected to the previous subject. It was as if she had had a private conversation in her head which linked the two disparate subjects for her but, given that he was not privy to this conversation, not for him. This mechanism now came to his rescue.

'Oh, I haven't told you. I've decided to start studying philosophy, just in general terms, nothing too difficult—I never got on with it much at school.'

'Excellent. That's a challenge for you. How are you going about that?'

'Years ago I read a book called "Le Monde de Sophie" by a Norwegian intellectual and it was about a man teaching a 15-year-old girl, the Sophie of the title, about philosophy, interwoven with a rather unusual story which I cannot remember. But the philosophy lessons were brilliant.

'I thought that would be about my level so I bought a second hand copy and pulled out all the different sections where Alberto Knox talks to Sophie about philosophers and their philosophies in terms I can understand. He starts off briefly talking about mythology—Norse, Greek—then gets into gear with the Natural Philosophers and ends up with Jean-Paul Sartre.'

'How far have you got?'

'The book only arrived a couple of days ago. I've stapled each section together and started reading last night. Nietzsche.'

'"The very word 'Christianity' is a misunderstanding—in truth, there was only one Christian, and he died on the cross.

Discuss."'

'Where's that from?'

'*The Antichrist*. But Nietzsche—that's almost at the end. You must have read all night.'

'Oh, I'm not reading it in order.'

'Ah.'

'I pulled out the index so I can look up who I want. And I looked up the bit on Nietzsche. And in it Alberto Knox mentions Kierkegaard who I'd never heard of so I looked him up next. A rather melancholy Danish christian. And there he refers to Spinoza and Hegel.'

'So you looked them up. You don't think it might be more, you know, logical to start at the beginning? To follow the progression of philosophic thought through time?'

Maddalena cocked her head to one side and looked at the priest, a slight frown on her brow. 'Yes, you're right. It was getting rather complicated. I was just so excited and anxious to get started. And I remembered a dancing quotation of Nietzsche which I read somewhere years ago—"I should only believe in a God that would know how to dance." I love to dance. So I started with him. Nietzsche. But you're right. I'll try to start from the beginning.'

They both remained silent for a while, looking out over the water. Not for the first time the priest found himself on the verge of telling Maddalena about his work, not particularly because he wanted to but for the simple reason that he knew Giacomo needed help.

He had spoken to the abbot about Maddalena a while back as a possible solution to the transport problem. Giacomo had not pursued it so the priest had let it drop. Recently, however, he had sensed a change. On his last visit to the monastery a few weeks earlier, while the two men were enjoying a nightcap of single malt whisky after Compline, the abbot had for the first time asked after Maddalena.

But the priest did not tell her. They finished their wine in the early evening sunshine, split the bill, and together walked along the seafront until their ways parted.

That morning in the market Maddalena had bought one of those pale green and white stripy courgettes she loved, still attached to its bright yellow flower, a dark purple trumpet aubergine about the same circumference, and a small yellow pepper. Now when she got home she rinsed several times a handful of long grain basmati rice, putting the first cloudy rinse water aside, about half a litre, for cleaning her face and rinsing her hair, and put the washed rice into a saucepan. From a bunch of marjoram tied with string and suspended from the knob of a kitchen cupboard door, she snipped off a couple of sprigs, popped them on top of the rice, added some coarse sea salt then covered the rice with water to a centimetre or so above the contents. When the water started simmering, she covered the pan, turned the heat right down and put on the timer for ten minutes.

She put a chair under the smoke detector, rinsed her vegetables briefly, dried them, and sliced them into bite size pieces while sesame oil heated up and started smoking in the pan. She loved the sharp sizzling sound the vegetables made as she emptied them into the pan. She shoogled them around a bit with a wooden spoon, scattered them with sea salt, turned off the heat and replaced the chair.

From the cupboard she took out a tin of tuna, changed her mind and put it back again. She took out of the fridge a chicken leg left over from a cooked free range chicken she had bought from the butcher a couple of days earlier. And put it back in the fridge. She would eat some of the rice and vegetables on their own, and keep the rest for lunch the following day with the cold chicken. Or perhaps the tuna.

She sensed, with the priest, there were things that had been left unsaid. She wondered whether he had been about to tell her about his work and if he had been, what had prevented him. The timer rang, the rice was perfect. She scooped out two or three spoonfuls onto a plate, added some of her stir fried vegetables on top, drizzled over some light and elegant Ligurian olive oil and ground some black pepper over the lot. She replaced the cover on the pan with the remaining rice, and put it into the sink to cool down quickly in cold water. She started eating her supper and, forgetting her recent resolution, started reading the pages on Descartes.

CHAPTER 8

They were sitting at a beach restaurant sipping cold beers. It was late afternoon in the back half of October. Mornings and evenings were chilly and the mistral had blown long and hard the previous day. Now the sun, which had been shining in a cloudless post-mistral azure blue sky, was beginning to lose its heat.

There were still lots of tourists around, and the owner had put out an extra couple of tables and chairs on the beach itself. One table was occupied. Maddalena had arrived first and sat down at the other.

'You can't get much closer to the sea than this,' said the priest, as he swiftly raised his feet to avoid one of those rare extra-energy waves that, now and then, took folk by surprise by coming in faster and stronger than the others, soaking unsuspecting sunbathers and their towels.

'The four o'clock wave,' she laughed, referring to a phenomenon oft reported in the local press.

'It's five,' he said, looking at his watch. 'It's late.'

'Maybe it's getting ready for the clocks going back,' said Maddalena. Then she frowned, not sure if she had got that right.

He was nervous. He picked up his glass of beer, did not drink, put it down again. He had decided to tell Maddalena about his work and the monastery. And he was nervous. Giacomo had called the previous evening. The abbot—always calm, un-ruffled, like the sea here some mornings when the water, crystal clear, resembled a lake, and the only motion was that of gentle ripples ending their almost invisible journey by quietly breaking onto the shoreline, followed by an almost inaudible and inexpressibly soothing and shushing sound as water was gently sucked through the smooth river-rounded pebbles back into the sea—the abbot had sounded a little stressed.

He had never been keen on the priest's idea of involving Maddalena in their work. But the situation was such that—thanks to the priest's tireless efforts—he could now do with some help. 'Could you talk to your friend?' The priest had texted Maddalena, she was free, they had arranged to meet.

He was nervous. There was absolutely no reason to think that she would not be delighted that he had finally decided to tell her about his work. He knew how patient she had been, holding back, often with difficulty, from asking intrusive questions, waiting until he was ready to talk.

Yet he had never intimated to her that one day he would be ready to talk. He had simply changed the subject or ignored any of her pointed, probing comments. He had no doubt that she would be pleased that he had finally decided to confide in her. And he was equally sure that she would be happy to help the community. Yet he was nervous with, it soon turned out, good cause.

He shifted in his seat. He cleared his throat. 'My work . . .' his voice tailed off. Maddalena looked at him expectantly. 'There is an aspect you could help with. You would need to go to a monastery.' He handed her a small thin booklet. 'I'd like you to read this first.'

Maddalena, who since he had arrived had been wondering what could be making the priest so ill at ease thought that, at long last, and not before time in her view, he had decided to take her into his confidence. She sensed she was about to discover the story behind the stamps.

She took the booklet. The cover was a pale dove grey colour. She read the title which was printed in a darker shade in plain typeface: "La Communità dello Spirito Santo". Underneath the title, a simple pencil sketch of three bending and overlapping ears of wheat—a minimalist design, just a few strokes, but the artist had managed to create such a sense of movement that you could almost feel the breeze blowing through the wheat field. She opened the booklet and started reading.

While she turned the pages, the priest watched her carefully for a reaction. There was none. Her end of summer deeply tanned face remained impassive. He turned away, looked out to sea, followed the path of a seagull as it flew purposefully above the water, wings flapping, its constant cry piercing the late afternoon air. He thought, *It's funny—the gulls are always squawking but often you don't hear them. And then other times that's all you hear, only their cry, nothing else.* He felt a certain relief now as he swallowed a good mouthful of beer. There was no going back. She was reading about the community. She would understand. She would help.

He glanced again at Maddalena, quickly, almost furtively, to see if he could gauge her reaction. Her glass of beer had remained untouched since she had started reading; he noticed that occasionally she turned back a page or two to reread something. *Good, that's a good sign,* he thought. The booklet was only a handful of pages but she was reading it carefully, taking it all in. Excellent.

When she had finished she took a large sip of her beer, now not warm but not ice-cold any more either. And reread the booklet from the beginning. The priest had the sudden feeling that this was not good. He started to feel slightly queasy. He looked at her while she read—her eyes never leaving the page—for a sign, an indication of what she was thinking, but there was none. Her face remained impassive.

Maddalena finished her second reading of the booklet, closed it and put it down on the table in front of her, looked at the priest and said, 'Let me see if I understand this correctly.'

In all the time he had known her he had never seen her face, her always smiling expressive face, he had never seen it devoid of all expression as it now was. Many times he had seen her laughing; when she had spoken to him about her spiritual experiences he had seen her crying. When they met he knew immediately if she was in carefree mood, had something on her mind, was tired; her face expressed her emotions before she opened her mouth. The face of the woman sitting opposite him on this autumn afternoon by the sea was blank, unsmiling, devoid of all expression.

'The Communità dello Spirito Santo was founded in the nineteenth century by,' she paused and reopened the booklet at the first page, 'by Amadeo of Marebosco who lived in Liguria,' she looked up and indicated to the east with a vague movement of her right hand. 'It is a small monastic community, a dozen monks I think I read.' The priest gave a confirmatory nod.

'The sole objective of this,' she paused and slightly emphasized the following word, '*unusual* community is to provide a discreet venue where senior figures from all world faiths—and interested atheists—can meet together with religious teachers to study in depth each others' beliefs. Very laudable.' The priest winced. 'Very laudable indeed,' repeated Maddalena, looking at him, her face remaining a blank canvas. The priest had expected a positive reaction, otherwise he would never have dreamt of telling Maddalena about the community. He was feeling more and more uncomfortable. He shifted in his chair but did not speak. This was not looking good.

She referred to the booklet again. 'In charge of this,' she paused again as if searching for the right word and having found it, again gave it a very slight but oh so noticeable emphasis, '*unorthodox* monastic community is Abbot Giacomo Ravasi.'

Maddalena continued without a pause. 'During my stays in various monasteries I have, as you can imagine, read a little bit about monastic life, in booklets we find in our cells or in the library. I know that most monastic communities live according to the Rule of Saint Benedict of Nursia. He was the Abbot of Monte Cassino, wasn't he, and lived in the sixth century, I think. From memory, there are just over seventy individual rules making up what is known as The Rule.'

She put down the booklet, and looking directly at the priest with an unfamiliar cold stare continued, 'I see Abbot Giacomo has managed to reduce that to a much more manageable five.'

The priest shifted yet again in his seat. This was not going at all well. He remained silent.

'And it seems that this *renegade*'—again the slight emphasis, again the priest winced—'this *renegade* monastic community operates in a completely autonomous manner. The pope appears to be just about aware of its existence, but the Communità dello Spirito Santo is responsible to no one.'

Maddalena continued looking at the priest who was looking for the waiter. He caught the young man's eye and indicated with the usual circular movement of his right index an order for another two beers.

'Which brings us to the financing of this *unconventional* monastic community.' *Oh, dear God,* thought the priest, *why did you let me think this was a good idea, this is your fault.* The waiter arrived at the table and opened the two bottles. The priest almost grabbed his beer out of the young man's hand, took a long swig straight from the bottle bracing himself for what he knew was coming next.

Maddalena poured her beer into her glass, took a sip, flicked through the booklet. The priest shifted in his chair, cleared his throat, and decided to remain silent until she had had her say. He rather wished he'd reread the booklet before giving it to her. It was in pristine condition. He had been the last—and indeed the only—person to read it years ago when Giacomo had given it to him. Since then the brief outline it gave of how the community worked had become second nature to him. He had forgotten how it must appear to new eyes, fresh eyes, Maddalena's eyes.

'Given that virtually nobody appears to be aware of its existence and that it is completely autonomous, the community has to be self-financing.' Maddalena referred again to the booklet. 'It says here that over the decades there have been occasional substantial donations. There have also been periods when the monastery's interfaith activities have been reduced to a trickle or have indeed ceased altogether due to world events. To keep the show on the road Abbot Giacomo and his monks have to raise money.'

Here we go, thought the priest, taking another slug of beer, and rather wishing God would transform him into the large gull skimming close by, low and fast over the sparkling blue water.

'All the monasteries I have visited have had shops,' continued Maddalena. 'They sell their own produce and they sell each others' produce. You know, things like honey, olive oil, essence of lavender, cheese, chocolates, that sort of thing. I bought a bottle of some amazing herbal elixir made by the monks at one monastery. And in true monastic tradition many of them distil liqueurs, don't they? Green Chartreuse, Yellow Chartreuse.'

She opened the booklet again. '*Your* monks distil high strength vodka.'

The priest, realising that God was not going to transform him into a gull and that he now really didn't have anything to lose, decided that attack was the best form of defence. 'It's very good vodka. Brother Aarne is Finnish.'

For the first time since she had started reading the booklet, Maddalena smiled. It was a tight-lipped smile radiating as much warmth as the tundra in Finnish Lapland. In winter. 'Of course,' she said, 'he's Finnish.'

'And he makes a really excellent cloudberry vodka, too.' A slight note of desperation had crept into the priest's voice. 'Wild cloudberries. His aunts send them . . .' His voice trailed off.

'Cloudberries,' repeated Maddalena, somehow making the word sound as if Brother Aarne was flavouring his vodka with reindeer dung.

They were both silent. The priest was looking at Maddalena who was gazing out to sea. She said, 'Some monastic shops I've visited sell icons. That's the kind of religious artistic activity you'd expect in a monastery, isn't it? The other main income stream of the Communità dello Spirito Santo appears to come from copies of well known works of art painted by,' she referred to the booklet, 'Brother Ange-Dominique, a Corsican ex convict.' She turned her gaze back from the sea to look at the priest.

'They're not copies. Or at least very rarely, sometimes he paints copies, but normally he creates a religious work based on a famous painting but painted in another artist's style. The canvas he was working on the last time I was there was based on da Vinci's "The Madonna of the Yarnwinder" painted in the style of Van Gogh, pink roses at her feet, olive trees in the background. And he recently finished one based on Gauguin's "Woman with a Mango", I can't remember the Tahitian title, where he's replaced the woman with the virgin and the mango she's holding with the Christ Child.' He paused for breath then added, 'Vivid colours. Blue dress, yellow background. It's beautiful.'

'I'm sure it is. Presumably he had plenty of free time to perfect his technique while he was inside.'

'That was a long time ago. Ajaccio prison—four years for a repeat offence, dealing in cannabis, ridiculous really.'

'And the other sixteen years?'

He should have read the booklet. Too late now. 'Ah. Well, I expect it was some island vendetta, perhaps a revenge killing, you know what the Corsicans are like, bit like the Sicilians.'

As the words came out of his mouth he realised, too late, his error. The look in Maddalena's eyes was about as murderous as that in the eyes of the Easter Monday protagonists in the Sicilian Vespers Massacre seven hundred years ago in Palermo, at the Spirito Santo church—that Holy Spirit again.

In his mind the priest was now backpedalling at furious speed. He had completely misjudged her reaction. Now it was a question of damage limitation. He knew her well enough, although obviously not as well as he had thought, to trust her not to speak of the community.

What would Giacomo say? How would he react? He'd never been keen on the idea of asking her to help. It was he, the priest, who had mentioned Maddalena to the abbot. She would be discreet, wouldn't she? Would she?

'Anyway, Brother Ange-Dominique's canvases sell throughout the world. Discreetly. Private clients.'

Maddalena looked unsmilingly at the priest. 'Yes, of course.

Through the auspices of your New York agent.' She leafed through the booklet. 'Mannie Morgenstern.'

'He's very good.'

'I'm sure he is. So, apart from occasional donations the monastery's income comes from the sale of high strength Finnish vodka—'

'Some flavoured with wild cloudberries.'

'—with or without wild cloudberries, and oil paintings of religious subjects—I assume they're in oils?'

'He paints in watercolours, too, I think.'

'Based on existing works of art but painted in other masters' styles. Have I got that right?'

'Yes.'

'And these transactions are, of course, all above board.'

'Absolutely. The vodka is despatched from the monastery cellars. All the canvases go through Mannie in New York. Everything, well, that is . . .' He stopped himself.

'That is?'

The priest hesitated. 'Sometimes, well, occasionally the financial situation has been such that . . .'

'Yes?'

'You mentioned them earlier, icons. Brother Ange-Dominique also creates icons. Very small, very beautiful, very portable. Sometimes, very occasionally, when Giacomo is really up against the wall . . .' He squirmed in his chair, drummed the fingers of his left hand on the table, picked up his beer with his right.

'Don't tell me. Let me guess. You smuggle them out. Cash only. No names, no pack-drill.'

'Only when it is absolutely necessary,' said the priest in a slow defiant voice, looking Maddalena straight in the eye.

Maddalena returned his gaze for a couple of seconds, closed her eyes, bowed her head and with her elbows resting on the white wrought iron table and her thumbs pressed against her cheek bones, gently massaged her forehead with the index and middle fingers of both hands.

The priest remained silent, gazing again out to sea and rueing his decision to tell Maddalena about the community. Where was the Holy Spirit when you needed her most, he thought. Oh, well, the monks would just have to carry on themselves fetching and carrying their visitors from the airport, wouldn't they?

As he turned his head to look again at Maddalena she raised hers, leant back in her chair and started laughing. She laughed and laughed, tears streaming down her cheeks. She laughed, unable to speak, her chest and stomach shaking up and down uncontrollably. People at neighbouring tables turned to look at her, the priest, his jaw slack, stared at her in astonishment.

She leaned forward to try to say something, but every time she started to speak laughter got the better of her and she collapsed back in her chair. The priest gave a tentative smile, tension faded from his face, replaced by a grin of relief. He started giggling and soon he, too, was laughing uncontrollably.

Maddalena wiped away the tears, regained control of herself, and in a voice still trembling with laughter said, 'I can't wait. When do we go?'

That evening the priest called the abbot to say that he had spoken to his friend and she would be happy to help. 'I've given her your number, she'll ring and come up for a few days. You'll like her, I know you will.' The abbot was not so sure. He had his doubts about this woman. Not about the work, she was presumably quite capable of driving to and from airports, but she was a "good" friend of the priest's. How good a friend would that be, he wondered? He couldn't put his finger on it, but he had this nagging suspicion that things at the monastery would never be the same once Maddalena arrived.

He also had other much more serious things on his mind. The priest, who knew the abbot well enough to sense this, said, 'Everything all right, Giacomo?'

No, everything was not all right. The Muse had deserted Ange-Dominique. It had been their agent Mannie Morgenstern who had pointed out that if you used the English word Brother rather than Frère, his initials spelled out BAD. The abbot had thought that hilarious. Whenever he referred to his artist monk by his initials it still made him smile even after all these years. BAD wasn't painting. At all. And that was not good.

'It's not the first time as you know, and it's never a good time when it happens but right now it's a disaster. He's there at Vigils, he's there at Lauds, he's there at mass—well, he usually turns up for that, and for Compline, even when he's painting—but he's there at Sext, None, Vespers... A disaster.'

The priest looked at his half-empty bottle of Mexican beer. He was not a great fan of monastic life and when he was at the monastery did not regularly attend the offices that made up the Liturgy of the Hours. If jetlag meant he woke early he might go to Vigils and he did always attend the last office of the day, Compline, but in between the church did not see much of him.

Now he said to the abbot, 'I rather thought that was an essential part of monastic life—attending the offices.'

'Not for Ange-Dominique when he's painting, it isn't. If the Muse is upon him, he has dispensation. Sometimes he paints through the night and rushes in last minute to Vigils reeking of paint and turps. Which is a bit hard to stomach at four in the morning but that's the way of it. For the past week he has been at every office. Early. It's a nightmare. The other evening I was just about to start Vespers and he hadn't arrived. You can't begin to imagine the sense of relief I felt—that we all felt, because everybody is well aware of the financial implications. If BAD isn't painting, things are not good. Then he rushed into church. I could have wept.'

The priest chuckled silently, grateful that they were talking on the telephone and not in person. The abbot needed to get this off his chest so the priest let him talk on. On one of his rare appearances at the first office of the day, he recalled seeing Ange-Dominique hurrying in last minute, folding back the long wide sleeves and adjusting the hood of the dark grey cowl the monks donned for the offices. He knew what the abbot meant about the turps.

'Mannie emails me daily. "Is the Dufy ready?" "Has he started the Manet?" "How far has he got with the *Agnus Dei?*" "I have a client for a Van Gogh." It's getting to the stage that I dread checking my emails. The boiler's on the blink again, we're half way through converting that barn into more accommodation, and creating another separate kitchen for the Muslims in the small cloister—why can't they all eat the same food? It would make life so much easier—and Ange-Dominique is not painting. It's a disaster.'

The priest did not think he had ever heard the abbot so worried. 'Giacomo, pour yourself a whisky, it's not the first time this has happened, and it won't be the last.' The abbot, who was already on his second dram, said, 'Unless this time the Muse has deserted him for good . . .'

CHAPTER 9

Maddalena and the priest would have gone to the monastery together but he was off again on his travels. She was too impatient to await his return. She wanted to meet the members of the Communità dello Spirito Santo as soon as possible.

The priest had explained that the abbot needed someone to meet visitors at airports and railway stations—those who had not made their own arrangements— and drive them up to the monastery.

The abbot knew that she did not have a car but there were always at least a couple of spare ones at the monastery, which had been bequeathed by various villagers in their wills. The priest had occasionally made the challenging journey to the monastery by public transport. Maddalena noted down the travel instructions. Someone would pick her up from her final destination—a bus stop in an isolated village in the middle of nowhere —and drive her up to the monastery, which made the middle of nowhere look busy.

Maddalena got out her map, found the towns and villages the priest had mentioned, and checked train and bus times. Timing was of the essence. There were few trains and only one bus a day, three days a week. On her map, she could see no symbol for the monastery. She bought an ordnance survey map of the area. There was no symbol on that, either.

She telephoned the abbot a couple of days later. A kind, gentle, deep voice, a reassuring voice, answered after a couple of rings. She introduced herself. He said how happy he was that she was prepared to help the community, noted down the date and time of her arrival and said he would send Brother Louis-Marc to collect her from the bus stop.

It was a bright, sunny morning. The air was clear and crisp when she set off with the section on Socrates on her day-long journey up into the hills to the Communità dello Spirito Santo. A main line train, a branch line train and a bus journey took her past olive groves. In a month or so, bright orange nets would be slung underneath branches for the olivade. Now, those thin branches were laden with still olive-green fruit. She passed pine forests, higher up, hillsides were splashed with red, gold and russet larches. Purple wild thyme and lilac Michaelmas daisies grew around pale limestone outcrops. There was snow on far-off peaks.

She travelled through tiny hamlets and villages that seemed deserted if it weren't for the aromatic wood smoke curling up to the heavens from old chimneys. A woman filled her plastic water bottles from a village fountain; an old man wearing a black beret sat on a rickety wooden chair in front of his terraced stone house watching the world go by, except it wasn't.

When the bus trundled into the little village where she would be picked up by the monk it was late afternoon. The sun was low in the sky, there was a distinct chill in the air. She pulled out a blue quilted jacket and long silk and lamb's wool blue scarf from her soft black travelling bag. The bus driver pulled up. She thanked him, said goodbye and climbed down into the deserted little street. There had only ever been a hand-ful of folk on the bus and for quite some time she had been the only remaining passenger.

She sat down on a nearby wooden bench and waited. A church bell chimed five times. A cock crowed. A couple of young men —tanned faces and necks, canvas game bags slung over their shoulders—walked by carrying fishing rods. 'Bonjour!' they said. She smiled and returned the greeting.

A car, small, pale grey in colour, screeched round the corner and came to an abrupt halt throwing up a cloud of dust and autumn leaves. The driver's door opened and out climbed a man around her age, average height, short greying hair, wearing roundish metal rimmed glasses, blue jeans frayed at the bottom and a checked brushed cotton shirt. They walked towards each other, smiling. 'Maddalena,' he said, 'Sorry I'm late.'

'Hello Brother Louis-Marc. Don't worry, I've only just arrived,' she smiled. They shook hands. He took her travel bag.

'I hope you had a safe journey.' Maddalena cocked her head to one side. The voice sounded vaguely familiar.

'Yes, thank you, Brother, a lovely journey.'

They got into the car and he started up the engine.

Maddalena looked at her watch. 'I think we're going to miss Vespers. Sorry.'

'Oh, not to worry. It won't be the first time,' he laughed, 'and it won't be the last.' Where had she heard that voice? She wanted him to speak more so she could try to place it.

'I'm so looking forward to my few days with you.'

'We are very grateful for your help, Maddalena.' So he knew why she had come. His shirt pocket started thrumming. He pulled out a middle of the range smartphone. 'Bonjour, Père Abbé. Yes, she's here,' he said, bestowing a beatific smile on Maddalena. He listened then said, 'OK. We didn't give them anything for the woodcock. Could you have a look in the book for me—and ring me back if there's anything else written down? Thanks. See you later.' As he terminated the call he said, 'Rabbits.'

'Rabbits?'

'A local farmer has been out shooting and he has some for us. We live in symbiosis with the villagers. We baptise, marry and bury—there hasn't been a parish priest here for as long as I can remember—and they provide us with food, equipment, a helping hand around the monastery when we need it.'

As they bounced along he waved at a pretty dark-haired girl in a wild orchard by the side of the road. She was perched on a ladder picking rosy-blushed apples, similar to her cheeks, and placing them in a wicker basket looped over a sturdy tree branch. Some of the old gnarled trees were covered with mistletoe. Maddalena could make out the small white berries. She wondered if they gathered it for Christmas and hung branches in the monastery refectory, but on reflection thought they probably didn't.

'Espérite, the mayor's daughter. She helps out sometimes at the monastery. She's training to be a hairdresser so she cuts our hair for practice. Those of us who still have some,' he laughed. He seemed to laugh a lot, Brother Louis-Marc. She liked that.

'What a pretty name—unusual, too, does it come from esprit, spirit?'

'Yes. It's an old name from these parts. When her father, the mayor, became an atheist he wanted to change it. But his wife wasn't having it. The mayor started calling her Cassandra. But she's still Espérite to everybody else.'

They arrived at a farm on the outskirts of a hamlet. They both got out—the monk to open up the boot and lay out a jute sack covered with a black plastic one, Maddalena to stretch her legs after the long day spent sitting down. A quacking duck waddled at speed across the courtyard, a cockerel in hot pursuit, followed by the farmer who appeared from the barn carrying a milk churn. He greeted them with a smile and a nod of acknowledgement.

The monk opened the rear passenger door and the farmer placed the churn, sloshing with milk from the evening milking, on the floor. He shook hands with Maddalena and the monk, who did not introduce her.

'We were out shooting early this morning.'

'Yes, I heard you across the valley, from the kitchen garden.' The farmer walked back to the barn and returned with four rabbits, forepaws tied together with string, which he laid out on the black plastic sack in the car boot. From a carton next to the rabbits the monk pulled out a clear glass bottle containing a colourless liquid and a second bottle containing a yellow liquid, both unlabelled and sealed with a screw cap. He handed them to the farmer. 'Thank you so much for the rabbits, Isnard. We'll enjoy them.'

Isnard nodded, disappeared with the two bottles and returned with the monastery mail—the postman left it with someone in the village, on this occasion Isnard—and two dark green bottles, corked and also unlabelled. 'For the marinade.' He was, like the monks, who lived in a contemplative community, a man of few words. Louis-Marc often thought Isnard would have fitted in well at the monastery.

They shook hands, said their farewells, Louis-Marc and Maddalena climbed into the car and, with a final wave to the farmer from each car window, they drove off. Where *had* she heard that voice?

'I'm guessing that one bottle was Brother Aarne's vodka. But the other one?'

'Pastis. The doctor was getting a bit concerned about the effect of the bartering. On the liver. So Aarne started making some pastis,' he laughed, 'which has a marginally lower alcohol content than his vodka.'

'You look after the kitchen garden, Brother?'

'Yes, I'm in charge of the potager, the orchard, the olive grove. We had a really good crop of greengages this year. And mirabelles and quetsch.' She racked her brains and in the depths of her memory she heard cicadas and birdsong and a church bell.

The monk chatted away, turning to look at Maddalena, smiling, driving slowly now that he had picked up both her and the rabbits. She listened to his voice and concentrated as hard as possible trying to remember. Every now and then she thought she was mistaken. Then the monk would say something and the tone, the expression, the timbre of his voice was unmistakeable. She was sure she had heard him on the telephone at SOS Amité. She had listened to so many people over the years that memories of any particular conversation were confused and usually impossible to recall. And there was no reason why she would want to recall them.

Nevertheless snatches of conversation started drifting up from her subconscious. *I have chosen a way of life—a free choice . . .* They eventually turned off onto a narrow unmade up lane, bordered by wild flowers and woodlands of holm oak, where potholes had been filled in with gravel to make the track less tortuous on car suspensions. 'I bet you can't hear yourself think for cicadas in summer,' she said.

'Oh, it's deafening!' he laughed. 'The only thing that shuts them up are the church bells—but not for long.' They rounded a bend and there was the monastery on the right-hand side and, further on, the abbey church, both built in ancient slabs of pale limestone. *I have not married, I have no children . . .*

The lane was a dead end although she could see paths leading off to the left and right beyond the church. *I have no regrets, except that . . .* The monk parked on the left alongside several other cars. She glanced at the number plates. They were local cars, apart from two which both bore the same northern department number, presumably rental cars.

It was autumn. No cicadas, little birdsong. The church bell chimed six. *Sometimes I feel an almost painful emptiness in my life. Just hearing a female voice has lightened my soul . . .*

They got out of the car. The monk carried her bag towards a one storey stone L-shaped building, an old barn by the looks of it. It adjoined the monastery wall and stood a short distance from the arched door leading into the monastery. Maddalena stopped so he stopped too. Now convinced that this was her lonely anonymous caller, she turned towards the monk, gave him a dazzling smile and said, 'I'd love to look around your kitchen garden, Brother Louis-Marc. Would you have time to show me while I'm here?'

The smile on the monk's face widened even further. 'Oh, yes, I'd be very happy to do that, Maddalena. You will find me there'—he indicated with a vague wave of his hand in the direction of the paths up ahead—'in the vegetable garden or the orchard.'

The old barn had been converted into a few small rooms for the occasional lay person who came to the monastery, he explained. Maddalena assumed, correctly as it would turn out, that Saint Benedict's rule about offering shelter to all visitors was not one of the five rules retained by the community's founder. Given that the monastery did not feature on any map, visitors must be as rare as hens' teeth, she thought.

Brother Louis-Marc opened the door at the far end of the building and ushered Maddalena into the room. It had a wooden floor, a crucifix on the wall, a lamp and a bible on the bedside table. A table, with another lamp and her room key, and a chair were placed under the window near a large old-fashioned radiator. He put her bag on the single bed, which had been made up. 'There are more blankets in the wardrobe,' he said, pulling back a floor length curtain to reveal hanging space, shelves to the right, and a couple of blankets on the shelf above. The wooden shutters were still open. She looked out onto a little clearing in the woodland interspersed with wild flowers, which seemed to have forgotten the season, and a carpet of fallen leaves in autumn livery. The lane they had driven up was off to the right. A door led into a tiny shower room. Private bathroom, thought Maddalena, this was luxury.

'Shall I close the shutters?'

'No, thank you. I'll leave them open.'

The monk stood by the door. He seemed reluctant to leave. 'I'll show you where the refectory is. There's not many of us, so we all eat together. The study groups have their own cloister, meeting rooms, kitchens, they're completely independent. We don't see them at all, really. I'll leave you to settle in while I take the rabbits to the kitchen. I'll be back in ten minutes.'

When he returned, he knocked on her door. As she left the room he said, 'The key?'

'Oh, I don't think there's any need to lock my door.'

They walked through the archway into a sheltered and tranquil limestone cloister where a small central fountain was surrounded by a patchwork of herbs—lemon thyme, Maddalena rubbed a sprig between her index finger and thumb, rosemary, mauve flower-headed chives, sage, plus clumps of verbena for tisanes, she presumed. 'I gather most of my herbs out walking,' said the monk. 'There's savory, a couple of bay trees, I've got branches drying in the kitchen, there's wonderfully scented marjoram, masses of wild thyme.'

'I'll help you skin the rabbits. Get them into the marinade. When will you do that? Tomorrow morning?'

'Oh, Maddalena! That would be wonderful! Yes, tomorrow morning. I'll get started after Vigils. It's normally a time for private prayer but preparing our food is a prayer in its way, isn't it?' Maddalena knew the first office of the day was around four in the morning and lasted about an hour. The monk seemed to take it for granted that she would be at it. She was not sure she wanted to be skinning rabbits quite so early in the morning, but having made the offer felt she could not now retract it.

As they walked along the first side of the cloister, the monk pointed out the abbot's office, the kitchen and in the first corner the stone steps which lead up to the first floor where the monks had their rooms, which she knew from other monasteries they referred to as cells. Along the second side of the cloister they came to a room marked 'Refectory.' He opened the door to reveal three rectangular wooden tables forming three sides of a square. Each table was laid out for supper with place settings only on the outer length of the tables. Maddalena presumed that having nobody sitting right opposite you made it easier to keep the silence.

'That goes through to the kitchen,' he said, indicating an adjoining door. 'Breakfast is self-service, between Vigils and Lauds.' He stopped suddenly and turned to look at Maddalena. 'The rabbits. We'll skin them after Lauds.' That would be around eight o'clockwas a relief, thought Maddalena.

The far windows of the refectory looked out onto another cloister. Brother Louis-Marc followed her gaze. 'That's the study groups' cloister. They sleep upstairs. We're restoring old buildings in the monastery gardens to provide more accommodation. Their meeting rooms and library are ground floor cells which we've converted. There's another smaller cloister the other side where we're creating the kitchens. Different dietary requirements, food preparation, you know, kosher, halal, the Buddhists, the Sikhs.'

'Do you have any groups here now?' As if on cue, as they continued gazing out onto the cloister, a flash of saffron flitted between columns, a colourful contrast against garden green cloister foliage and the whiter shade of pale limestone.

'Of course they used to be interconnecting, the cloisters, but as things started expanding we decided to close off theirs. That wrought iron gate over there is locked. So we have our privacy. And they have theirs. When they arrive, they come in the main entrance to meet the abbot—and again at the end of the session to say goodbye. If there are any problems, you know, housekeeping, maintenance, that sort of thing, someone will telephone the abbot who sends over Matteo or Gianni.'

For a member of a contemplative order, thought Maddalena, Brother Louis-Marc was remarkably chatty. Or maybe it was precisely because he spent most of his days not talking. They left the refectory and continued walking round the cloister. The room next to the refectory was the chapter house where they met once a day to discuss monastic matters, he explained. They walked past the corner wrought iron gate leading into the visitors' cloister. Their library was located along the third side of the cloister, which backed onto the monastery gardens which she would see later, the monk told her. The fourth side was downstairs cells—and they were back at the main entrance.

She was to meet the abbot outside his office after Vespers which would be over in ten minutes, he said, looking at his watch. Maddalena said she would go back to her room to unpack. Brother Louis-Marc walked back with her. He stopped outside her room and just stood there smiling at her.

'Thank you so much, Brother Louis-Marc. I'll see you later.' He continued standing there, smiling, then he turned and walked back to the car for the mail Isnard had given him. If he hadn't been a monk in a monastery, he would have been whistling.

He started flicking through the handful of envelopes extracting letters not addressed to the abbot. This was yet another of the many rules of St Benedict that had fallen by the monastic wayside. The abbot had long since ceased reading the incoming mail to his monks and, frankly, had also got fed up licking down the envelopes of their outgoing mail. Among the letters for the abbot Louis-Marc noticed one postmarked Rome.

Louis-Marc was a gentle and holy man who loved God. The Holy Spirit had wafted into his life some thirty years ago when he was between girlfriends. He had been ordained, but soon realised that parish life was not for him. He assumed it was thanks to the same Holy Spirit that he had come across a rare mention of Amadeo of Marebosco and the Communità dello Spirito Santo. With great difficulty he tracked down the monastery, arrived one blisteringly—even too hot for the cicadas—August day, and never left.

He loved working outdoors—in his kitchen garden, looking after the olive trees, tending his orchards—and he loved discovering what was going on in the outside world through the internet. He was constantly looking up information on the myriad things that interested him.

At one point, in his constant search for outside stimulus, he had joined Facebook and checked religiously each day to see if he had any friends. He eventually ended up with three—a young niece, an old girlfriend, and a friend from the seminary with whom he had lost contact. Then one morning he received a friend request from the abbot.

A great-nephew had emailed the abbot to say that while searching for someone with the same surname he had come across Brother Louis-Marc. He just wanted to tell his great-uncle how fantastic it was that they were all so modern at the monastery.

The abbot, a free spirit if ever there was one, felt Facebook was a freedom too far. Having read the email after Compline he did what he always did when he had a problem to solve, or thought he might be about to have one. He poured himself a single malt whisky, splashed in a drop of spring water, and thought.

Before he retired for the night, having done some online research, he had joined Facebook and sent a friend request to his boundary-pushing monk. When the abbot checked a couple of days later Brother Louis-Marc had closed his Facebook account. That same evening, the abbot closed his—happy to have avoided a face-to-face confrontation. He celebrated this felicitous face-saving solution with a small dram. The Facebook fiasco had, albeit temporarily, curbed Louis-Marc's desire to reach out for contact with the outside world.

Then Maddalena came to the monastery. And he had somebody to talk to. She listened, she asked him questions, she was interested in what he did, she offered to help him in the kitchen, she asked him to show her around his domain—the potager, orchards, olive groves. Just the thought of her company skinning the rabbits filled him with joy. It seemed that the tiny but growing empty gap in his otherwise peaceful and fulfilling existence here was about to be filled.

He had never heard of SOS Amitié.

When the abbot passed the still beaming Louis-Marc in the cloisters his heart sank. Giacomo had been uncomfortable right from the beginning about the involvement of the priest's friend. He loved the young man as a son and his intuition had told him that a good female friend of the priest's was bad news for his monastic community. His intuitions were rarely wrong.

When he saw her waiting for him outside his office, his worst fears were confirmed. Olive skin, dark shining hair, smiling brown eyes, radiating joy as she went to meet him, hand outstretched. He gave an inward groan. This was bad news indeed.

'Benvenuta, Maddalena,' he smiled shaking her hand, and showed her into the room that served as his office. Maddalena thought, *This is how I imagine God looks.* Abbot Giacomo, mid seventies, was tall, his beard and hair—he still had plenty of it—were not grey but white. His smiling blue-grey eyes were accentuated by his habit, a dove grey full-length wide-sleeved linen robe cinched with a dark brown leather belt. Leather-sandaled bare feet and around his neck a wooden cross hung from what looked like a long brown leather shoe string.

He indicated a chair and sat down behind a desk of dark chestnut. The room was simply furnished, wooden crucifix on the wall, an icon of the virgin. On his desk, in a small frame of pale wood, was what looked to Maddalena like a newspaper cutting. It was a quotation from Mahatma Gandhi. *"Mon exigeance pour la vérité m'a enseigné la beauté du compromis."*

The abbot spoke briefly about their work in a gentle melodious tenor voice—he was the mainstay of the polyphonic singing in the abbey church. The Communità dello Spirito Santo appeared to operate on a need-to-know basis. And it appeared that nobody needed to know very much. He asked nothing about her.

It reminded Maddalena of an article she had read in *La Croix*, the French national daily newspaper, in another monastery. The columnist had led a varied life including a spell in the French Foreign Legion where, he had written—as in the navy— you saluted everything that moved and painted the rest white. That did not apply here, of course, but what he wrote further on did, she thought. You never ask a fellow legionnaire questions about his past. If he wants to tell you about it, he does.

Abbot Giacomo confirmed what Brother Louis-Marc had already told her: that the small monastic community did not get involved in the day-to-day running of the interactive study groups. 'We provide the location, accommodation and facilities. And, when needs be, the transport, which is where you come in.'

This required the utmost discretion due to the extremely delicate nature of the community's work, he explained. 'We now have very senior people coming here to get to know each other and to learn about each other's beliefs, together with interested and thoughtful non-believers. In some cases, if their presence here was known, well, I don't mean to sound dramatic, but lives could be in danger.' So no waiting at Arrivals holding up one of those little boards with a name written in capital letters, thought Maddalena, but refrained from saying so out loud.

'Up until now, one of us has driven down to collect people when necessary but none of us likes being away from the monastery. This is our home where we live the traditional simple monastic life of prayer, work, and rest. However, thanks to the ceaseless work of our—' he paused a fraction of a second '—mutual friend the number of gatherings is increasing, which of course is excellent news. And a monk will go when I ask him because I am the abbot and they all know how important our work here is. But they aren't happy about it. And my first duty, above all others, is to my monks.'

A bell chimed to signal the end of the Adoration which took place after Vespers in the abbey church. 'We'll talk again, Maddalena.'

'I hope I'll get to meet the rest of the community while I'm here. Brother Ange-Dominique, Brother Aarne . . .'

'Ah, yes,' smiled the abbot. 'You are with us for a few days, I think. Tomorrow you will have a walk around, get your bearings, you'll find you way to the distillery, to the atelier. And you've met Brother Louis-Marc, of course.'

They parted company. Maddalena returned to her room and was walking back to the refectory as she heard the supper bell ring out. It was being rung by a young fair haired man who blushed crimson as he smiled at her. Maddalena did not notice in the cloister half-light. But the abbot, who had arrived behind her, did. *Wretched woman,* he thought.

In the refectory they each stood by a laid place setting, the abbot said grace, there was a shuffling and scraping of chairs as everyone sat down—the monks in their dove grey habits, and Maddalena. A young girl from the village helped one of the monks bring out dishes in turn from the kitchen and place them at the head of each table—a rather good leek and potato soup, slices of salmon quiche, an apple—and they ate in silence listening to Dinah Washington.

They could have managed without help from the youngsters in the village and surrounding hamlets, and indeed quite often had to at harvest time, when their parents needed them in the fields and orchards. But the abbot paid the young folk for their work in the kitchen and laundry and grounds. It was not much but in these parts work was scarce. The young tended to leave for the larger towns and cities as soon as they could. This was part of the community's contribution to their symbiotic relationship with the villagers.

Maddalena glanced around her as surreptitiously as possible. The priest had told her briefly about the various members of the community. The young bell-ringer was clearly the novice Luca. She decided that the monk with the swarthy complexion and stocky stature, dark grey-flecked hair grazing the neckline of his habit, who kept staring at her, was the Corsican artist, Brother Ange-Dominique.

She had noticed occasionally in other monasteries that— perhaps it was the result of living in a male-only community— the monks appeared to have no understanding that staring at people, particularly women, could be conceived as rude. If they saw something unusual, out of the ordinary, it seemed perfectly natural to them to stare at it.

The four terribly old bearded monks who sat together and kept falling asleep between courses were the monks collectively referred to as the Ancients. Nobody could remember when they had arrived at the monastery. They had just always been there.

In fact, they had joined the Communità dello Spirito Santo when it was still based in Liguria in Italy. The Holy Spirit had breezed into the lives of two of them when they were in their late teens. The other two arrived in their late twenties having had careers, one as a submariner in the navy, the other in teaching. They were now the only remaining members of that original community which had come to France to restore the deserted monastery in its isolated location, much better suited to the nature of their founder's work. They were young and vigorous then and with their now departed brothers had moved heaven and earth to fix roofs, rebuild walls, weed overgrown cloister gardens.

Now, they did not always attend all the offices and had moved down to ground floor cells. The village doctor called in regularly to check on them, and if one of them had not been seen for a while a monk would pop along to his room to check he was still alive.

The fifth elderly monk—but not nearly as old as the Ancients —with the remnants of what looked as if it had been sandy-coloured hair was Brother Séamus. He hailed from the Outer Hebrides. You would think the gentle breeze of the Holy Spirit would be lost amidst the howling Atlantic gales of the Western Isles. But no. One day decades ago, Séamus MacNeil had abandoned his lobster creels and set off from his Catholic island home in search of a southern French monastery that a visiting Irish priest had told him about. It was the first time Séamus had left the island and it had been a great adventure, not least because he did not know the name of the monastery or exactly where it was.

He did remember that it was in a department with the word Alps in its name. Unfortunately he was unaware that three neighbouring departments had the word Alps in their names. When he eventually arrived at Marseille, he set off, taking two trains, for a little town that sounded vaguely familiar to him but was, sadly, not the right town, and was in the wrong department.

Séamus had alighted at a tiny one-track station, long since close down, and made his way to the ramshackle café opposite where he enquired how to get to the monastery. Nobody knew of any monastery in the vicinity. An old man wearing blue denim dungarees and a black beret shuffled over and said that there used to be one up in the hills, nobody ever went there, perhaps that was the place he was looking for. Séamus agreed that it probably was and asked how he could get there. The old man cocked his head and looked at Séamus for a moment, then offered to drive him.

And that was how Séamus had arrived at the Community of the Holy Spirit, with his bagpipes and a bottle of an island single malt whisky in his luggage. He still played the pipes and had also taught young Brother Matteo. He would sometimes play just before Vespers and the other monks had grown to love the strange skirl of the pipes resonating through the early evening air. But they never saw the tears well up in Séamus's eyes because he was dry-eyed again by the time he entered the church.

Every year, for his birthday (and Christmas and Easter), a bottle of single malt would arrive from his Hebridean family and friends. Although only five of St Benedict's rules had been retained by Amadeo and his successors, most of the others remained unwritten rules which were dutifully followed by the community. Séamus would obediently hand over the hooch to the abbot who would dispense drams on high days and holidays and to himself on most days.

Over the years, usually in June, glisteningly fresh wild Scottish west coast salmon would also arrive, complete with sea lice, in large white polystyrene ice-packed boxes. These were always moments of great joy and celebration at the monastery. The first one would be prepared with all the love and attention that was its due, poached gently in a court bouillon and served with a rich deep yellow mayonnaise which Matteo made with day-old eggs from one of the farms; the following arrivals were put in the freezer and enjoyed over the following months.

The abbot, sipping one of the single malts or savouring a mouthful of succulent pale pink salmon, occasionally wondered what he would do when Séamus died and the whisky and salmon, but particularly the whisky, stopped arriving. Perhaps he simply wouldn't tell the family—at least not immediately. It never occurred to him that he might predecease his Scottish monk, which would have resolved the dilemma.

The two young dark-haired men, mid thirties, with designer stubble—presumably they were normally clean shaven but they had been up since before dawn, Maddalena reasoned—were the Italians Matteo and Gianni, in charge of repairs and maintenance. The priest called them the inseparable twins. That meant that the monk she was sitting next to and couldn't really get a good look at must be the distilling Finn, Brother Aarne.

"September in the Rain" came to an end, grace was said, and everyone stood up to take dishes through to the kitchen.

The monks lunched listening to a reading and dined listening to music. To ring the changes in a daily life that didn't have many, the abbot had decided that when a particular novel was finished they would reverse the order and lunch listening to music and dine listening to a reading.

There was no shortage of religious readings and music but their founding free spirit, Amadeo, believed they had a duty to listen to great profane works, too, produced by those of God's children endowed with creative genius. As well as a fair smattering of Ave Marias, Stabat Maters, Requiems, and sung Masses, each monk in turn could choose a piece of music and a novel of their choice, within reason.

For example, although Nabokov's "Lolita" would be out of the question, everybody had thoroughly enjoyed his funny-sad novel about Russian émigré "Pnin". The abbot did not share Gianni's enthusiasm for Queen but Matteo had managed to slip into a playlist of operatic duets Freddie Mercury singing "Barcelona" with Montserrat Cabballé, one of the abbot's favourite sopranos. A felicitous choice which pleased, partially, both parties.

Every now and again Abbot Giacomo also asked his monks to choose music and readings from their own countries. They were all reasonably proficient in each other's languages except that nobody spoke Finnish apart from Aarne. Brother Ange-Dominique occasionally mused that he had had enough time on his hands in his earlier life to learn the language, if he had known he would be spending the rest of his life with a Finn.

They had recently all enjoyed Aarne's choice in English translation of "The Year of the Hare" by Arto Paasilinna. The abbot had felt the choice of a Piedmont dish of hare in wine sauce to accompany one of the lunchtime readings had perhaps been inappropriate. It turned out that the choice had not been deliberate but had simply coincided with the delivery by villagers of part of the bag of a morning's shooting. It had been a truly delicious dish. Matteo had simmered in red wine pieces of young hare for half an hour or so with softened chopped onion, carrots, garlic and celery, plus bay leaves, cloves, cinnamon and seasoning. He had used the livers to thicken the sauce, and had added some Marsala towards the end.

Nobody understood a word of Séamus' readings of the poems of Rabbie Burns. Nevertheless they loved listening to his Western Isles accent which even after all these years had not lost its shushing softness, like the sound of gentle waves breaking on white shell-crushed Hebridean beaches.

Just as the monks told the time by reference to the daily offices—'I'll see you just before Vespers,' 'He's leaving after Lauds,'—so certain events were recalled by the readings. The priest always remembered that his first visit to the monastery was on the night Rodion Raskolnikov was murdering the pawnbroker Alyona Ivanovna, and then her half-sister, with an axe in Ange-Dominique's reading of Dostoyevsky's "Crime and Punishment". During the artist monk's lengthy incarceration in Ajaccio he had become a great fan of Russian literature. Over the years he had regaled the community not only with serious works but also with Gogol's funny tales, short stories, and—a particular favourite with the monks—his novel about his anti-hero Chichikov's search to buy up "Dead Souls".

The first visit to the monastery of Aarne's atheist aunts, an event indelibly imprinted in the abbot's mind, would for him be forever linked to Cervantes, Don Quixote, and Sancho Panza. The evening of their arrival Brother Louis-Marc was reading, in French translation, the chapter in which the man from La Mancha—the Knight of the Sad Countenance—confuses two Benedictine monks with wizards abducting a princess.

And the abbot had just started a reading of Graham Greene's "The Power and the Glory" the day he received the first anonymous letter from Rome.

Abbot Giacomo's idea of pushing out the musical boundaries had not been a success. He had suggested that each of them should also choose, now and again, a more challenging contemporary piece of music. So they struggled through Stockhausen's "Elektronische Musik", tried to make sense of "Four Pieces on a Single Note", a piece for chamber orchestra by Giacinto Scelsi chosen by Brother Gianni, and generally rather liked Aarne's selection, "Laterna Magica", a sort of dream-like orchestral piece composed by a compatriot, Kaija Saariaho, and based on Ingmar Bergman's autobiography.

Then one lunch time the novice Luca put on, with a certain sense of pride in his innovative choice, the three movements of John Cage's 4'33" for piano. During the meal murderous looks were directed towards the novice. The abbot had taken him aside later to gently explain that while he appreciated Luca's diligence in searching out boundary-breaking pieces of music, given that theirs was a contemplative order where verbal communication was kept to the strict minimum, this had perhaps not been a judicious choice.

Things finally came to a head over another of the novice's selections. One evening—the priest happened to be at the monastery that night and still cried when he thought about it—Luca, who during his earlier research had retained John Cage's comment that "Everything we do is music," hunted down a symphonic poem for orchestra by the American composer Alan Hovhaness, "And God Created Great Whales." Not only was he thrilled with the title—a quotation from Genesis—but the piece also featured recordings of songs by bowhead and humpback whales. It had actually been rather soothing, they all agreed afterwards.

During the meal, one of the Ancients suddenly woke up, and, upon sensing the sonar-sounding song of the humpbacks, cried out, 'Dive! Dive! Dive!' This woke the other three Ancients from their slumbers with a start. They looked in confusion and not a little panic at their fellow brother shouting out what to their impaired hearing sounded like 'Die! Die! Die!' Luca looked as if he rather wished he could do both.

The abbot, who had forgotten he had an Ancient submariner in the community, put his elbows on the table, his head in his hands and closed his eyes. Everybody else froze—soup spoons, pieces of bread, glasses of water, half way to gaping mouths—staring at the Ancient who was staring back at them with a wild look in his eye. And so it came to pass that the song of the whale was the swan song of the community's foray into the world of contemporary music.

Between supper and Compline was chapter so now, while Maddalena went for an evening stroll, the monks left the refectory and made their way around the cloister to the chapter room. Here they would normally listen and meditate on a rule of St Benedict but given the community had only retained five of them, if they started the cycle on a Sunday, say, by Thursday they had finished and were ready to start over. Instead, the abbot just made any necessary announcements, and dealt with any issues that needed dealing with. It was at the previous evening's chapter that he had announced Maddalena's imminent arrival. He had explained that she was a friend of the priest, and the purpose of her visit, and had asked Brother Louis-Marc to collect her from the village.

It was the last Saturday in October. The monks took their seats and waited for what they knew was coming. The novice Luca shifted in his seat looking very uncomfortable, as well he might, thought the abbot. 'Tonight,' he said, looking straight at Luca, 'the clocks go back. When we turn out the light tonight, we will all turn BACK our watches ONE hour. We will do this only ONCE. And we will all have an extra hour's sleep—unlike last year.' Everybody tried, with varying degrees of success, to keep a straight face although those that had suffered sleep deprivation the previous year had been far from happy at the time.

If a bell had to be rung in the monastery, Luca the novice was in charge of ringing it. The first bell to clang out was reveille at 03:55. The previous autumn Luca had got himself into a terrible pickle—the abbot blamed the presence of Espérite who had spent the afternoon in the monastery orchard helping him pick apples. Luca rang reveille all right but unfortunately the bell started clanging through the cold night air at 02:30.

Most of the monks were heavy sleepers who relied on alarm clocks to get up so they had slumbered on in the arms of

Morpheus; others who relied on the bell to get up, which unfortunately for Luca included the abbot, had got up, and stumbled bleary-eyed to the abbey church. 'Luca, are you sure this is the right time?' yawned the abbot, 'we're supposed to have an extra hour's sleep.' Luca pulled out from his deep pocket a small mobile phone he never used but always carried with him, and then retrieved his small old-fashioned alarm clock. He showed it to the abbot. It had a cracked face and no battery.

In silence, the abbot marched the novice outside and they both looked up at the bell tower clock which Matteo had turned back an hour the previous evening. The dark cloud that had been obscuring the moon moved on. The time was now 02:45. They returned to the church where Aarne, Matteo and Séamus were sitting in the choir fast asleep. The abbot woke them up. Luca opened his mouth to try to explain. 'Don't say anything, Luca,' said the abbot. He instructed Aarne to ring reveille at the correct time and they all went back to bed.

Much later that morning, Aarne and Matteo had frogmarched Luca, in gentle monastic fashion, to the distillery. Brother Séamus arrived a few minutes later. They sat themselves down on the bench, chairs and stools at the end of the building where cases of vodka were stacked up awaiting despatch. 'We are just curious,' said Aarne. 'In your own words, what exactly happened?'

'Well, after Compline I went to my cell and knelt down for private prayer...'

'We're not interested in the praying, Luca, we want to know about the alarm clock,' said Brother Séamus.

'I think we are interested in the praying,' said Aarne rather sharply, glaring at Séamus. Aarne was Novice Master and although he only had one—but hope springs eternal—he took his job very seriously.

'Well, yes, of course we are interested in praying, it's a very important part of our lives,' said Séamus quickly, 'in fact the most important, I'd say. Yes, praying, private prayer. Essential. What I meant was, could you just talk us through...'

Luca started talking. He explained that he had decided to turn his alarm clock back an hour during the afternoon so he wouldn't forget to do it later. Then after his private prayer—Aarne nodded encouragingly at this point—he had been gnawed with doubts and thought he had meant to do it earlier but hadn't in fact done it so before he turned out his light at nine o'clock he turned it back an hour again. Matteo who was sitting at the table with paper and pencil crossed out -1 and wrote down -2.

'And what about the alarm, Luca? What time did you set the alarm for?' asked Aarne.

Luca seemed not to have heard the question and continued, 'I sat on my bed and I started to panic—you know how I do sometimes—had I turned it back one hour or two? There didn't seem any point in setting the alarm if I hadn't got the actual time right. I was very tired so I decided I would sleep for a bit then go downstairs and look at the bell tower clock because I knew you had already turned it back,' he said, looking at Matteo who was nodding and replied, 'Good idea, Luca. Mind you, it was a cloudy night, I'm not sure . . .'

Luca, unused to but rather enjoying all this attention, carried on talking, 'My alarm clock showed 19:00 so I set the alarm for midnight. When it went off I got up and set off for the bell tower. When I got to the cloister I saw lights under the Ancients' doors so I thought I'd ask one of them instead.'

'O, Cristo!' muttered Matteo, knowing that the Ancients often fell asleep with their lights on, and inadvertently reverting to the blasphemous language of his pre-monastic youth at the thought of Luca waking up an Ancient—irascible at the best of times—in the middle of the night to ask the time. Aarne gave Matteo a murderous glance.

'I put on my dressing gown and sandals and went downstairs, but when I tapped on the first door there was no answer, so I went in and he was fast asleep. So I just stood by his bed and hoped he would wake up. You know, like you do, if you know someone is there watching you . . .'

The other monks remained silent imagining the picture of what would happen if the Ancient did indeed wake up and found young Luca just, well, standing there looking down at him. It did not bear thinking about—and yet it had to be thought about because it seemed highly probable that it had come to pass.

The distillery telephone broke the silence. Aarne answered. It was the abbot. 'I can't get hold of Matteo. Is he with you?'

'Yes, he is, Père Abbé. We're with Luca. We'd just like to understand what happened this morning.'

'So would I. I'll be right over.'

Luca should by now have finished his period of discernment and either be making his final profession or leaving the monastery. He gave no indication to Brother Aarne of doing either. But they were such a small community and, although Luca often drove the abbot to distraction, he was, usually, a much appreciated extra pair of hands.

The abbot occasionally mused that he might one day end up marrying Luca and Espérite in the village church. As well as the purveyance of game, another element of the community's symbiotic relationship with the villagers had been the decision, as soon as they had arrived here, to ensure the celebration of Sunday mass in the small Romanesque village church where there had been no parish priest for as long as anyone could remember. The abbot also celebrated the other sacraments which were an integral part of village life for both believers and non-believers. It always saddened him that baptisms outnumbered weddings. Both were outnumbered by funerals.

They could have used the abbey church, of course, but then the village one, which had been the focal point for the village and outlying hamlets for centuries, would have fallen into disrepair. So the ordained monks—the abbot, Louis-Marc, Aarne, and Matteo—took it in turns to celebrate mass in the village church on Sundays and high days and holidays.

The priest, when he was there, sometimes walked down to the village on a weekday, ringing the church bell to announce that he was about to celebrate mass. Those villagers who could—more out of courtesy to the priest who had made the effort, and for the aperitif afterwards than a deep-seated faith —downed tools and made their way to the church. Tractors would trundle into the small main square and farmers in muddy wellington boots would march into the church. Even the atheist mayor would leave whatever he was doing on his farm when he heard the weekday bells.

Now, the abbot yawned, left his office, walked round the cloister and through the door into the monastery garden to hear what young Luca had to say for himself. He could see smoke curling up into the crisp morning air from Ange-Dominique's atelier. The autumnal odour of the wood-burning stove pervaded the garden. He was very tired.

As he entered the distillery, Matteo jumped up to offer him a chair but the abbot waved his hand in refusal and perched himself on a nearby pallet of vodka. Before he sat down he glanced briefly at the address label on one of the cases and did a double take. The order, which he was pleased to see included a few cases of cloudberry, was destined for Abu Dhabi. He looked across at Aarne and raised his eyebrows. Aarne gave a little shrug. Yet another example of the mysterious ways in which God moves, thought the abbot, settling himself on top of the order.

'So Luca, figlio mio, talk us through it,' he said.

'Well, Padre Abate, after Compline I went to my room and knelt down for private prayer.'

'We're not interested in your private prayer, Luca, we want to know why you were ringing the bell at half past two in the morning.'

There was a terrible silence. Aarne coughed and looked down at his finger nails. Matteo and Séamus fidgeted and shifted in their seats. The abbot looked around at his monks, his brow furrowed. 'What is it?' Then he realised what he had said.

'What I mean, of course, Luca, is that private prayer is an essential part of monastic life. We're monks. That's what we do. We pray. A lot. However, right at the moment, what we are interested in is why instead of everyone gaining an extra hour in bed SOME of us were woken over two hours earlier than normal. That's what I mean, Luca.'

Brother Aarne picked up the tale and brought the abbot up to date with the story. 'He saw lights under the Ancients' doors, thought they were awake and decided to ask one of them what the time was.'

'O, Dio,' said the abbot. Aarne's jaw muscles tightened, the other two monks shifted in their seats again and avoided looking at Luca, the abbot, and each other.

'But he was fast asleep so I just stood by his bed. He seems to use his prie-dieu as a clothes horse, Padre Abate—his robe, belt, dressing gown were all hanging over it. Anyway, suddenly he woke up and let out a terrific scream. I'm surprised none of you heard it. "Luca! Cosa c'è? What are you doing in my cell? Have you any idea what time it is?" he yelled. Well, of course I didn't, that's why I was there. I tried to explain and showed him my alarm clock. He grabbed it out of my hand and hurled it against the wall. I went to pick it up and the back piece had sprung open, the battery had fallen out and I couldn't find it. "Fuori, fuori, fuori! Get out, get out, get out!" he yelled. So I did.' The abbot closed his eyes and had a great deal of difficulty reopening them.

Luca had been genuinely upset by the Ancient's outburst. He was fond of the old men and once a week, sometimes helped by Gianni, he gently combed through and cleaned their beards which were of biblical bushiness. It was like a trip down a culinary memory lane as they recalled all the meals they had eaten that week.

'Ah, here's some of Gianni's penne, that was delicious wasn't it? With the tuna and olive sauce—look, here's a piece of tuna and . . . yes, half an olive. Now, what's this? Oh, that's the apple compote Matteo made. And that looks like—did Séamus make you some porridge this week? This piece here is well chewed, isn't it? I'm not sure what this is. Let me think, it could be a piece of the guinea hen Louis-Marc cooked. He said I could easily make that—let's see if I can remember. You season the bird, put it on a large piece of foil, bit of lemon juice, olive oil, crushed garlic—oh, here's a piece here—some rosemary and sage and—' He stopped searching for food and searched instead for the missing ingredient, 'bay leaves, that's it. Then you just wrap it up in the foil and cook it in the oven.'

'How long for?' enquired the Ancient.

'Oh, I don't know, probably for an hour or so, I expect. I think most things are cooked for about an hour or so, aren't they?'

The abbot usually called by when the beard-cleaning took place. He derived a primal pleasure from these grooming sessions which reminded him of an online video he had once seen by mistake. He had been searching for information on the Primate of an Eastern Orthodox Church who was sending a representative to attend a study group, and had come upon a gorilla combing a mate's fur for fleas, or whatever got lodged in gorilla fur. An Englishman dressed in what looked like a safari suit was crouching in the undergrowth giving a whispered account of what was going on. It had been fascinating to watch, far more interesting, the abbot thought, than the Primate, when he eventually found him.

The abbot had also felt the same comforting sense of back to nature on a walk out on the hills one July afternoon.

It was the week that Brother Louis-Marc was reading in the evening "To Kill a Mockingbird". Louis-Marc had loved both the book and the film with Gregory Peck playing Atticus Finch. Very occasionally the abbot chose a film for the monks to watch and, following the reading of the book, Louis-Marc had high hopes that the abbot would agree to show the film version.

The community's venture into film had had a chequered history. The first film the abbot had chosen was a James Bond adventure. It had been a disaster. The "romantic" bits hadn't worried them at all. But all the gadgets and gizmos invented by Q gave the cloistered monks nightmares for weeks.

The next film, chosen by Matteo, was much more successful. With Pier Paolo Pasolini's "Il Vangelo secondo Matteo" they were on much more familiar ground. They had all liked the fact that the cast were not professionals and that Pasolini had included his mother playing the older Mary. The abbot had been surprised that they already knew, before he told them, that Pasolini was a homosexual and had been murdered at Ostia near Rome in 1975.

Brother Louis-Marc chose the third film. He had been a great fan of the French film director Louis Malle and the actor Michel Piccoli. He knew the abbot was a fan of Stéphane Grappelli. He had suggested they watch "Milou en Mai" directed by the first, starring the second, sound track by the third (with a little Mozart and Debussy.) It was a delicious comedy filmed in the Gers in south west France and everybody had enjoyed it. Louis-Marc had remembered the bit about the joint being passed around but didn't worry too much given everyone but the abbot knew about their pot-smoking painter. Sadly, he had forgotten the bit when Milou's niece starts stripping off revealing her breasts, albeit briefly.

The abbot's other back to nature experience was also on the day that Aarne had chosen to play at lunchtime a selection of songs from "Änglanatt" by the Pro Musica Chamber Choir. Aarne particularly liked "Härlig är jorden" and had included it at the beginning, in the middle, and again at the end of his compilation.

True, these were Christmas songs and it was July but they were sung in Swedish so he didn't think anybody else would notice. The only thing that gave it away was the occasional mention of Bethlehem. Aarne didn't think the others would be paying attention but the abbot, of course, was and had glanced at his monk with almost imperceptibly raised eyebrows.

So it was with the pure voices and melody of "Härlig är jorden" ringing round his head that the abbot headed for the hills and encountered four naturist ramblers wearing nothing but rucksacks, walking boots, sunglasses and sunhats. The naturists had come round a bend in the track to find the abbot, in the dappled shade of a rowan tree, sitting on a large limestone boulder beside a bunch of wild lavender he had picked for the little chapel, and eating a couple of melting squares of 73% dark chocolate with cranberry.

They had scrabbled for their pareos but the abbot had said, 'No, please, my children, not on my account. It is a fine day for rambling unencumbered by clothes.' The two women looked undecided, but upon the abbot's entreaties everybody tucked their pareos back into their rucksack straps. The women's hands however hovered over the material like a gunslinger's hand hovers over his holster.

They stood in the sunshine, the scent of boot-crushed wild thyme perfuming the air, with just the hint of a breeze providing some respite from the summer sun. The abbot had never gone walking in the hills naked but seeing this foursome brought back memories he had thought long buried. He and Livia had often sought out deserted beaches in creeks and inlets, either at weekends or on holidays, where they had lain naked on rocks like lizards basking in the sun then sliding into cool water to lazily swim and embrace.

The abbot gave his head a little shake and returned his attention to the walkers. The hikers explained that they belonged to a Provencal naked rambling association which had been created by a group of naturists.

'We set off fully clothed and then those that want to, start stripping off,' said one of the men.

'The organiser chooses walks that are well off the beaten track, where we are unlikely to meet other hikers,' continued the other man.

'And we always have our pareos to hand if we do,' added the younger of the two women. 'The group walks are on Sundays but today we decided to go off on our own—it's such a lovely day.'

They chatted about flowers and herbs and shrubs they had seen along the isolated hill path the walkers had taken. He was the only person they had met all day. 'Don't you get criss-cross marks on your backs—from the rucksacks?' asked the abbot. (Livia and he would be brown all over by the end of the summer).

'Not really, we took them off for lunch a while back,' said one of the men, 'and now we're heading for the lake over there for a swim.' It wasn't the monastery lake, that was well hidden away, but one of the larger ones up in the hills.

'Ah, mes enfants!' exclaimed the abbot with delight. 'There is nothing, absolutely nothing, that beats swimming naked in a lake. Or in the sea.'

The foursome looked with growing curiosity at this old man with his twinkling grey eyes, white hair and beard and battered straw hat protecting his head from the sun's rays, who called them "children." He carried no rucksack. They knew from their map that there was no hamlet or habitation nearby.

They had already walked fifteen kilometres. They had listened to a skylark, heard the occasional chirp of small invisible heath land birds, they had walked past a couple of bories, those ancient dry stone huts which provided shepherds with seasonal shelter in days gone by, but they had seen no sign of human life.

If this old man was a shepherd, where was his flock? They had seen no sheep. Or goats or cows, for that matter, although the younger woman, who had studied animal droppings as a child, had pointed out to her companions that wild boar had passed this way. The old man appeared to have been spirited here from nowhere. The hikers could not know that there was a tiny track nearby that meandered down to the monastery. It was overgrown and completely invisible to walkers unless you knew it was there. A large gorse bush and a small limestone boulder marked the spot. In his early days as a young monk at the monastery he had got hopelessly lost up in the hills and they had had to send out a search party.

The ramblers had each noted what looked like a dark brown shoestring hanging around the old man's scraggy neck. He had tucked whatever was on the end of it between the buttons of his short-sleeved blue denim shirt. The older woman momentarily mused that it might be one of those emergency bright red call buttons that she had got for her elderly and fragile mother. She was supposed to press it in an emergency but when the emergencies arrived—as they did with increasing frequency—her mother always forgot to do so because she forgot she was wearing it.

She looked at this old man who every now and then gazed off into the distance, like her mother used to do, a gentle smile playing around his lips as his attention wandered away into another world, his world. A ridiculous thought, given their location, entered her head. She wondered whether he had made a bid for freedom and bolted from a home for the bewildered.

'Et vous, Monsieur, you are . . .?' said the woman, indicating with a general gesture the surrounding landscape and leaving the unfinished question hanging in the air just as the mid-afternoon July heat hung heavy around them at what now seemed the hottest part of the day.

'Me? Oh, I'm an abbot,' said the abbot, fishing out from inside his shirt his wooden cross.

The effect of this response on the naked ramblers was electric. Pareos were whipped out and wound round bodies quicker than a magician conjures a white rabbit out of his hat. The abbot was most distressed and remonstrated with them but to no avail. The pareos remained in situ.

'Well,' said the abbot, sensing it was time to move on, 'it has been a pleasure talking to you. Enjoy your swim. And may God bless you, mes enfants.' They bid each other farewell. The nonplussed naturists stood staring after the abbot as he turned and ambled away. Then, shaking their heads and smiling to themselves they removed their pareos and set off towards the lake further up in the hills. The abbot paused in his tracks, turned and watched the four brown bottoms walking away. Then, thrilled with what had been a most unexpected but delightful encounter, he headed back with his wild lavender to the monastery.

The abbot's mind had wandered. He now turned his attention back to Luca and the irate Ancient. 'But before I left I wanted to turn off his bedside light,' Luca was explaining, 'so I walked back to his bed. He was sitting up, clenching and shaking his fists in a rage like an angry child. Then he suddenly calmed down and lay back down again. So I covered him up, turned off the light and made for the door.'

As Luca had opened the door, he turned around to check again on the Ancient, backed out of the cell, quietly closing the door —and bumped straight into another Ancient against whose wall Luca's alarm clock had been hurled.

'He was just standing there, Padre Abate. I let out a shriek he gave me such a fright. He just stared at me and then he said, "Let he who be without sin not live in a greenhouse" and went back to his cell. I don't think that's quite right, is it, Padre Abate?'

The abbot opened his eyes and said, 'Aren't we supposed to be in church?' Everyone looked at their wrist watches except Luca who saw no need to have one. The church clock automatically struck the hours, the quarters, halves and three quarters, except during the night when the timing mechanism kicked in to turn off the chiming.

The bell for mass, however, should have been rung ten minutes ago but Luca was in the distillery. 'You can never turn a bad day into a good one, my grandma used to say,' said the abbot. 'Go and ring the bell, Luca. Scappa! Scappa!' Luca, slightly taken aback by what the abbot had said because he seemed so old that Luca couldn't imagine him having a mother far less a grand-mother, scarpered. By the time the others arrived, the bell rope was being pulled with more vigour and for longer than usual, as if the novice thought that that might make up for it being rung late.

That was last year. Now in the chapter room, the day of Mad-dalena's arrival, the abbot looked long and hard at Luca and, now that this particular chapter was closed, the monks filed out and made their way round the cloister and into the abbey church for the last office of the day.

Maddalena was already sitting in a front pew, copies of the Liturgy of the Hours and Psalms open at the right pages. She sat in the half-light, waiting. She loved Compline. The monks filed silently into the choir and took their places in the carved wooden stalls which faced each other below the altar. They removed their copies of the Liturgy of the Hours from the shelves in front of them and placed them on the slanted top. The abbot, in his stall facing the altar, lifted up the thin piece of wood attached to the left of his shelf and tapped it against the pew to signal the start of the office.

At the conclusion of the office, the few lights that were on were extinguished leaving only a spotlight on the tall statue of the Virgin sculpted out of a piece of linden wood standing in a niche to the left of the altar. The monks started singing the "Salve Regina", the haunting more complicated of the two modes. For a second, she hesitated—they were so few in number, her contralto voice would stand out—then joined in.

The abbot now stood at the foot of the altar holding a branch of boxwood with Luca at his side holding a dish of holy water. Dipping the boxwood into the water, he blessed his monks as they bowed their heads in front of him and filed out of the church through the door leading directly back into their cloister. Then he and Luca walked over to Maddalena. The abbot blessed her, Luca blushed, and everybody went to bed. It had taken twenty minutes from start to finish.

By nine most lights around the cloister were out; half an hour later the only light came from twinkling stars. Maddalena walked along a path in the moonlight, breathing in the cold night air, returned to her room, set the alarm on her phone for 03:50, and fell into a deep sleep.

CHAPTER 10

Luca rang the bell at the right time. Maddalena made her way under the stars to the church. An hour later she was sipping black coffee from a bowl and eating slices of baguette spread with butter and quince jam. Instead of going for a walk she went back to bed and slept again until the bell rang for Lauds.

Afterwards, when she arrived in the kitchen, Brother Louis-Marc was already there. He smiled, offered her an apron and they went outside into a small walled area where the two pairs of rabbits were hanging from nails in the wall. It had been many years since Maddalena had skinned a rabbit but she thought it was probably like riding a bicycle—once you knew how to do it, you never forgot. The monk handed her another small sharp kitchen knife and they silently set to work in the morning sunshine, making incisions to cut the fur in the right places allowing them to then simply pull off the skin. She found she enjoyed working in this companionable silence. Now and again, he would turn to smile at her and she would smile back.

They rinsed their hands under the garden tap, took the carcasses inside, and set about jointing them, putting the pieces into a large oval cast iron dish that sat ready on the work table. Louis-Marc uncorked the two bottles of local red wine farmer Isnard had given them and poured in enough to cover the pieces of rabbit. Maddalena snapped off a few bay leaves from the string-tied bunch hanging from a nail and put them into the marinade. She found the peppercorns, crushed a dozen or so with the back of a wide and heavy kitchen knife and added them. She followed Louis-Marc back outside and watched him cut sprigs of thyme. He rubbed one between his fingers and as he gave her the herb their fingers touched briefly. The aromatic scent brought back memories of many hillside walks, of wild purple-flowered mountain thyme releasing its heady scent as it was crushed under her boots.

Back inside he pointed to the large upright fridge. She opened it and took from the door a glass jar of flat-leaf parsley. He extracted a few sprigs and added them, too, to the marinade. Maddalena found coarse sea salt and scattered some into the oval dish.

She was reminded of a line from one of the Gospels something about us being the salt of the earth. In Matthew, or perhaps it was Mark, or it might have been Luke. Maybe it came up in all four Gospels. In any case it seemed to have been taken to heart here. There was a tub of wet coarse grey sea salt from Guérande on the Atlantic coast; there was fine sea salt, fleur de sel, from Noirmoutier in the Vendée to the south; more fleur de sel from the southern salt marshes of Aigues-Mortes in the Camargue; and crystals of rose-coloured salt from the Himalayas, perhaps donated to the monastery kitchen by visiting Tibetan Buddhists, she mused.

Standing next to each other, they both pushed down the herbs with their hands and gently mixed them into the wine.

Chalked up on a blackboard on the wall were the menus for the coming seven days and on a second one, tasks for the day. She saw that the rabbits, which had arrived unexpectedly, were now scheduled for Tuesday lunch. As Louis-Marc put the lid on the oval dish and carried it into the walk-in larder, the bell started ringing for mass.

They tidied up, wiped down surfaces, washed hands and parted company. Smiles they had exchanged, eyes had sparkled, but not a word had passed their lips. Shortly after mass—where she was surprised and delighted to see that the communion wine was a deep rich red—everyone was back in church for Sext, which was followed shortly after by lunch listening to a reading of "Pride and Prejudice".

The abbot had decided to have Jane Austen's novel read at lunchtime to avoid a repetition of what had happened with Charlotte Brontë a couple of years back. Gianni had been reading "Jane Eyre" in the evening. He had got almost to the end when Jane returns to Thornfield to find it an abandoned and blackened ruin, and learns that Rochester was injured in the fire.

The community had finished their fruit, nobody made a move to clear the plates, Gianni who should have stopped reading at the end of that chapter, started the next one and read on to the end, uninterrupted by the abbot who had read the novel decades ago but wanted to hear the happy ending again, too. By the time they had cleared up they were running so late that the abbot skipped their own chapter and they had all gone straight to church for Compline.

All that first morning, every time Maddalena looked up—from her mass book, from her psalms, from her lunch—she would meet the dark brown eyes of Brother Ange-Dominique staring at her. Initially she had given him a gentle smile and looked away; now under his continuous gaze she felt the colour starting to rise in her cheeks.

The monks in general—with, it had to be said, considerable exceptions—behaved in a suitably monk-like fashion with eyes usually downcast. They entered and left the church eyes downcast; they ate with eyes downcast; they walked around the monastery eyes downcast—yet very little escaped their notice. They had acquired over the decades the ability to take in a huge amount of visual information each time they did raise their eyes. Rather like the children's party game when you had thirty seconds to memorise twenty objects on a tray before it was removed.

So everybody was aware from the first moment he stared at her that Maddalena had caught Ange-Dominique's imagination. They held their collective breath. Was this the manna from heaven they had been praying for? Was this woman, the priest's friend, going to lead their fellow monk, their main breadwinner, out of the artistic desert?

He had had models before but it had always ended badly. Espérite, the mayor's daughter, had sat for him. So had Isnard's daughter, Jaumette. And Honorade, the doctor's daughter. And their female cousins, mothers and aunts. But it had always ended in disaster. None of them could sit still for more than five minutes, said Ange-Dominique. They got cramp, they couldn't stop chatting to him while he tried to paint. He felt he couldn't smoke a joint. They simply just didn't inspire him. So he had painted from his imagination. And he had painted beautiful things.

Now Ange-Dominique wasn't painting anything and unfinished canvases were stacked up around the atelier. Not only had the lamb for de Zurbarán's *Agnus Dei* been taken back to Isnard's farm, it had probably been butchered and eaten by now. Mannie Morgenstern was frantically emailing the abbot who had put all building projects on hold.

On Sunday afternoons, after lunch and siestas, the monks spent a fraternal hour or so together talking before Vespers. After lunch Maddalena spent an hour with the empiricists Locke, Berkeley, and Hume then left her room to visit the monastery garden. She let herself in through the gate opposite the cemetery and wandered past various shrubs and dark glossy-green leaved orange trees. As she approached Brother Ange-Dominique's atelier she saw that the door was open. The monk, his smock covering old jeans and a pale grey sweater, was standing at his easel. On a large sheet of paper clipped to his easel he had drawn a dramatic charcoal outline sketch of Maddalena, draped in the Virgin's hooded cloak with strands of dark hair falling across her brow, rosary in hand.

He turned round, saw her, and smiled. He indicated a solid wooden chair with a cushion on the seat. Maddalena walked slowly into the atelier, sat down, found a comfortable position, looked around her, found something to settle her gaze on, and, lost in her thoughts, remained immobile. It was only much later that she noticed the framed poem hanging from a nail on the wall:

Seul est Mien
by Marc Chagall

Mine alone
Is the country in my soul
I enter there without a passport
As if it is my home.
It sees my sadness
And my solitude
It lulls me to sleep
And covers me with a heavy perfume.

For the next few hours, with sure, rapid strokes the monk sketched, filling sheet after sheet. 'OK,' he said, and she would change position, turning her head in a different direction, re-arranging her legs, her arms, into a new but still natural position, again settling her eyes on a focal point, and then she would freeze into her new pose. She stood up and rested a hand lightly on the chair back, she sat on the floor on an old rug resting her elbow on the chair seat, she picked up a bible, settled into a reading pose, then at the last minute she raised her eyes and looked straight at the monk.

The bell rang for Vespers. If he heard it he showed no sign. There was a spark in his eyes, a half smile on his lips. As the sun went down he closed the door and lit the word-burning stove. At dusk, he turned on lights. He connected his iPod to his little speaker. Maddalena recognised the emotive polyphonic singing of Corsican voices.

Every now and then he paused to give her a break. He indicated the small shower room at the back of the atelier, just past the single wooden bed, while he wandered out into the garden. He poured them both a glass of cool spring water. He prised open a tin and offered her a dark chocolate biscuit—and started work again. The powerful voices of I Muvrini started singing "A Tè, Corsica". It wasn't her island but it nevertheless sent shivers down her spine.

Charcoal, pencil, Indian ink, acrylics, water colours, oil . . . Full length sketches in broad strokes, sheets filled just with individual details—hands, eyes, a section of wavy hair, a foot.

The bell rang for supper, for chapter, for Compline. The sense of relief in the church when neither Ange-Dominique nor Maddalena turned up for the final office of the day was almost palpable. The other monks, who had arrived as usual in dribs and drabs, cast their eyes surreptitiously towards the cloister door. There was no sign of Ange-Dominique. They cast their eyes surreptitiously towards the main door of the church. There was no sign of Maddalena.

The abbot arrived. Wood tapped against wood. The office of Compline commenced. Everyone expected to see Ange-Dominique rush in last minute with cowl swirling and adjusting his hood. But he did not appear. The little community breathed a collective sigh of relief. The Muse had returned. Her name was Maddalena.

Later, the abbot, who perhaps had not fully realised the stress he had been under, wanted to weep tears of relief. He settled instead in his study for a Speyside single malt.

When Brother Ange-Dominique finally decided it was time to call it a day, it was well into nighttime. Apart from his occasional, 'OK,' they had not spoken. Now he took off his smock which, she noticed, had roundish black marks on the deep pockets, smiled at her and said, 'Merci, Maddalena. I must finish these,' he indicated the unfinished canvases propped up against the studio walls. 'Then we will work together. I have ideas, so many ideas.'

'Frère, on one of my visits to your island, to Corsica, it was many years ago now, I went to the Fesch Museum in Ajaccio.'

'Ah, oui! Cardinal Fesch, Napoleon Bonaparte's uncle. One of my ancestors was a cardinal, you know, Tommaso Maria Zigliara. We produced another cardinal not so long ago—first one in decades—the son of a good friend of my mother's.'

Maddalena, smiling at the thought that this ex-convict was, albeit distantly, related to a red hat, continued, 'Along a ground floor corridor there was an exhibition of works painted by local prisoners. It was part of a programme. They had been allowed to choose a work from the collection and either reproduce it in its entirety or just paint a detail. Some of the paintings were, well, very naive, but there were others that were amazing. I remember saying to the museum warden that some of the prisoners could start new careers as forgers when they got out.'

The monk laughed as he poured out two glasses of red wine from a dark green unlabelled bottle. 'Salute!' With his small folding knife he cut a few slices of dried saucisson which she had noticed earlier on a small wooden board on the table. 'You may well have seen some of my paintings. I signed them with my initials AD. That's how I got started.'

'Bon appettitu, Maddalena.' They sat down at the table and ate and drank. Maddalena realised she was starving. Earlier, in anticipation, Ange-Dominique had removed from the small freezer compartment in his little fridge slices of crusty wholemeal bread which had now defrosted. If he was the main breadwinner at the monastery, the abbot was the main breadmaker.

Ange-Dominique opened up the wood-burning stove and toasted in turn two slices on the end of his toasting fork. He drizzled pale green olive oil (another unlabelled bottle so presumably their own production, thought Maddalena) over the bread. Then he sprinkled over each slice a teaspoonful or so of a mixture taken from a small plastic bag—darkish brown in colour intermingled with small white grains.

'This is delicious. What's the mixture?'

'Zaatar, a mixture of wild thyme, sumac and sesame seeds. Many of our visitors come from the Middle East. They often leave us some of their dried herbs and spices. Someone from Lebanon left this.'

The monk sliced more saucisson, looked around him, got up and came back with a little lidded glass jar of small dark shiny olives and a piece of dried string-wrapped and slightly wood smoke-scented charcuterie. 'Coppa! Delicious. I thought I saw a piece of prisuttu hanging up in the kitchen, too,' said Maddalena.

'Yes, my family sends supplies—we should be getting some figatelli over the winter. I grill them on the barbecue over vine cuttings.'

Maddalena, who was not a great fan of figatellu, a fresh liver, gelatinous fat and offal sausage, but fully recognised the value of using up just about every part of the pig, said, 'Well, you know what they say: "Cu' si marita sta contentu 'nu jornu, cu' ammazza 'u porcu sta contentu n'annu'."' The old saying came from Basilicata —where, like Corsica, there was also a preponderance of pigs—who marries is happy for a day, who kills a pig is happy for a year.

Corsica had spent five hundred years under Genoese rule, preceded by two centuries under Pisan rule. Their language was closely related to Italian so the monk had no trouble understanding the dialect. He threw back his head and roared with laughter.

From a table drawer he pulled out a heavy sharp bladed knife and cut a few thin slices of coppa. Maddalena told him about the first time she had seen them, the Nustrale pigs, driving cross country to Corte. She had suddenly passed huge black and dark grey animals, tiny identification labels in their ears, snuffling along the road side eating acorns and chestnuts. The car in front had pulled over and the occupants had got out to take photos of them.

She told him about her walk from the hillside village of Soccia to Lake Creno, partly covered by water lilies and surrounded by Corsican Laricio pines. While she was picnicking on a flat rock just above the water she had heard snuffling and then watched mesmerised as one large pig followed by two smaller ones clambered down the rocks just a few metres from her.

On another day, she had driven through a little village, rounded a corner and come upon a stone smoke house in the bend, curls of smoke from smouldering chestnut, or perhaps it had been beech wood, spiralling up into a cloudless blue Corsican sky.

Maddalena paused, gazing silently into the distance thinking of another dinner with another Corsican. It was Bastia in November. They had been to an A Filetta concert, the first time she had heard traditional Corsican polyphony. On the Saturday they had visited the mushroom festival in the Place Saint-Nicolas, Bastia's main square, where folk had brought in baskets of fungi from woodland forays for identification. That night they had dined in a restaurant in the citadel. She had thought—for a while—that she could, would, spend the rest of her life with this man. But it was not to be.

'Where are you, Maddalena? Where do you go? I could see earlier that you were far, far away. I'm not complaining, mind, because you don't move a muscle—it's wonderful for me. If you had any idea of the trouble I've had with models in the past.'

She snapped out of her reverie and turned to smile at the monk. 'It's a special place, your island.' He went over to the little fridge and returned with a truly tangy and tasty hard cow's cheese. 'Local,' he said.

She opened her mouth to ask him how he had become a monk, remembered the article about the Foreign Legion, and remained silent.

As if reading her thoughts, Ange-Dominique said, 'Plenty of time to think, in prison.' So he assumed she knew his background, thought Maddalena. 'I'd grown up as a Catholic, of course. It used to amuse me that we would be at loggerheads with certain families—usually for the most ridiculous reasons, a wall built twenty centimetres from where it should have been built, for example, a thoughtless remark made at a family gathering—and they would go back for generations, these disputes. But as soon as someone died, there we all were in church together for the funeral as if we were the best of friends. The following day we weren't talking to each other again.' He stopped talking to eat some more charcuterie with a few olives, putting the small stones on his plate.

'The prison chaplain used to visit regularly, nice man, I liked him. And then there was the painting. That really changed my life—when I realised that I was good. That was quite something.' He took a sip of wine. 'A little voice started nagging, niggling inside my head—perhaps I wouldn't have heard it if I'd been in the noise of the outside world, or if the libeccio had been blowing—then it would disappear, the little voice, and I would carry on preparing my requests for parole, having them turned down, painting, reading, listening to music.'

She wanted to ask what crime he had committed but remained silent, sipping her wine.

He said, 'Our island culture is—well, Corsicans can be hot-blooded, vendettas, I was young but no excuse. I served my time.'

Maddalena, staring into the fire, said, 'I'm Sicilian.'

He smiled. 'Ah. Right.' As he looked at this woman who had suddenly entered his life he felt a profound sense of—of what? Not happiness but rather a profound sense of peace, of tranquillity. He knew why she was at the monastery. He knew he would not see her all the time. He knew he had works in progress that he must finish. But he also knew that from now on he would have plenty of opportunities to draw her, to paint her. At this realisation, an immense sensation of satisfaction filled his soul.

That first evening, he had no way of knowing that what would happen later to the priest would inspire him to create some of his greatest Marian masterpieces. Right now, sitting in his atelier on this late October evening, the Muse had returned and he offered up a silent prayer of thanks to his God.

They rinsed plates and glasses in his little sink, tidied up and walked out into the night. Maddalena said goodnight to the monk and turned to walk towards the door in the wall but Brother Ange-Dominque murmured, 'This way, it's quicker.' He led her through the door into the cloister and walked round it to the monastery entrance on the opposite side. He opened the door, they shook hands.

'Thank you for a delicious supper, Brother Ange-Dominique.' Maddalena delved into her memory for another Corsican phrase from those bygone times. 'Bona notte.'

'Thank you for coming into my life, Maddalena. Bona notte.'

The next day, Monday, was the equivalent to a monastic day off. All offices were held in private apart from Lauds which included mass, and Vespers at the end of the day. The Ancients stayed put; the kitchen was abuzz with chatter as packed lunches were prepared; Gianni and Aarne went fishing in one of the streams higher up that fed their lake; the others went off walking in the hills; and Brother Ange-Dominique—to the continued joy of all, not least the private buyer who had commissioned it—returned to his atelier, his oils, and his virgin Mary painted in the style of Raoul Dufy's "Jeanne dans les fleurs."

Maddalena spent the day reading and thinking. She walked along paths, discovered the kitchen garden, fruit orchards, olive groves. The abbot had told her to make free use of the kitchen so she made herself a sandwich with bread, cheese and slices of ham. She walked down to the village passing the time of day with the various villagers she met. She returned taking a different path which eventually brought her back via the lake. It was a bright sunny crisp and cloudless autumn day.

As she walked, she smiled to herself about the irony of it all. She, with her serious doubts about the necessity of a virgin birth, was now to be, or so it seemed, the Muse for Brother Ange-Dominique's paintings of the virgin. God did indeed move in mysterious ways.

Vespers, supper listening to Jean Sibelius's Symphony No 2, chapter for the monks, Compline and bed for everyone apart from Brother Ange-Dominique who, much to the abbot's relief and celebrated with a small dram, continued to paint into what Brother Séamus would call the wee sma' hours.

CHAPTER 11

Early the following morning the abbot received an unex-pected and, for them, large order for fifty cases of Brother Aarne's vodka. *This*, thought the abbot, *is beginning to seem like Christmas and Easter rolled into one.* Although the Dufy was now coming on in leaps and bounds, the community was not paid for paintings until they had been shipped to Mannie in New York. The vodka, however, was paid for before it left the monastery.

Brother Aarne started labelling up before mass and carried on straight after the lunch of wild rabbit. Louis-Marc had floured and sautéed the pieces then cooked them slowly in some of the wine with shallots, fresh herbs, carrots and celery, and served it with trofie, a short thin twisted Ligurian pasta beloved by the abbot.

During the afternoon, Maddalena knocked and popped her head round the distillery door. Brother Aarne—above average height, fair skin, dark blonde hair, almond-shaped light grey-blue eyes with a hint of turquoise— was busy labelling up the bottles. 'Can I help?' she asked. 'Come in, come in,' replied the monk, stopping his work.

She walked in, looked around, and went over to look at a frame hanging on one of the walls. It contained a quotation in French by the Portuguese poet Fernando Pessoa: "Nous voulons une Europe qui parle d'une seule et même voix; mais dans toutes ses langues, de toutes ses âmes. "

'Died of cirrhosis of the liver,' said the monk.

'Is that why he's here?' she said, glancing around at the still and the bottles.

'No,' he laughed. 'It's what he said about the European Construction—sums it up nicely, doesn't it? We want a Europe which speaks with one and the same voice but in all its languages, with all its souls.'

Maddalena walked over to the old-fashioned hand labelling machine, watched how the monk operated it, and then took over while he started boxing up the bottles already labelled and placing the sealed cases on the pallet. Together they worked in silence, exchanging the occasional smile.

Supper had included a fricassee of fungi—cep, chanterelle, wood hedgehog—gathered on the previous day's walk, cooked gently in butter, garlic and sprinkled with chopped flat leaf parsley. It had been accompanied by accordionist Richard Galliano, a great favourite of Louis-Marc's, playing Bach's No. 1 violin concerto in A minor.

Brother Aarne caught Maddalena's eye. He raised his eyebrows, she nodded discreetly, and they both returned to the distillery. The sooner the order was ready to leave the monastery for onward despatch from the village, the sooner payment would be made.

They worked on silently and by ten o'clock had completed the order. Maddalena was shattered. They walked out into the monastery garden which was bathed in moonlight. 'The Hunter's moon,' said Aarne.

'Why is it called that?'

'It usually rises thirty minutes later on each successive night rather than the usual fifty minutes. The September Harvest moon is the same. So there is less time between sunset and moonrise and therefore longer periods of light at this time of year for hunters and farmers to finish their work.'

Maddalena looked across to Ange-Dominique's atelier. It stood in darkness. Back inside the distillery Aarne produced a couple of small glasses, some small dark black olives, and a bottle of vodka. He plugged his phone into a small speaker and with Django Reinhardt and Stéphane Grappelli playing "Sweet Georgia Brown" quietly in the background, they sat down at the small corner table, and he poured them both a glass.

'Kippis!'

'Kippis!' said Maddalena, imitating his accent.

Brother Aarne downed his vodka in one swallow. Maddalena did the same. He refilled their glasses.

'How did you arrive here, Brother?' She would not have made a very good legionnaire, she thought. He told her that he had been born and brought up in southern Finland in a family of hedging-their-bets agnostics. His father had two sisters who had never married, had no children, consumed astonishing quantities of vodka with no obvious effect on speech or behaviour, were atheists with a capital A, and adored their nephew Aarne.

His life's path had taken a sharp turn one day in Lapland. He had decided to move to the north to stay with a relative after an unfortunate affair with a married woman. It was possibly not the wisest of destinations. He went in November. Daylight was scarce in those parts. It got light about ten and was dark by mid afternoon. 'My alcohol consumption, already heavy, increased,' he continued, replenishing their glasses.

He lived near Lake Inari. One of his sources of income came from taking visitors out to see the Northern Lights, and in daytime onto the frozen lake and through pine forests in a sleigh pulled by a snowmobile. He would kit the tourists out with protective clothing against the considerably sub zero temperatures, wrap them up in reindeer skins in the sleigh, jump on his machine and set off across the snow white lake.

When they reached the forest on the other side he drove them through small snow-covered birch trees to a sheltered spot near a small stream. Here they would stop and he would make them coffee which they would sip listening to complete almost unnerving silence. All the time he was in Lapland he never tired of listening to the silence.

On the day his life changed, he had as usual walked over to the stream, had broken the surface ice and scooped water into an ancient metal container. He gathered twigs made a small fire, boiled up the water, made the coffee and poured it through a sieve into three one-handled birch wood bowls for his two visitors and himself. Oh, it smelled so good, that freshly brewed coffee after the freezing ride across the ice.

The monk refilled their glasses and continued his tale. He sat on reindeer skins with the two visitors. They cupped their hands around the birch mugs, sipped their coffee, and listened to the silence. Nobody spoke. Suddenly Aarne felt an almost imperceptible breath of wind on his cheek. He looked around him, nothing stirred, the dwarf birch trees remained motionless yet the gentle breeze continued to caress his face. He looked over at the couple who sat silently entranced by the winter landscape.

At that moment if Aarne had had to speak he would have been unable to do so. A strange, almost painful sensation seemed to rise up inside him from his very soul, his throat tightened, he thought his head was going to explode. Then just as suddenly the breeze ceased, the sensation inside him subsided. He looked around him. The couple was still mesmerised by this silent world of white. Aarne thought, *Does God exist? I don't know. I have no proof. But I believe he does.*

That afternoon, as he watched a herd of reindeer race across the barely distinguishable snow-packed road, he knew he had to leave Lapland. He didn't know where he was going to go but he would start by going home.

Aarne refilled their glasses. 'I packed my bags the following day and headed back south. I had this terribly strong sensation that there was something missing in my life. I felt I needed to find a place—a silent place like Inari but not Inari—where I could have time to think, to reflect, to work out where my life should be going.'

He loved his aunts as much as they loved him. They had other nephews and nieces but he knew he held a special place in their hearts. He felt comfortable with them. He told them what had happened, that he wanted to find a place where he could spend a quiet time of reflection.

The aunts gave the matter some thought. The elder one, Tuulikki—Tuuli means wind in Finnish, he said—called him a few days later. Although she had calmed down somewhat with the arrival of old age, Tuuli had led what can perhaps best be described as a Bohemian verging on gypsy way of life which had caused her brother, Aarne's father, much grief over the years. Among the extraordinarily disparate collection of contacts she had made over decades of travelling the globe was an Indian Sikh who had befriended a Russian Orthodox priest who had met a senior Islamic philosopher who had been to the Comunità dello Spirito Santo and knew Abbot Giacomo.

'I arrived here and in a comparatively short space of time realised that this contemplative life was the one I was looking for. I left for the seminary and once I had been ordained I returned to the monastery.'

Maddalena did not hear the end of the story. She had laid the side of her head on her folded arms on the table and was fast asleep. Brother Aarne yawned, stretched, and could not resist doing the same.

This was how the abbot found them, together with two empty glasses and an almost empty bottle of vodka (not the more expensive cloudberry, he was relieved to note). The owl had woken him in the night with its single plaintiff high-pitched little hoot, he had got up, looked out of the window, seen the glow of the distillery light and wandered down to investigate.

Wretched woman, he muttered to himself. His dilemma now was what to do. If he covered them both up with a couple of blankets and turned off the light they would know that someone had been in, and they would know that it was him. If he left them, they would no doubt wake up in due course and head off to their beds. He saw that the order had been completed and was sealed up on the pallet. He decided on the latter course.

The following morning the abbot was astonished but pleased to see both Brother Aarne and Maddalena at Vigils. The woman could easily have slept in, and Aarne knew he always had dispensation if he had worked late to prepare an order for despatch.

The monk sought out his abbot immediately after Lauds who listened carefully as Aarne explained that they had completed the order late the previous evening and had then celebrated with a couple of glasses—*a couple of glasses!* thought the abbot—of vodka.

By mid-morning the espresso machine had taken such a hit the abbot had to empty another pack of beans into it. By late morning the van arrived from the village, the distillery doors were opened up and Aarne forklifted the pallet of vodka into the van. By early afternoon the much needed payment was in the monastery bank account. The abbot, on balance, all things considered, was a happy man.

After lunch—pan fried brown trout, following a good Monday catch by the fishermen augmented with a couple of extra fish offered to them by a villager fishing the same stretch, sautéed potatoes and braised chicory—Maddalena who was not feeling at all well had a siesta. In the afternoon she walked down to the village to clear her head. Suddenly, as if the great egg-layer in the sky had raised his baton, a hen started cackling ecstatically, immediately followed by, it seemed, every other hen in the neighbourhood. There was, reflected Maddalena, absolutely nothing like a freshly laid egg. She chatted to villagers she passed; she greeted the young folk coming off the school bus.

When she returned to the monastery she headed down towards the kitchen garden where she found Brother Louis-Marc pottering around among his leeks and onions. His face lit up when he saw her and his eyes sparkled. 'You look a little pale, Maddalena. Are you feeling all right?'

'I'm fine,' she smiled. 'Your mâche looks lovely,' she said, pointing to a raised bed of dark green lamb's lettuce. She opened the thin cotton bag she was carrying to show him the hazel nuts and walnuts she had gathered in the woods on her way back from the village.

He took a couple of walnuts, prised open their partially

split greenish-brown husks and removed the dark moist walnut shells, placing them in Maddalena's cupped hand. He opened each one up with his pocket knife, extracted the kernels, peeled off the papery pale yellow skin, easy to do when they are fresh, handed a whole white kernel to Maddalena and ate the other one. He loved fresh walnuts.

They strolled together past garlic, shallots, broccoli and carrots, cauliflowers, marrows and chicory, small purple-topped turnips, onions, and potatoes. In a sheltered corner, hardy rosemary, thyme and parsley, and a few plants still of coriander.

'And that?' said Maddalena. 'That looks very much like cannabis.'

'Ah. Yes. That's not for us, it's for Ange-Dominique,' he said hastily, as if that made it all right. 'Prison, you know. He was in prison for a long time and acquired the habit. Well, actually, now I come to think about it, I think he must have acquired the habit before he went to prison. I think his first spell behind bars was for dealing. Repeat offence.'

'Does the abbot know?'

'Oh, dear no,' said Brother Louis-Marc.

The abbot was perfectly well aware that his monk was growing cannabis in the herb garden. Indeed, every now and then, he took what he knew to be a really very unchristian-like pleasure —but it was so much fun—in walking over to join Brother Louis-Marc to have a look at what he was growing.

Slowly but surely he would make his way towards the raised bed of herbs relishing the monk's desperate efforts to steer him away from the offending plants. 'Come over here, Père Abbé, I must show you the courgettes, a fantastic crop this year. They're in flower so I thought I'd make some beignets de fleurs de courgettes this week, I know you enjoy that dish.'

The abbot would move away towards the courgettes, then stop and say, 'How's the basilico Genovese coming on?' half turning back towards the herbs. 'Oh, it's doing really well, Père Abbé, just wait till you taste the pesto tomorrow night with the linguine—you'll think you're back home in Liguria.'

And the abbot, happy to know that two of his favourite meals were on the menu, let himself be led away to the bright yellow-flowering courgettes, which were indeed a sight to behold.

Now the bell rang for Vespers. Louis-Marc and Maddalena parted company. She walked to the monastery kitchen and left the bag of walnuts and hazelnuts on the table. Brother Louis-Marc, with a quiet smile, gave himself a little hug, and put his spade and fork back into the potting shed.

That evening, after a soup thick with vegetables pieces and supplemented with white haricot beans, there was a salad of lamb's lettuce dressed with a walnut oil vinaigrette and sprinkled with a handful of fresh white walnut kernels.

On the Thursday morning Maddalena went to the kitchen to see if she could help Brother Louis-Marc and found instead Brother Matteo. She glanced at the blackboard. He was making chicken stock, for a risotto, from a couple of old hen birds, plucked and ready for the pot, which the mayor's wife had delivered earlier that morning.

They smiled at each other. While he broke up the carcases, put them into the large stock pot, covered them in water and started bringing it up to the boil, she grabbed an apron and started peeling a couple of onions, roughly cutting up leeks and carrots, flattening unpeeled cloves of garlic, crushing black peppercorns.

With the exception of study groups, teachers and interpreters, who operated completely independently, there was only the occasional odd visitor at the monastery itself, usually a family member of one of the monks. Some visitors were odder than others.

Brother Matteo had been born and brought up in Genoa the capital of Liguria. He had acquired at birth, through a complicated family history and his parents' strong desire to keep its various family branches together, a Calabrian godfather, who was also an older cousin.

Matteo had not had any contact with his cousin godfather since he had joined the Communità dello Spirito Santo. His cousin had chosen a different path through life and had become a member of the very discreet and very dangerous and most powerful of the three Mezzogiorno mafias, the 'Ndrangheta, also known as La Santissima.

Some time back, Orazio Condello, presumably unfamiliar with the fact that Matteo had to ask permission from the abbot for any visits, had announced his imminent arrival at the monastery, giving barely twenty-four hours notice. Matteo had briefly explained the situation, the abbot had briefly hesitated, gave his permission and Don Orazio, who was not in the habit of asking permission to do anything and so would have come any-way, drove up to the monastery in time for lunch the following morning. He would stay overnight in one of the ground floor rooms reserved for the occasional male visitor and leave the following day.

Brother Matteo, nervous, greeted his godfather with a smile and an outstretched hand which Don Orazio ignored, hugging the monk and kissing him on both cheeks. Matteo had not seen the man standing before him for almost twenty years. As a child he had adored his holidays in the Mezzogiorno with his Calab-rian cousins. The family would drive down from Genoa to Reg-gio di Calabria and head east to the family village of San Luca. They would stay in a big old family house in the Parco Nazion-ale dell'Aspromonte and all summer long the young cousins would run wild. They swam in the Ionian sea and in rivers. He remembered that there was one nearby called the Fiumare Bonamico. In those days they were all good friends. He would return north as brown as a berry desperate for his next carefree holiday in the toe of Italy.

He would not have recognised Orazio—short, dark-skinned, receding hairline, a thin livid scar down his left cheek—if he had passed him in the street. Although his skin was weathered by a life lived under the Calabrian sun, his features were drawn, the eyes seemed sunken, hollow, inexpressibly sad. If eyes are the mirror of the soul, Don Orazio's soul was in torment, he thought.

The two men had walked and talked in the monastery garden, calling in briefly at the atelier and the distillery where Ange-Dominique and Aarne respectively acknowledged Orazio's presence with a smile and a nod. They both knew who he was. The abbot was always interested to see how quickly word got around in what was supposed to be a contemplative community.

They left the garden by the wooden door in the wall near the cemetery. 'What are those black marks on his smock pockets?' said Don Orazio. 'They look like gun shots.'

'No, no,' said Matteo with a nervous little laugh. 'He often puts his joints in the pockets without putting them out properly and only realises when they start smouldering. I'm always worried that one of these days he's going to go up in flames, what with all that turps.'

As they passed the small walled cemetery on the left, on their way down to the lake, Don Orazio walked towards the little cemetery gate and raised the horseshoe metal lever to enter.

'Your work, Matteo?'

'Yes. Gianni made the lever.'

They walked slowly round the cemetery. Don Orazio paused to read the inscriptions on each simple wooden cross, the names and dates of the men who had devoted their lives to God and to the work of the Communità dello Spirito Santo. They sat in silence on the circular bench Matteo and Gianni had built around the old elm tree. The Ancients often came to sit here when the weather was mild and sunny, as if wanting to get used to what would soon be their final resting place.

As they continued along the path towards the lake Matteo asked after cousins, aunts and uncles. He said how sad he had been to read in the papers about Sebastiano's death. His closest cousin, in terms of both age and affection, had been murdered in an internal 'Ndrangheta vendetta. He didn't ask what Don Orazio had been doing since he last saw him.

His godfather asked, politely, after the Genoese family members, but he was much more interested in Matteo's life at the monastery, how he had become a monk, what he had done be-forehand in his life.

'You never wanted to marry, settle down, have a family?'

Matteo laughed and said, 'Oh, no,' a little too quickly which made his godfather turn to look at his godson. When they reached the lake, Matteo pointed out an area and said, 'That's where Aarne wants to build his sauna. There, by those birch trees.'

Don Orazio laughed. 'A sauna—you'll be the first monastery in the world with a sauna.'

Matteo chuckled and said, 'It wouldn't be just for us, of course, but for the visitors, too. Aarne says it's a way of life in Finland. I think it's probably the only thing he misses about his previous life. He won't get it. Every now and then he produces a plan of how it will be and gives it to the abbot. But he won't get it. I don't think the abbot is against it in principle, but all the money goes towards increasing capacity and facilities for the visitors.'

The monk bent down to pick up a small pebble and threw it into the lake, creating circles of ripples. 'Our work here is like that,' he said. His cousin turned to look at the younger man, a slight frown on his face. 'Throw another one in, over there,' said the monk. Don Orazio threw in another pebble, far enough away from Matteo's pebble, and it too formed circular ripples as it hit the water. 'Our work here,' said the monk indicating the ripples of his pebble. 'The work of one of our sister communities, let's say the one in Lebanon,' he said pointing to the ripples from his cousin's pebble.

He threw in a third pebble which landed in the lake more or less equidistant between the first two. 'The small monastery in Pakistan.' The ripples of the third pebble quickly spread out and joined up with the others. 'You see how it works. How we hope and pray it works,' said Matteo. They both felt the wind stir—the mistral was due—and a brief breeze blew across the lake quickly pushing the ripples into each other and away across the water in the same direction. 'And sometimes we have a bit of extra help.'

In silence, they stood gazing out across the lake. 'What's that over there?' said Don Orazio pointing to a small stone building the other side of the water.

'That's an ancient chapel. We can walk around the lake to it, if you want.' They two men set off along the narrow path. 'We don't know who built it so we call it Amadeo's chapel. I really hope that one day we will have sufficient funds to repair it—it doesn't need that much work, the roof is sound and the walls are thick limestone.'

As they walked, the enchanting silvery sound of bells jingle-jangling around necks of browsing goats, hidden from view among the hills, carried on the wind to the two men.

They arrived at the chapel, Matteo opened the door and they walked in. 'The door needs work, we need to fit windows, you can see that the interior needs patching up.'

'Lovely marble altar,' said his cousin. 'And the crucifix . . .' He looked up at the large figure of the Christ on cross hanging behind the altar. The Messiah's mouth was open. The pain and suffering reflected in his face and tortured limbs was terrible.

'It's magnificent, isn't it? Sculpted out of linden wood, and astonishingly, the paint has hardly faded. Makes a change from all those easy-on-the eye crucifixes you see so often. You know, our Saviour just hanging there looking as if it was the most natural thing in the world to be nailed to a cross. I suppose they came into fashion because the suffering Christ was deemed too distressful to look at by the faithful. Ironic.'

As Matteo gazed at the wooden figure on the cross, his thoughts went back to when he had looked at another crucifixion in another place with another man. He had travelled to Alsace in eastern France with Werner, a young German he had met and fallen in love with on a skiing holiday.

Werner worked for his father who owned a vineyard and had arranged for his son to spend a week visiting the vineyards across the border in Alsace. Matteo had made the long journey by train to join Werner in Colmar. The young men had spent an idyllic week driving through the ridiculously picturesque half-timbered, red-geranium bedecked villages—Riquewihr, Turckheim, Eguisheim, Guebwiller—tasting elegant rieslings, gently aromatic gewürztraminers, scented muscats, stylish pinot gris.

To the west, behind the villages on the lower slopes, rose the ancient round-topped Vosges mountains and the three silent brooding medieval pink sandstone dungeons, all that remained of the three chateaux of Haut-Eguisheim. To the east, the Rhine and the Black Forest of Werner's homeland.

In Colmar they had strolled along the Lauch, through the Petite Venise, over cobble stones and past medieval half-timbered buildings, stopping here and there for a glass of pinot blanc or edelzwicker or one of the many artisanal local beers.

Werner wanted to see again the fifteenth century altarpiece "Madonna in the Rose Garden" which he had seen as a boy and which was displayed in the Dominican church by the market. It was the work of Colmar-born artist Martin Schongauer and the young Werner had been mesmerised by the Madonna's red gown and cloak, usually depicted in blue, the little birds—warblers, chaffinches, goldfinches—and the wild strawberries at her feet.

They had walked over to the Unterlinden Museum. And that was where Matteo saw Grünewald's terrible crucifixion of the Christ, part of the magnificent Issenheim altarpiece painted in the sixteenth century. Matteo thought on reflection that it was then, gazing at the man on the cross, his suffering depicted in shocking detail, the Baptist pointing to him, the tiny lamb, head turned towards the crucified, he thought it was then that the seeds had been sown.

After their week in Alsace Werner returned to his vineyard, Matteo returned to his studies in Genoa. They wrote, they met when they could which was not very often. Over time, the relationship, which had seemed to the young men so strong and invincible, died down like the mighty mistral when it has blown itself out.

The spark kindled in Matteo that Colmar day remained buried among the ashes of his love for Werner. Then a gentle movement of air, the beginnings of the wind again, stirred the spark, rekindled it and Matteo began the journey that would end here at the Communità dello Spirito Santo.

As the two men left the chapel Matteo turned back to look again at the Christ on cross. He smiled. His cousin, slightly raising his eyebrows, gave him a quizzical glance.

'I was just remembering a visit to a jeweller's with a friend. A woman at the counter was asking to see some gold crosses. The young assistant said, "Do you want a plain one, or one with the little man on it?"'

Don Orazio smiled, too, and they started walking back round the lake.

Matteo said, 'If we ever get the work done, I'd love to use the chapel for the Shepherd's mass. Way back the pope used to celebrate three Christmas masses in three different churches in Rome—the Angel's mass at midnight, the Shepherd's mass at dawn, and the King's mass on Christmas day. We celebrate the Christmas Vigil and the midnight Angel's mass at the village church, and the King's mass on Christmas day at the monastery. Perhaps one day we can celebrate the Shepherd's mass at dawn here in Amadeo's chapel. It's tiny, I know, but I don't think they'll be queuing at the door at that time of day.'

As they turned to walk back to the monastery Don Orazio said he would like to speak with the abbot before he left. Upon their return Matteo went off in search of Abbot Giacomo leaving his cousin walking slowly, thoughtfully, up and down on the gravelled area outside the main door.

The abbot received Don Orazio in his office. He had had an intuition that Matteo's godfather would want to see him. He had quickly looked up the 'Ndrangheta—the word apparently meant heroism and virtue—on the Internet. He had been horrified. As so often happens, one becomes hooked on the horrific. The quick look had turned into a longer one as he skimmed through various articles and newspaper reports.

Cocaine, vendettas, what became known as the "first" 'Ndrangheta war in the mid 1970s. Originally a horizontal structure of local groups, now known that there also existed a vertical structure, appropriated Catholic terminology for different grades of members—santisti, vangelisti.

Like Matteo, the abbot also saw sitting before him a tormented soul. Don Orazio told Abbot Giacomo that he had heard a little about the monastery's work and asked the abbot to tell him more. The abbot hesitated for a fraction of a second then explained how they provided a secure, discreet venue for liberal open-minded influential members of other faiths to learn about each others' beliefs.

He explained that there was absolutely no question of proselytising, that the whole ethos of their work was that a better understanding of each other's religions, beliefs, non-beliefs, sacred texts, could, would, should, play a small part in easing worldwide tensions created by those differences. Don Orazio occasionally nodded as he listened to the abbot. His gaze did not leave the abbot's face.

'It's a very long-term project,' he smiled. 'But thanks largely to the work of a colleague, a priest, who works with the Community, we have some pretty influential people coming now, including interested atheists, which encourages us.'

'How do you pay for it?' said Don Orazio, more interested in material matters.

Not with any of your money, thought the abbot. He said, 'We manage. Our visitors pay for their own travel here and in general provide their own food, or they tell us what they want, we get it and they reimburse us. We thank God daily that numbers are increasing. And we trust that He will provide the wherewithal to continue converting buildings into accommodation, meeting rooms, kitchens. *Unless we can ever get them all to eat the same food prepared in the same kitchen,* thought the abbot, *Oh, what a joy that would be.*

Don Orazio remained silent, looking around the room, and looking desperately tired, thought the abbot. Mind you, if he's driven up from the Mezzogiorno. And so little warning. Very odd, he thought.

'I congratulate you, Padre Abate. Your work is important. You are doing something worthwhile, so much violence and killing in the world.' He paused then, as an afterthought, said, 'In the name of religion.' The abbot thought that was a bit rich but said nothing. Don Orazio picked up the framed photo on the abbot's desk and read out loud the Gandhi quotation. "My demand for the truth has taught me the beauty of compromise," smiled and ran his finger around the frame, slowly, feeling the wood.

'Matteo made that.'

'I remember as a youngster when he and his family came to Calabria. We spent the summer in the old family house in the Aspromonte, he was always playing around with bits of wood, sticks, twigs, making things. Those were happy, carefree days...'

He replaced the frame and said slowly looking straight at the abbot, 'I chose . . .' He paused, searching for the right word. 'I chose a different path. Now I need to ...'

Oh, dear Lord, thought the abbot, *please, please, don't let him ask me to hear his confession.*

'I need to put things in order. Yes...'

The two men remained in silence for a minute. Then the abbot took a deep breath and said, 'Is there anything you feel you would like to say? Would you like me to hear your confession, figlio mio?'

Don Orazio looked at him and chuckled. 'You're a brave man, Padre Abate. No. I wanted to see Matteo, to see where he was living, to meet you, to hear more about your work. I have done those things. I will leave tomorrow morning as planned.'

'You look tired. Rest perhaps before supper.'

'Grazie, Padre Abate, grazie mille.'

As the abbot accompanied Don Orazio to the door, Matteo's godfather paused in front of a small table. It was a most unusual table, entirely made from pieces of silver birch bark—the top and the legs. He picked up the newspaper lying on it so he could examine the table in more detail. 'Matteo's workmanship again.' It was a statement rather than a question. The abbot nodded.

As Don Orazio replaced the newspaper he glanced down at the headline: "You cannot believe in God and be Mafiosi, says pope." He turned and gave the abbot a rueful smile. The abbot, who would have removed the paper if he had remembered about the headline, gave a slight shrug, raising his hands, palms upward as if to say he wasn't responsible for the newspaper's front page headlines.

They parted company. Later, Don Orazio dined in the refectory and retired to his room straight afterwards. The following morning, although he woke when Luca rang the bell for Lever, he did not attend the early offices. He spoke again briefly with Matteo in the morning and attended mass.

It was only when the abbot, who was celebrating that day, started giving communion to his monks that the horror of the situation dawned on him. If Don Orazio came up to receive the host, the abbot could not in all conscience, knowing what he did, give him the body of Christ. The abbot felt sick. But Don Orazio had the good grace not to take communion. After mass, having accomplished what he had set out to do, he thanked the abbot for receiving him, and left the monastery.

'He's dying,' said the abbot as they watched him drive off down the bumpy track. 'Yes,' said Matteo. 'I think he is.'

A few months later Matteo received a call to say that his cousin had died of cancer. A week or so later he went to tell the abbot that he had received an email telling him that in his will Don Orazio had left him the old house they used to stay and play in as children, and the sum of fifty thousand euros. For "tax reasons" Matteo would have to come to Calabria to collect the money, which would be handed over to him in cash in a suitcase.

At the time the monastery finances were in one of their periodic parlous states. Brother Ange-Dominique, deserted again by the Muse, was not painting. It happened now and then, there was nothing to be done but wait. Orders for Aarne's vodka had dried up so they had been using up existing stock and he had not been distilling for a while. Two large orders had just come in, one for the cloudberry, so he was now cranking up the distillery to restart production.

The Community was beginning to reap the harvest from seeds unstintingly sown by the priest since he had joined the community. Increasing demand meant more accommodation and facilities. There was no shortage of old stone buildings around the place—in the monastery garden outbuildings had already been converted into the distillery, atelier, workshop and laundry.

There was no shortage of potential only an enormous shortage of money. Money to finish converting into accommodation the large old house in a quiet far corner of the garden, to continue redeveloping ground floor rooms in the small cloister into meeting and study spaces, and kitchens, to continue upgrading the upper floor cells adding small but functional private showers, to repair rickety radiators and parlous plumbing.

While Matteo was telling the abbot about his inheritance there was a knock at the door. 'Avanti', said the abbot and a spectral-like figure covered head to toe in a white powdery material walked in. It was Brother Aarne. The very second-hand still had just exploded.

That evening, when his monks had retired for the night, abbot Giacomo returned to his study. He had no problem with the concept of suitcases of cash. He was Italian. A long time ago, he had left the monastery to drive to a hillside Ligurian village to pick up his share of a family inheritance. Bundles of cash in a suitcase.

It was the origin of the cash which made it impossible to accept. The proceeds from the sale of his monk's old holiday home was a different matter because Matteo had explained that it had been built by earlier generations. But could he take the risk? Although he knew the few lines by heart, he reached into the drawer, took out the envelope, and re-read one of the handwritten unsigned notes from Rome. He replaced the envelope in the drawer, turned to God, turned to Gandhi, turned to the drinks cabinet.

The following morning he asked Matteo to come to his office. 'Of course we cannot accept the cash. Perhaps you can arrange for it to be given to a local priest or a local organisation? As for the house, it seems to me that your old family home could perhaps continue to provide happy holiday times for youngsters in Calabria.' Matteo nodded in silence, left the abbot's office, and sent the email he had already drafted confirming how he wished to dispose of his inheritance.

A few weeks later, Brother Louis-Marc came to see the abbot. He was carrying an old battered anonymous brown leather suitcase with old fashioned metal locks that one of the village girls had found. The abbot raised his eyebrows and indicated to his monk to place the suitcase on his desk. The abbot clicked open the two catches, raised the lid, and found himself looking at bundles and bundles and bundles of used euro notes.

'Which bedroom?' enquired the abbot, already knowing the answer.

'Oh, she didn't find it in a bedroom, Père Abbé. It was right at the back of a cupboard—in the laundry.'

The abbot closed the suitcase. He picked up the telephone and told Brother Aarne to get in quotes for replacing the still. Then he called Matteo and told him and Gianni to go ahead with the building works that had been put on hold and to start repair work on Amadeo's chapel. 'And you, Louis-Marc, can now sort out your greenhouse.'

He would announce the windfall to the community at chapter that evening although he knew perfectly well that by then everybody would already know. The following morning, Aarne came to see him with yet another proposal for the sauna which the abbot put in the drawer on top of all the others.

Now, as the chicken stock came to the boil and Maddalena skimmed it, Matteo went outside for thyme and parsley. She found the cloves and stuck a few into two onion halves. They put everything into the stock pot with a few bay leaves, and Matteo turned the heat down low. They left it on the back of the stove, barely simmering, for an hour and a half or so, skimming off the fat now and then, while Matteo peeled, quartered and gently cooked in a little butter with a split vanilla pod a compote of apples, and Maddalena peeled and poached whole pears in red wine with a couple of sticks of cinnamon.

They stopped for coffee which the monk made in an old Bialetti Moka pot. 'This belonged to my grandmother—look, the hinge broke and Gianni managed to repair it,' he said as he poured the coffee into two mugs. They went outside to sit on the bench in the little garden. Speaking in Italian, he thanked her for her help, using the familiar *tu* form of address. He was a good-looking young man, tall, clean-shaven, dark brown hair, gentle brown eyes. He seemed reticent, happy enough to sit in silence listening to occasional birdsong. Maddalena was getting used to this way of living where exchanges were kept to a minimum and idle conversation was virtually non-existent.

They heard a car draw up. The wooden door in the monastery wall opened and the mayor's wife stepped through and greeted them. 'Could I possibly borrow some pasta, Brother Matteo? I've run out.'

'I'm not sure whether we can spare any.'

The mayor's wife laughed. 'Oh dear, is Gianni still stock-piling?' In reply, the monk bowed graciously and waved his arm in the direction of the kitchen. 'Spaghettini, orecchiette, cavatelli, tortellini, fettuccine, capellini. Please help yourself, Signora.'

Matteo's litany of pasta reminded Maddalena of a fishmonger she had heard in the fish market in the Rialto in Venice —"Gamberetti, cozze, vongole! Roba fresca, pescata stanotte"— a time when another love had blossomed and faded leaving her with happy memories and a very good recipe for risotto and tender young peas.

She had noticed that even though the community consisted of twelve men, eight of whom were Italian, there did seem to be an astonishing amount of pasta in the pantry. Shelves were stacked with all conceivable shapes and sizes—and there were several boxes and packets of each type.

The mayor's wife returned with a packet of linguine. 'Is that all? Please, take some more—for your friends, neighbours, relatives.'

'I'm picking up a kilo of fresh yeast for the abbot when I'm in town next week. I'll replace the linguine then.'

'Oh, no, please don't,' said the monk. 'I have a theory that he must have been traumatised as a child because his mother ran out of pasta for a couple of days. Every time we use a box or packet he adds at least two, TWO, to the shopping list. We take it off the list, he puts it back on. I've had to put in an extra shelf in the pantry, just for his pasta.'

The mayor's wife left, laughing, with her linguine. As Maddalena and the monk went back into the kitchen Brother Gianni walked in. Similar height and colouring to Matteo, and growing a beard by the looks of it. A lot of girls must have rued the day the Holy Spirit breezed into the lives of these two attractive young men. Or perhaps not, she thought, as she saw the gentle look they exchanged.

Gianni also came from Liguria. He had been born in Sanremo not far from Marebosco, the native village of the community's founder, Amadeo. He knew of the Communità dello Spirito Santo and thought that might be the right place for him. It was. He had worked in hospitals and had a little medical background so he looked after monks if ailments were minor and called in the village doctor if they were not.

He had come to the kitchen to rescue some chicken broth before it went into the risotto. One of the Ancients was a bit under the weather and had remained in his room. It was easier for Gianni, and the others, to keep an eye on them now they occupied ground floor rooms.

A few months back, the Ancient for whom the chicken stock was destined—Gianni would add some coarse sea salt, a handful of vermicelli and perhaps a couple of small pieces of the poached chicken to it—had had a near death experience. He had been bedridden with a fever, slept most of the time, was eating little, they had to force him to swallow liquids. The doctor called in daily. They all thought he was dying.

Sometime earlier, Gianni had decided to compile a playlist of "Ave Marias". As with the pasta, he could not content himself with just a few different "Ave Marias". He strung together the usual Schubert and Bach/Gounod compositions, of course, and versions by Donizetti, Verdi and Rossini, by Dvorzak, Tresch and Liszt, by Brahms, Bruckner and Bortrivansky, by Mozart, Palestrina and Rachmaninov . . .

Frankly, after he had played it in the refectory—several times—everyone was thrilled when he discovered the young Italian trumpeter Fabrizio Bosso and started following him around, in the musical sense. They were even more delighted when Louis-Marc introduced him to the flamenco guitarist Paco de Lucia, neither of whom appeared to have recorded anybody's version of "Ave Maria".

Given the gravity of the Ancient's state of health, Gianni decided that only the Ave Marias fitted the bill. He put his playlist on repeat and it played continuously for the duration of the Ancient's illness. This added a sense of urgency to the community's prayers for their fellow monk's speedy recovery (or demise), given that they took it in turns to keep a constant vigil at his bedside.

One sunny morning Brother Gianni had opened the window to let in a little warm spring sunshine and had then left his patient sleeping. A little later, the Ancient opened his eyes. He could see nothing but bright white light streaming onto his face warming his whole body. He could hear nothing but heavenly voices continually singing "Ave Maria."

He lay there blinded by the eternal light streaming down upon him and thought, *I have died.* He became aware of dark shadows advancing towards him, saw his parents and other long-dead relatives. A beatific smile slowly spread across his old and wrinkled face as he held out his thin bony arms to greet them. As the mistiness in his mind melted away, and his sight gradually cleared, he realised it was Gianni and the doctor. His eyes filled with tears. 'Welcome back,' said Gianni with great tenderness and sincerity, mistaking the Ancient's tears for tears of happiness.

Now, while Brother Matteo prepared a tray for the broth, Gianni smiled at Maddalena. He placed his hand on her shoulder.

'Grazie, Maddalena, we are so happy to have you here with us.'

'Anch'io sono contentissima di essere qua con tutti voi.'

The bell rang.

In the afternoon Maddalena walked to the kitchen garden hoping to find Brother Louis-Marc. She could not see him and so walked further on and found him in the olive grove. Among the dense foliage some of the small green olives were beginning to turn purple.

'They are mainly Aglandau, very resistant to cold, but we also have some much older varieties—Filayre, Estoublaïsse, Grappier. We'll normally harvest them at the end of November, early December and take them to the village mill for pressing.' Maddalena hadn't heard of any of these varieties.

On some of the less laden trees, you'll see olives partially wine-coloured, mottled with pale green, he continued. 'We keep back a few black Tanche olives for eating but most go for oil. Have you tried it?'

'Yes, I have,' said Maddalena, remembering her impromptu supper with Brother Ange-Dominique, 'a pretty green colour, elegant, I liked it.'

'Artichokes, apple, cut grass...'

'I'm not sure I got all that,' she laughed. 'I'll have to pour out a spoonful in the kitchen and taste it properly.'

'Some say they've been here since Roman times. The olive groves. But we can't find any written reference. They've certainly been here for several centuries. Probably planted when the first priories were founded in the tenth century.'

They walked through the olive grove. The sun, now low in the cloudless blue sky and losing its heat, was burnishing the far-off mountain tops which would soon be snow-capped. There was a crisp chill in the air and occasional birdsong. Somewhere, a cock crowed.

They walked and talked under the long and thin and silvery-green leaved branches growing out of old, thick, gnarled trunks. A week ago they had not met. Now, thought Maddalena, it seemed as if they had known each other all their lives. As they made their way back towards the kitchen garden, they paused and carried on their quiet conversation, turned towards each other.

The abbot, who wanted to speak to his monk, could have telephoned him but felt like a bit of fresh air. As he made his way towards the two figures they became aware of his approach and turned towards him, smiling. But it wasn't their smiles that caused a little stab of pain inside him. It was their eyes—their shining, sparkling, happy eyes. Long-buried memories flooded back into the abbot's consciousness.

The Holy Spirit had left Giacomo her calling card when he was in his teens, and he had briefly dallied with joining the priesthood. It had then sat on his mantelpiece for the next ten years or so. He became an architect. He fell in love with a young woman, Livia Di Pietro, and they made plans to marry.

He no longer went to church but she did, so he started accompanying her. Gradually, his earlier desire to dedicate his life to God returned. It had been the happiest and it had been the hardest time of his life. He loved Livia but he loved God more. He had never regretted his decision. But now seeing those two pairs of shining eyes he wondered where she was now, the woman he had loved and left.

He pushed thoughts of those earlier times out of his mind and mused on what might be more immediate cause for concern. *Wretched woman*, he thought to himself. He had forgotten what he wanted to see Louis-Marc about, remembered, and Maddalena left them to their discussion.

During their silent supper that evening they listened to some famous operatic duets. When the abbot heard the voice of Maria Callas he smiled in remembrance of the "Norma" debacle. Brother Ange-Dominique had compiled a playlist of La Callas's greatest hits which they had listened to with great pleasure.

The final aria on his playlist, which had mesmerised them all, was "Casta Diva". The orchestra played the last couple of chords —the monks listened in rapturous silence. Even the Ancients had stayed awake. Then the spell was broken as an appreciative Covent Garden audience broke out into tumultuous applause. Ange-Dominique, who had inadvertently included a live performance on his playlist, had pushed back his chair which crashed to the stone floor, adding to the cacophony of sound, and had sprinted over to turn off the music. He and the priest, who had been with them that evening, still laughed about it now.

After supper, the abbot asked Maddalena to come and see him the following morning. Before retiring for the night, he went briefly to his office. The telephone rang. It was the priest calling from an airport somewhere in the Middle East.

'Ciao, Giacomo. How's it going? With Maddalena? She must have been with you almost a week now, I think.'

'Is that all?'

He thought about all that had happened since the woman had arrived at the monastery. She had drank the best part of a bottle of vodka with Aarne and they had both fallen asleep in the distillery; Louis-Marc was wandering around with a silly star-struck smile on his face; Luca blushed beetroot-red everytime she looked at him (he must speak to Louis-Marc about beetroots, they hadn't been on the menu for a while). On the plus side, and it was, he had to concede, a very big plus, she had proved an inspiration to Ange-Dominique; she had helped Aarne get out the order and get in the cash in record speed; they had got drunk on the plain vodka, not the wild cloudberry.

'Somehow it seems much longer.'

The background airport noise was such that the priest did not pick up on the weary tone in the abbot's voice.

'Has she met everybody?'

'She certainly has.'

'I'm so glad. I never really had any doubts. I knew you'd like her. She'll be a real asset to the community.'

'Mmm. It's rather as if Maddalena has been with us always.'

'When does she start?'

'I'm seeing her tomorrow morning to talk about that. When are you back? When will you come to the monastery?' He really should tell him about the letters from Rome.

'Back in a week or so I think. I'll let you know.'

The following morning Maddalena arrived five minutes early and made herself an espresso. At the appointed time she knocked on the door. 'Avanti.' The abbot was sitting at his desk.

'Buongiorno, Padre Abate.'

'Salve, Maddalena, come stai oggi?'

'Benissimo, grazie.'

He indicated a chair and she sat down opposite him.

'I think you have met most of our small community, Maddalena. Now I need to talk to you about how you can help us.'

He explained that there had been a slight change in plan and that some of the current visitors would need to be taken to the airport at the weekend. While he was talking he opened a desk drawer, slid his fingers inside the outer wrapping of a chocolate bar, counted six remaining squares. The 47% dark chocolate with lime zest. He left the drawer open.

More visitors were arriving during the week and he hoped that she would be in a position to drive both groups, keeping the car in between times. Maddalena, who had already been working on translations in her room, occasionally in the small library, and, on the philosophy front reading about Renaissance humanism, smiled and said that that would not be a problem.

The abbot put his hand into the drawer again and fingered the other bar. Fair Trade DRC and Peru 70%, only three squares left. Maddalena had seen him open the drawer but these were the early days of their relationship. She didn't know what was in it. Watching the abbot, she was aware that there was an internal tussle of some sort going on inside his head. She was also aware when the abbot had resolved it. He stopped talking, smiled at her, and removed from the drawer the remains of a chocolate bar. He laid it on his desk and closed the drawer. From within

the outer wrapper he removed the silver foil-wrapped chocolate and snapped off one of the three remaining squares. He
hesitated —for really only a fraction of a second— then handed
two squares to Maddalena.

CHAPTER 12

And so it came to pass that Maddalena started her chauffeuring duties for the Communità dello Spirito Santo. She drove the current visitors—two Buddhist monks, one Hindu and an interpreter—back to the airport, and drove a Greek Orthodox priest, two Sikhs and an imam to the monastery.

Arrivals recognised her from her photograph. She recognised them from theirs. Everything was carried out with the utmost discretion. Conversation was minimal. Apart from initial greetings, Maddalena, always smiling, never spoke unless she was spoken to, which was rare. Some visitors did not speak any of the languages she spoke. Others did but chose not to, burying themselves in their holy books or gazing out of the window at the unfolding Mediterranean scenery. They rarely spoke to each other.

Abbot Giacomo said she was to make herself at home in her room. On each visit to the monastery she brought clothes and toiletries and books and music until she had created a little home away from home. Her philosphy studies continued apace. She had heard about lectures given by a Dominican brother and attended his series of talks in town on Nietzsche (a firm favourite of the Dominican philosopher and of Maddalena's), the Stoics, Edith Stein and Epicurus, Hegel, Aristotle and company. She often struggled to understand everything. She would buy a copy of each lecture for five euros and reread them when she was at the monastery. The environment certainly provided a peaceful place for philosophical reflection. It did not necessarily clarify matters. Maddalena's mind would wander. She found it hard to concentrate. She persevered. The thumbed state of the stapled lecture notes were a testament to her determination. At worst, she reasoned—and reasoning was where she came unstuck—she would have a brief background about some of the world's great thinkers. At best, she reckoned if she continued rereading the talks, she might end up with a clearer idea of what they were thinking about.

She enjoyed her time at the monastery—attending the offices, inspiring Brother Ange-Dominique to paint, working in the kitchen garden with Brother Louis-Marc. All these tasks were carried out—most of the time—in a companionable silence. There was no idle chitchat. What little they knew about Maddalena and she about them—think Foreign Legion, she kept telling herself—was, occasionally, revealed in those rare moments of conversation.

She loved working in the kitchen with whoever was in charge of preparing meals that day or week. Since her arrival, the other monks, who shared out culinary duties, had at some moment or another asked her, rather shyly, if she could perhaps, possibly, if it wasn't too much trouble, teach Brother Gianni a few simple dishes that didn't contain pasta. Maddalena recalled the visit of the mayor's wife and Matteo's comments.

The problem had arisen some time back when Brother Gianni had been obliged to cook all week. This had never happened before but was due to an unfortunate combination of circumstances—the muse was upon Ange-Dominique, Aarne was attending the study group on Islam (the abbot required all his monks to take advantage of the teaching available), Louis-Marc was replacing the abbot who had left rather unexpectedly for Rome, (nobody quite knew why, probably something to do with the letters, no doubt he would tell them in due course); Luca was too young, Séamus too old, and Matteo was battling against a deadline to finish off rooms before the arrival of a study group.

Brother Gianni could only cook pasta. The first course might be a salad of cold pasta with the addition of whatever came to hand—slices of the Corsican charcuterie sent by BAD's mother, pieces of cooked cold chicken, chunks of tuna. The main course would be a different type of pasta served hot with a tomato sauce with the addition of whatever came to hand that he hadn't used for the first course.

He cooked the pasta well and everyone enjoyed it because he was normally only required to produce it once a week. However, during this particular week the community ate nothing but pasta for lunch and dinner.

The crunch came when on the third day the Ancients, who were always destabilised on the rare occasions that the abbot was absent, had refused, in protest, to come to the refectory. Matteo went to find out if they were all right. He went into the first room and the Ancient, who was traversing one of his less lucid periods, said he was fed up with eating pasta every day and he was going to report the matter to the Union.

Matteo popped into the next room and tried to persuade the occupant how important it was to eat something. The Ancient opened his bedside drawer to reveal his small mobile phone, two yoghurts, apples, bananas, biscuits, pieces of bread. He then slammed shut the drawer and said in a loud voice, 'Basta con la pasta!'

At this point, the other three Ancients shuffled in chanting, 'Basta con la pasta! Basta con la pasta!' Brother Matteo didn't know whether to laugh or cry so he just left.

On one of her visits, Maddelena had a word with Brother Matteo. 'I'm happy to help Gianni but, you know, it will be difficult to teach him if we can't communicate. Perhaps I should ask the abbot if it's OK to talk...'

'Oh don't worry about that, Maddalena, it was the abbot's idea in the first place. Gianni's on duty tomorrow. Buona fortuna!'

The following morning when she arrived in the kitchen she found Brother Gianni looking very disconsolate in front of a dozen large shiny peppers—red ones, green ones, yellow ones.

'Salve, Gianni, I'm here to give you a hand. What are you going to do with those?'

'I don't know,' replied the mournful monk. 'I've never done peppers with pasta before.' He put the coffee pot onto the stove.

'Perhaps we could forget the pasta and make an entrée with just the peppers.'

'What do you mean—forget the pasta?'

'You could make a pasta dish for the main course,' said Maddalena, realising that it would possibly be too traumatic to remove pasta from both the first and second course.

'Well . . .' said the monk. He did not sound very convinced.

'It's really simple. We wash the peppers then roast them in the oven. Can you put it on at 240°C? Shall we have coffee outside while it's heating up?'

They walked out into the small garden area and sat on the bench. 'I expect they've told you. That's why you're here,' said the monk.

'I love working in the kitchen with you all.'

'Yes, but they've asked you to teach me because they're fed up with the pasta. I expect they told you about the Ancients. When the abbot went to Rome. I do different pasta, you know, if it's long thin or ribbon pasta for the main course, then I use small twists or tubes—trofie, the abbot likes trofie, or strozzapreti or rigatoni—for the first course. It's always a different type of pasta.'

'Yes, I'm sure it is. And you cook it perfectly. But it's still—well, it's still always pasta, isn't it?'

The monk sipped his coffee. 'Yes, it's always pasta. I can't cook anything else. They take bets when I'm cooking on which type of pasta it's going to be.'

'I'm sure the monks don't bet, Gianni.'

'Not proper bets, we haven't got any money. But you know what I mean. I happened to see Aarne and Ange-Dominique exchanging glances once when I'd cooked some capelli d'angelo. Ange-Dominique was grinning and Aarne wasn't looking very happy. At the end of lunch, he did the washing up but it was Ange-Dominique's turn to do it that week. That's just one example. I could give you plenty of others.'

Maddalena tried to temper her smile. 'Maybe we can find some simple things for you to cook.'

'That aren't pasta?'

'That aren't pasta.'

They went back in and put the peppers on a tray into the oven and roasted them for half an hour or so, turning them over half way through. Then Gianni took the tray of soft and blistered peppers out of the oven.

'Parts of them are black,' he said.

'Don't worry about that. Now we put them into these two plastic bags—we won't get them all into one—and seal them. We'll leave them for a quarter of an hour—they'll be easier to peel.'

The monk went to the pantry for some tins of chopped tomatoes and started chopping up some onions to make his sauce for the main course, comfortable now he was back on home territory.

When the peppers were cool enough to handle, they peeled them, removed the stems and pips and sliced the peppers lengthways into strips. Under Maddalena's supervision, Gianni arranged them in two dishes and poured over the juices left in the bags.

'They look very colourful, don't they?' he said, as he followed Maddalena's instructions and sprinkled on fine sea salt, added a few grinds of fresh black pepper and drizzled over some olive oil. Maddalena removed a sliver of pepper with some juices, cut it in two and they both ate a half.

'Do you think it needs any more seasoning, Gianni?'

'È perfetto, Maddalena. I just wonder if we shouldn't add some penne? Or maybe some linguine—thin like the pepper strips—that would look nice, don't you think?'

This was like weaning someone off an addiction, she thought. She said, 'I think the dish should be served just as it is, Gianni,' and I hope to God they all like it, she added silently.

Gianni had sweated his onions, added his tomatoes and Maddalena had found some cold chicken in the fridge. While he carefully removed the meat and cut it up into pieces, she quickly wiped over some firm, unblemished, dazzling white mushrooms—a villager grew them in old wine barrels—and halved or quartered them depending on size. She popped outside and returned with some thyme and parsley. He watched her carefully as she removed the thyme leaves and with a sharp heavy kitchen knife chopped up the flat leaf parsley.

'This is really an entrée dish which you can serve hot or cold but you'd need more mushrooms. I'm just using what I found in the pantry. Now, heat up some olive oil in a pan and pop in these cloves of garlic. I've peeled them for you. When you start smelling the garlic, put in the mushrooms and thyme leaves, then turn up the heat for a couple of minutes.'

She instructed him to add some salt and pepper while she poured in some white wine. 'This smells good, doesn't it?' said the monk, watching the pan bubbling away until the wine had almost evaporated and the mushrooms were cooked.

'Sprinkle over the parsley—that's it. Taste it. Now add it to your tomato sauce with the pieces of chicken.'

A bell rang. They quickly tidied up and cleaned work surfaces. 'What pasta are you going to cook, Gianni?'

'I thought I'd cook some strozzapreti.'

She smiled. The word meant priest strangler.

'Or you could do rice.'

'Rice?' The monk looked at her as if she had used an obscenity.

'It was just a thought. No, you're right, pasta's good.'

Later on when the lunch bell rang, everyone filed into the refectory and sat down. Maddalena suddenly felt very nervous. Grace was said—often a particularly pointed reading was chosen from the booklet when Brother Gianni was in the kitchen—and the monk appeared with the trolley and placed a dish of the red, green and yellow peppers at the head of each table. Everyone stared at the peppers, then stared at Gianni. Apart from Matteo and the abbot nobody knew that Maddalena had been helping in the kitchen. They did now.

The peppers with a spoonful of the dressing were served to

everybody and eaten, as usual, in silence, listening to Luca, who would eat later, reading "The Man who Planted Trees" by Jean Giono. Along with "Animal Farm" it was a great favourite and it wasn't the first time they had heard the story, set not so very far away from where they now sat. But rather like little children who never tire of hearing the same fairy tale read over and over, they never tired of hearing about Elzéard Bouffier planting his trees.

When Gianni stood up to collect the two dishes one was empty. One of the Ancients was endeavouring to help himself to the two remaining strips of pepper in the other dish. 'But you don't like peppers—that's why I didn't give you many to start with,' whispered Aarne, trying to take the serving spoon and fork off the Ancient. 'I like these ones,' hissed back the Ancient, wrestling back the cutlery with a force that belied his venerable age.

Brother Gianni looked around, caught Maddalena's eye and a large smile slowly spread across his face. He disappeared with the trolley and returned with two large oval dishes of strozza-preti with its tomato, chicken and mushroom sauce—another triumph. Not for the first time, Maddalena marvelled at how expressive silence can be. Nobody spoke but the refectory radiated with a palpable sense of gastronomic contentment.

That afternoon, the flush of his lunchtime success had faded. Maddalena arrived in the kitchen to find Brother Gianni standing looking, again, disconsolate in front of a basket of fennel bulbs that Louis-Marc, or perhaps it was a villager, had left on the kitchen table.

'Ciao, Gianni,' said Maddalena. 'Ooh! Fennel—I love fennel.'

The monk turned to look at her, his face a picture of misery. 'I've never cooked pasta with fennel before. In fact I've never cooked fennel.'

'Perhaps we could just use the fennel.'

The monk's jaw dropped. Maddalena went over to the vegetable rack and picked out half a dozen medium sized potatoes. 'We could make a fennel and potato soup. That's a tasty winter dish.'

Brother Gianni looked as if he was about to burst into tears.

'I'll help you. It's easy and quick and very tasty. Then we'll make up a chicory salad of something or other. What do you think?'

They peeled the potatoes and cut them up into chunks. They washed the fennel bulbs. Gianni watched as she cut off the hard end of one the bulbs, and then the bright green feathery stalks and laid them to one side. 'We need the feathery bits for later,' she said, cutting up into chunks the remaining bulb. 'Now you do one.'

When the vegetables were all cut up into pieces, Maddalena popped a sufficiently large pan onto the stove, heated up some virgin olive oil and threw in the fennel pieces. 'Now just stir those around gently, they must soften but not take colour.' The monk took the wooden spoon and followed instructions.

Maddalena added the potatoes, sprinkled grey sea salt over the vegetables, filled up a measuring jug with water and added enough liquid to just cover the pan contents. 'We bring that just to simmering, put on the lid, turn the heat right down and let it cook for twenty minutes or so.'

When the potatoes were cooked but not mushy Gianni, under Maddalena's watchful eye, crushed them , which thickened up the soup. 'Mmm, smells good,' said the monk, 'and tastes delicious. Is that all there is to it?'

'It's garnished with some freshly ground pepper, a pinch of cumin—that adds some colour—the feathery fennel leaves, a drizzle of olive oil and thin shavings of parmesan. But that means we need to plate it up here in the kitchen before serving it and I know you normally ladle out soup at table. I think we'll have to forget the garnish.'

'No. I'll get everything ready here and I'll plate it up, like you said.'

He shaved off slivers of parmesan onto a plate, lined up all the other ingredients so he didn't forget anything, and snipped off a saucer full of feathery fennel fronds.

While grace was being said, he ladled out the hot soup in the kitchen, careful not to overfill the bowls, garnished it as Maddalena had told him and very carefully wheeled the soup plates into the refectory. It was all rather impressive, thought Maddalena, giving Gianni an approving nod and a smile as he placed her plate in front of her.

The monks ate their soup savouring slowly the pieces of fennel and crushed potatoes and listening to Joseph Canteloube's "Songs from the Auvergne" sung by Sara Macliver with the Queensland Symphony Orchestra. Their favourite was "Bailero" so Brother Louis-Marc had made up a playlist which started and finished with that song. And then on reflection, he had added it again in the middle.

Every now and then one of the Ancients would pause, spoon halfway to mouth, and raise up his eyes as if to thank the Almighty for this manna from heaven. Matteo caught Maddalena's eye and mouthed, "Thank you." Aarne, when he thought the abbot wasn't looking—but he was, not much escaped the abbot —discreetly gave her the thumbs up.

Gianni, who had started suffering from withdrawal symptoms, had wanted to serve after the soup a salad of penne, left over from a previous meal, mixed up with not very much— he thought perhaps he could add some chopped up hard boiled eggs he had found in the fridge and, given that it was still sitting on the kitchen table, a sprinkling of cumin "for colour".

What was actually served was a salad of sliced raw chicory with a lemon juice and olive oil dressing and the cheeseboard. The monks were relieved and delighted to see the abbot help himself—for the first time in weeks—to a generous portion of both cheeses. Brother Séamus had brought in the mail that day which included a letter from the doctor's surgery for the abbot. His cholesterol level was obviously under control again.

The following morning Gianni sought out Maddalena. They walked in silence out of the monastery and sat in the sunshine on a bench under an olive tree. He was clutching a notebook.

'Ti ringrazio, Maddalena. Guarda, I've written down the recipes. Would you check them for me?' He handed her the notebook and a pencil. She made a few corrections and handed them back.

'The potato and fennel soup was really delicious, Gianni, well done. Perhaps you could make these dishes again the next time it's your turn to cook—give you a bit more practice.'

'You know, even the Ancients said how much they enjoyed the meals when I went to check on them last night. Will you help me again, Maddalena? Just simple things like we did yesterday. Next time you're here.'

'Certo, certo! It will be a pleasure, Gianni.'

Maddalena was leaving the following day for the airport then home. The abbot had asked Matteo to cook one of Séamus's salmon which he had removed from the freezer the previous day.

'In your honour, I think, Maddalena,' said Matteo, who was due to replace Gianni in the kitchen. He asked Maddalena if she could help Gianni make something that wasn't pasta to accompany the fish.

Gianni arrived and headed off to the pantry for pasta. Suddenly, Maddalena had a Damascene moment. She loved eating a rice dish that a Lebanese friend had introduced her to many years ago. The perfect rice dish for Brother Gianni – a rice dish made with vermicelli.

She joined Gianni in the pantry. It was well stocked with bags, indeed sacks, of rice of all description thanks to pantry donations left behind by the visitors' cooks. Maddalena had already seen some long grain Punjab basmati rice. There were six packets of vermicelli.

'Rice, Gianni,' said Maddalena. The monk looked nervous. 'You will love this dish,' she said, reaching for the basmati.

'I'm not so sure, Maddalena. Couldn't we do some bucatini? Or perhaps some maltagliati?'

'No, Gianni, we are going to make some rice to go with Matteo's salmon. But,' and here she paused for effect, 'it is made with,' another pause, 'vermicelli.'

The monk's eyes lit up. He called out through the pantry

door. 'Did you hear that, Matteo? It's rice, yes, but it's got vermicelli in it. Fantastico! Andiamo!' Matteo, who was preparing the bouillon, smiled.

'Right, first we need to wash the rice,' said Maddalena, pouring a large bag or so into a large pan and covering it with cold water. She was used to making this dish just for herself, with some left over for the next day. She was not at all sure about the quantity for twelve. 'Swirl the rice round a bit in that, pour off the water, and do it again another couple of times—to get rid of the surface starches and any debris.'

The monk followed her instructions. 'Heat up some olive oil in this pan here—we need one with a tight-fitting lid—and then put in, oh, I don't know, a couple of handfuls of vermicelli, perhaps a bit more.' The pan sizzled gently. 'Now stir that gently until the vermicelli takes a bit of colour.' The monk assiduously followed her instructions, adding the basmati rice when the vermicelli started to turn light brown.

'Put in enough water to cover everything, plus a good centimetre—you have to do it by eye, really—now add some of the coarse sea salt, a couple of grinds of pepper, a few bay leaves.' Matteo walked over to have a look at the contents of the pan then returned to his fish. 'OK, bring that up to the boil. As soon as it starts simmering, put on the lid, turn the heat right down and put on the timer for—we'll check it after ten minutes or so.'

The two of them went outside, admiring on the way Matteo's splendid salmon which he was about to put into the huge fish kettle which the priest had picked up for a song, well, a couple of songs, in a second-hand market in Marseille. They sat on the garden bench in silence in the sunshine, each wrapped in their own thoughts.

'I'll write the recipe down later,' said Gianni. 'This is marvellous, Maddalena, I can't thank you enough for taking the time to help me. And pasta with rice! Who would have thought?'

'It's rice with pasta, Gianni,' said Maddalena, worried that in her absence the monk would have a tendency to reverse the quantities.

'Certo, certo.'

'The timer's gone off,' said Matteo from the kitchen door.

'When you write out the recipe, Gianni,' smiled Maddalena, 'make a note that if you go outside while the rice is cooking, and nobody else is in the kitchen, you should take the timer with you.'

Back inside, following instructions, Gianni took the pan off the heat, removed the lid, and with a fork moved the rice around a bit, scraping the bottom of the pan. They both tried a little and decided it needed a minute or so more. Maddalena replaced the lid, put the pan back on the stove and turned off the heat.

The bell rang. Matteo's salmon was poached and cooling in the court bouillon. He had not filleted it because they always brought in Séamus's salmon whole on a large silver platter. It was such a special occasion. Maddalena wondered if maybe Séamus would pipe it in like the haggis on Burn's Night.

'We'll keep the first course simple. What about some slices of lonzo with some salad leaves?' They had a word with Louis-Marc who provided them with some lamb's lettuce which they dressed with hazelnut oil and a cider vinegar made by the doctor's wife.

The following day Maddalena left the monastery. As usual, everyone was sorry to see her go—even the abbot.

CHAPTER 13

The priest and Maddalena, who rarely found themselves at the monastery at the same time, continued to meet in town when they could, which was not very often. He seemed to be travelling more and more; she was busy ferrying monastery guests and spent Christmas and New Year with her son and daughter with the family in Sicily.

'Thank you for the book—very interesting. I enjoyed it, I really did. Especially this bit.' Maddalena handed him back the Varillon book he had lent her months ago, opened at page 112 where a passage on the virgin Mary was underlined in pencil.

They were sitting outside on a café terrace in the February sunshine. Laden orange and lemon trees lined streets and filled gardens, forests of fluffy fragrant mimosa flowers had turned slopes of surrounding hillsides yellow, white-flowering branches of almond trees heralded the return of spring.

The priest put down his mint tea, took the book and read the lines. In the passage the author, Jesuit theologian François Varillon, says that a particular theologian thinks (although he adds that not all theologians share his opinion) that the doctrine of the divinity of Jesus would not be put in doubt if Jesus was the issue of a normal marriage, if he had been conceived, as we all are, by the sexual conjunction of a man and a woman. Varillon continues that the theologian is certainly right in the sense that the apostles believed in the divinity of Jesus thanks to the resurrection, thus independently of the virginal conception.

'Ah,' said the priest, who shared the opinion, although he didn't remember reading that bit. 'I bet he wishes he hadn't said that.'

'I dare say he does but he did and it makes me feel a whole lot better that my own thoughts on the matter have at least been expressed by such an illustrious personage.' The theologian in question at the time the book was published in 1981 was Cardinal Joseph Ratzinger, who would become better known to the world in general as Pope Benedict XVI. The priest recalled very well when he was at the seminary in Rome being told something similar by one of their theological professors. He did not mention this to Maddalena.

'He gave me some chocolate. Did I ever tell you? The abbot, when I first met him. Dark chocolate. It was delicious. He keeps it in his desk drawer.'

'Yes, I know. He must have taken a liking to you pretty quickly. I didn't get any until several weeks after we first met.'

She and the priest had other animated discussions—the animation was more on Maddalena's side than on the priest's side, it had to be said—about other issues relating to their religion.

'I hope I won't get bored,' he said one afternoon, pouring hot water onto the dried verbena leaves in his cup at a beach café. 'You know. Eternal life,' he said, slightly stressing the "eternal".

'Oh, heavens, no, I don't think we will be. But what will we look like? Will we be resurrected looking like we did when we died—old and wrinkly if we have lived to a great age? Suppose you've had a leg amputated, for example? Will you be resurrected with one leg or two?'

The priest, who had not given much thought to this aspect of eternal life, listened as Maddalena warmed to her theme.

'I think we might be like kaleidoscopes,' continued Maddalena, 'diaphanous figures constantly changing in appearance to reflect how we looked at different stages of our lives.'

The thought of being surrounded by eternally evolving friends and family made the priest feel slightly queasy. He sat in silence then said, 'So that snotty nosed four-year-old sitting on his cloud playing the harpsichord could be Mozart.'

Maddalena ignored his remark and continued, 'We will float

around surrounded by those we have loved plus everybody else, in a blissful state of just, well, being, existing, no feelings like boredom or anything else. Just a sublimely joyjul sensation, you know, how you feel when it's blowing a hoolie outside and you are snuggled up warm and safe in bed.'

A particularly challenging exchange—not really an exchange, Maddelena talked, the priest listened—took place over an early evening April supper down by the port. They had gone there to enjoy some plump Marseillan mussels raised in the Bassin de Thau in the Hérault, and so they had ordered Noilly-Prat as an aperitif.

'I could say that I think Saint Paul—nothing worse than a convert for preaching to others, but a great letter writer, I grant you that—I could say that he was a misogynist, quite possibly impotent, which is why he suggested that everybody should live a celibate and chaste life like him—although I don't believe Christ ever spoke on the subject,' said Maddalena.

The waiter arrived with the two glasses of vermouth. Not for the first time he wondered, as did the staff in other places the couple frequented, about the exact nature of the relationship between the man and the woman. They were obviously very fond of each other. He had often seen the woman put her hand on the man's arm during an animated discussion but had never noticed any behaviour of a romantic nature.

She looked older than him—a relative? Yet their physical appearances were completely different—she was olive-skinned, dark-haired and Italian whereas the man was French. They obviously enjoyed each other's company, sometimes deep in conversation, other times laughing, occasionally he had seen them looking at foreign stamps.

Two steaming black ceramic pots of mussels in their blueblack shells cooked simply with shallots and white wine arrived together with a large bowl of long thin pale straw coloured salted French fries.

'I could also say that I wonder if the Catholic Church would have accumulated its enormous wealth if priests had been allowed to marry and wives and children had had to be housed, fed, clothed—well-to-do men, however devout, may well not have bequeathed property and land to the Church when joining a religious community if they had a family to look after.'

The priest listened, wondering what had brought on this particular outpouring as he poured out a glass of water and one of a crisp sylvaner from the two carafes on the wooden table. They each used an empty bivalve shell to extract the juicy mussels—the same deep ochre orangey colour as some of the old town terraced houses—and a fork, or their fingers, for the fries.

'I could say that I think the dogma of the virgin birth, which subsequently led to the much later add-ons of the Immaculate Conception and the August feast of the Assumption—try removing *that* public holiday from the Italian or French calendar —I could say it is the frustrated response of a male-only group of humans who can thus channel their renouncement of earthly female companionship into adoration of a young Jewess, who I have always thought of as rather a revolutionary woman, who gave birth to the Messiah—but was born and lived her life just like the rest of us.' Maddalena emphasised these last words—and paused for breath.

She asked for a couple of spoons so they could drink up some of the liquid and continued, 'I could say all of these things. But I won't because you have been travelling and are suffering from jet lag.' She gave the priest a warm wide smile. 'Instead I will tell you about the Cézanne exhibition I went to and my night at the opera with the Pearl Fishermen.' The priest never asked her who she went with; Maddalena never proffered the information.

She told the priest that she had asked the abbot if she could come to the monastery a few days before she was needed. He had replied that she could come for as long as she wanted, whenever she wanted, provided she continued to help Brother Gianni improve his culinary skills.

The priest was delighted that everything seemed to be going well. However, it seemed to him, when the two of them did manage to meet up and she told him about her stays at the monastery, that she spent rather a lot of time in the kitchen garden with Brother Louis-Marc.

He didn't mention that, of course. And when they met in May at the port, she didn't mention that earlier that month at the monastery, on a rather overcast and cool afternoon, there had been a knock at her door. Louis-Marc, dressed in his frayed blue jeans and a checked shirt, stood there with a small white china bowl full of wild merisier, small deep red-black cherries still attached to their stalks. 'Oh, how lovely. Come in.'

He had shown her the wild cherry tree a few weeks earlier. '*Prunus avium*—the cerisier des oiseaux. Have you ever eaten them? Then I'll bring you some when they ripen.' Now here he was with a bowl full of cherries. He placed it on her table and sat down on the end of her bed as if it was the most natural thing in the world to do. Maddalena pulled out the chair and sat down facing him and they started eating the small firm-fleshed cherries, dropping the stones into the waste paper basket she had placed between them.

'Not the sweetest, we'll have to wait for the burlat, but I quite like that hint of acidity,' said the monk.

'You should have called me to give you a hand.'

'I climb up into the tree with my basket. It has a long rope handle which I hang round my neck. Do you like them?'

'They're delicious. Thank you, Louis-Marc.'

They sat chatting, comfortable in each other's company, until the bell rang for the end of work. Beaming, the monk got to his feet and walked to the door. They said goodbye and as he walked back to the monastery a cockerel crowed, followed by a second one. His face, like the sky above, clouded over. Perhaps he should not have gone to Maddalena's room, he thought.

As she watched the monk walking away, Maddalena's face, too, clouded over. Various villagers had hens and ducks but to the best of her knowledge, which was by now quite substantial given her regular trips into the valley, the only cockerels you heard as clearly as the two which had just crowed were at Isnard's farm. That morning, she had walked down to the village and Isnard's wife had invited her to supper the following evening. She had been about to dispatch the two young cockerels to make a coq au vin. They should have been in the marinade by now.

Maddalena and the priest chatted on in the May sunshine, never short of things to talk about. He tried hard to make time on his travels to visit museums and art galleries. She always enjoyed listening to him describe what he had seen. They talked about the books they were reading. He asked how she was getting on with her philosophy. She made him laugh as she recounted the story of Brother Gianni, the Ancients and the pasta. 'Everyone was busy so Brother Gianni had to cook all week and it was pasta, pasta, pasta.'

'What, even the abbot wasn't around?'

'No, he'd gone to Rome apparently.'

The priest, who had been refilling their glasses with a pale, refreshing rosé, looked up sharply. 'Rome? He never told me about that. What was he doing in Rome?'

'I don't know, something to do with a letter, I think.'

CHAPTER 14

The abbot walked out of his office to the delicious aroma of freshly ground coffee and found the priest making himself an espresso ristretto from the machine on the wooden table in the cloister. He had arrived late the previous evening and had made his way to his usual ground floor room. The main door was closed at night but never locked.

'Successful journey? You look tired.'

'Yes on both counts,' said the priest, smiling and downing his coffee in one go. He rinsed out his cup under the cloister garden tap and the two men walked out of the monastery. As they strolled around the church and along the path which led down to the lake the priest spoke briefly about his latest trip to the Middle East. Then he said, 'The last time I saw Maddalena, she mentioned something about Rome.'

'Did she? Is she planning on going?'

'No. But she said you had.'

'That was ages ago. How on earth did she know that?'

'She was recounting the story of when Gianni was in charge of the kitchen and cooked pasta all week.'

The abbot laughed. 'Oh yes, that was a disastrous week, apparently.'

'Matteo had explained to her how it came about, that everybody was busy doing something or other. And you had left for Rome. Something to do with a letter.'

'We thank God daily for the arrival of Maddalena at the monastery. Not just for the fetching and carrying, but for having taken the time to teach young Gianni a few simple dishes that do not include pasta.'

'What took you to Rome, Giacomo?'

'She had her family send us a delivery of artichokes, those small purple spiky ones that you eat raw, I love them—I don't think you get them here in France. She showed Gianni how to prepare them, slice them thinly and dress them with a little olive oil, vinegar—it was earlier in the year so they were using lemon juice in the kitchen instead of vinegar. They were truly delicious. Yes, we give thanks daily for Maddalena's arrival.'

He doesn't want to tell me, thought the priest, *now why is that?* Mind you, those artichokes sounded delicious.

Although they were somewhat sheltered from it, the mistral had blown long and hard for the past two days leaving a brilliant cobalt blue cloudless June sky. They paused when they reached the gnarled and twisted olive trees growing round the large, gravelly and sun-baked piece of ground, marked out by roughly hewn and spliced tree trunks.

These tree trunks had been at the root of a most unmonastic stushie, to borrow again from Brother Séamus's evocative Scot's vocabulary. To mark out the ground, Aarne and Louis-Marc had helped themselves to pieces of timber—oak, elm, walnut, lime wood—that Matteo and Gianni were seasoning for various purposes—picture frames, furniture, statues, coffins. For a couple of days there had been a noticeable cooling of relations between the two sets of monks. It always amazed the abbot how even in a community where silence was the order of the day—every day — you could always tell when people weren't talking to each other.

In the monks' cemetery a little further on, the Ancients, who hadn't left the monastery while the mistral was blowing—it would possibly have blown them over, they were now so frail— now sat on the circular bench under the elm. The abbot opened up a wooden box in the corner of the marked off area, took out two sets of boules and stuffed into the deep pocket of his robe his magnet, attached to a polyester strap, for picking them up, while the priest traced a semicircle in the sandy gravel with the toe of his shoe. The abbot threw the target, the small white wooden cochonnet.

'What's the weather forecast for Sunday?'

'Excellent,' said the abbot, continuing the priest's semicircle to make a full circle—it infuriated him that the priest never did that. He then stood within the circle, feet together, les pieds tanqués, which gave the game its name. He concentrated and, holding his boule palm down, flicked his wrist and launched it into the air. It landed well short of the cochonnet and stopped dead.

They both recalled the mid-morning downfall of biblical proportions the previous year during mass in the village church, attended by believers, non-believers and the not sures, which had threatened to turn the annual fête into a wash out. Trestle tables and benches had been hastily moved under the canvas awning which had been hastily erected following the previous evening's weather forecast.

But as so often happens in these parts, by the time mass was over the rain had eased up. By the time aperitifs had been served the rain had stopped and by the time everyone had finished eating the sun had come out and dried off the village pétanque terrain. The final results, chalked up on the blackboard, bore witness to the inevitable monastic white wash, and everyone trooped back to church for Vespers.

'You know I wish just once, just once, we could give them a run for their money. Have a team make it into the second round. It's not much to ask,' said the abbot in a rather wistful way.

The priest laughed, squatted down on his haunches balancing on his toes, knees akimbo, and as he launched his boule held his bent left arm slightly behind his back. 'But Giacomo, they play pétanque week in, week out. Some of them play almost every evening. All these boules of yours go back into Matteo's box after each feast day and don't come out again until the following year. What do you expect?'

This was not strictly true. The abbot and the priest quite often played when the latter was in residence. These comparatively infrequent sessions, however, made little impression on the abbot's game.

The abbot attempted to dislodge the priest's boule, which was perilously close to the cochonnet, by shooting a tir devant. Standing upright, he looked at his objective, his face marked with concentration. His aim was to launch his boule high and far to cover most of the distance in the air. It would then hit the ground less than thirty centimetres short of the objective, and roll at sufficient speed to knock the priest's point-scoring boule away from the cochonnet.

The boule flew out of the abbot's hand, landed close to its destination but on a hard piece of ground and bounced back up again. It continued its journey over both the priest's boule and the cochonnet, landed again on the other side and sped away towards the olive trees until its progress was halted by Aarne's and Louis-Marc's tree trunk boundary.

Sadly, the abbot was as good a pointeur as he was a tireur. He tried his hand at a demi-portée. His next boule should land halfway, with sufficient élan to then roll right up to the cochonnet. Brow furrowed, he launched his boule. It sailed up too high, hit the ground with a thud, rolled perhaps ten centimetres and stopped dead.

Once he got his eye in, the priest who had played pétanque as a youngster, was not a bad player. He was a pointer and headed up the monastic team on the great day with Brother Ange-Dominique, a milieu who could both point and shoot and had once reached the Triplettes finals in the Corse du Sud championship before his incarceration.

The annual fête, held turn and turn about in the village and at the monastery, was in honour of their founder Amadeo of Marebosco. It had been initiated, in consultation with the mayor, when the monks had arrived from Liguria. It was known from the sparse literature extant that Amadeo had not been keen on the canonisation process deeming that there were already far too many saints. So he was presumably not disappointed when he died and went to heaven that successive popes did not make him one. In any case, although the mission to which he had dedicated his life may have merited sainthood, the extremely discreet nature of his work meant that even the pope, who did the canonising, had hardly heard of him. So there was no official saint's day to celebrate.

The monks knew the year of Amadeo's death but he had died in February which by general agreement was not deemed a good month for a fête. They tried to get hold of a copy of his birth certificate but without success. When they contacted the commune of Marebosco they received a reply stating that they held no records prior to 1866.

The monks thought that this might have had something to do with the nineteenth century Risorgimento movement which had finally resulted in the unification of the various peninsula states—including the Republic of Genoa, capital of Liguria—and the establishment of the Kingdom of Italy in 1861.

The community of the day had left Liguria for France in September but that was harvest time so not a good time for the villagers to forsake fields for festivities. So they had settled on the third Sunday in June.

As their second game progressed, the priest attempted a carreau to dislodge his opponent's boule. The abbot—he could no longer crouch down on his haunches so he remained upright—decided to pointe à la roulette and had launched his boule low to hit the ground within the first few metres of where he was standing and roll the rest of the way towards the cochonnet. The terrain was not particularly flat and it had stopped short about half a metre from the cochonnet.

When successfully performed, the carreau was a spectacular shot. The priest, standing upright, concentrated hard on the interloper he wanted to replace. Then, holding his boule in the palm of his hand, the back of his hand uppermost, he extended his arm and launched it into the air. It landed with a sharp cracking sound of steel on steel knocking away a boule and taking its place. It was text book stuff—if it had been the abbot's boule and not one of the priest's earlier ones.

'It's funny how they always look like their smiling even when they're not,' said the priest. Both men had noticed the arrival of the Buddhist monk who had been watching the game from a distance for some time and was now walking towards them. The general rule, unwritten—like most of the community's rules—was not to initiate contact with visitors. So they waited to see whether the Buddhist wanted to speak to them.

'I remember seeing a television programme about a Tibetan monastery. They were interviewing a young American Buddhist. It was his eyes—they just shone and sparkled. It was quite extraordinary. I've never forgotten it,' said the abbot.

The Buddhist monk made it clear in a combination of broken English and French that he wanted to join in. The priest removed another set of three boules from the box and gave them to the Buddhist monk who knotted up his saffron robe revealing a pair of thin muscular legs covered to the knee by an undergarment.

The priest picked up his boules, the abbot's magnet picked up his. He handed the cochonnet to the Buddhist monk who moved to a different part of the terrain and traced a semicircle in the gravel, paused, looked at the abbot and carried on with his sandal to make a full circle. The abbot immediately warmed to the Buddhist who now threw the cochonnet then crouched down on his haunches imitating the priest and copied the abbot's last throw. The three men, the Buddhist monk still squatting, watched the boule move smoothly at speed to stop about two centimetres from the cochonnet. 'Beginner's luck,' said the abbot, smiling at the Buddhist who smiled back.

They played on. It wasn't beginner's luck. The Buddhist, who had realised the importance of studying the terrain, who had carefully watched how pebbles in the way could deflect the trajectory of a boule, and who, thanks to a lifetime of meditation, had concentration in spades, was a natural.

He may not have been familiar with the terms, but he was both a pointeur and a tireur. Depending on his shot, he stood or squatted down, blanked out everything from his mind and launched his boule. It went up, came down where it was supposed to and rolled either right up to the cochonnet or knocked an opposing boule out of the way. He produced two spectacular carreaux that left the priest and the abbot flabbergasted. In brief, the Buddhist played a blinder.

At the end of each game the points were totted up—a player gaining a point for each boule he had closest to the target. The winner was the first team or player to reach thirteen. By the end of their third game, the Buddhist monk had racked up a maximum nine points.

The abbot turned to the priest and said quietly, 'Do we know how long he's staying?'

The priest, who was as vague as the abbot about the length of stays, said, 'I don't know, but I do hope he's not leaving before Sunday.'

Although the abbot was advised of study group arrivals so that rooms could be prepared and collection arrangements made if needed, the teachers were in charge of the duration. Sometimes study periods were extended, sometimes they were curtailed, usually when there had been some new outrage perpetrated in one of the attendees' countries.

The monastery hosted visitors over the Christmas period—an important festival for christians but not for everyone else. Repairs and renewals and renovations were carried out in between study sessions. The abbot, with the priest's agreement, had decreed that the only time they would close was during Holy Week, the seven days between Palm Sunday and Easter Sunday.

The abbot walked over to the beaming monk and said, 'Well done, brother!' and paused. 'We were wondering how long you are staying with us.' The Buddhist beamed. 'When do you leave the monastery?' He repeated his question, this time walking away from the monk, carrying an imaginary suitcase and turning to wave goodbye. The Buddhist monk waved back.

The abbot said to the priest, 'Have you got a diary on you?' The priest did not have one but fished out of his jacket pocket a notebook and quickly wrote down on a blank page the day and date of the next few days through till the following week.

The abbot showed it to the monk and said in that unfortunate way people have when they speak to foreigners who because they do not speak the same language are assumed to be hard of hearing, 'WHEN – DO – YOU – LEAVE?' He pointed at the Buddhist monk, waved again, and pointed to tomorrow's date in the notebook, paused, and repeated the gestures for the following days. The monk continued beaming in silence, then pointed to himself, waved to the abbot, and pointed to Saturday.

'He can't leave Saturday. He must stay till Monday,' murmured the abbot to the priest.

'Yes,' said the priest.

'We must explain to him that on Sunday we have the fête, that the whole village comes here for the day, that we picnic outside, have music, dancing—and a pétanque competition. And that he must be on our team. He cannot leave on Saturday.'

The Ancients, who had been sitting separately like four points of the compass on the bench around the elm tree, were now huddled up together looking over the low cemetery wall towards the three men by the olive trees.

They watched as their abbot raised his arms in the air in a wide movement encompassing the area around him and then raised ten fingers in the air, closed his hands, and repeated the gesture three or four times with a large smile on his face. They watched as the abbot then drank from an imaginary glass and ate imaginary food. They watched as he wiggled his fingers and rocked from side to side playing an imaginary accordion and then started executing a curious little jig, turning round in a circle.

While he was miming this, the abbot said to the priest, 'Draw a picture of a pétanque match, would you please, figlio mio.' The priest opened his mouth to protest that he had no idea how to draw a pictorial representation of a pétanque match, thought about Sunday, and opened up the middle pages of his notebook.

On each page, he drew several little stick men, in groups of three, holding a round black circle in each hand, with a large V drawn in the join of the pages. The abbot looked at the drawing, looked somewhat askance at the priest, sighed, and showing it to the Buddhist pointed repeatedly at him then at the stick men holding their boules. The Buddhist monk looked at the drawing then looked up at the abbot who flicked back through the priest's notebook and jabbed his finger at Sunday and proceeded to give an encore of his earlier performance.

At this point Brother Ange-Dominique, who had been taking a break and smoking a joint down by the lake, came up the path and saw the three men standing on the pétanque terrain. He stopped in his tracks, took the remains of the spliff he had extinguished earlier out of his paint-smeared smock pocket and looked at it, slowly shaking his head. The Ancients had by now vacated their circular bench and had slowly made their way across the small cemetery to stand by the low wall for a better view.

Meanwhile the Buddhist monk had reached the stage of enlightenment. He let out a long 'Aaah' and beamed even more, if that were possible. He walked away carrying an invisible suitcase, turned to wave to the abbot and the priest, returned and pointed in the notebook to Monday. 'Yes!' said the abbot almost weeping with joy. 'Yes!' he repeated, approaching the Buddhist monk with arms wide open.

The Buddhist held up his right hand to indicate that these celebrations were premature. He produced from somewhere within his blazing saffron-orange robe a state-of-the art smartphone, opened it up, tapped it a couple of times, waited a handful of seconds then spoke briefly into it in his own language. He listened, closed his phone and returned it to the deep recesses of his robe. Turning to the abbot and the priest, he gave the thumbs up sign and this time allowed himself to be enveloped in the abbot's fraternal embrace.

The following day Brother Aarne's atheist aunts were due to arrive from Finland. The first time the abbot had met them they had served vodka in their honour which the aunts had downed as an aperitif and continued to down throughout lunch. By the end of the meal, between them they had finished the bottle yet showed none of the signs normally associated with the consumption of such a quantity of high strength spirit.

Tuuli was of above average height with a mass of auburn hair which she wore swept up and held in place by various combs. Her younger sister Olga was a smaller, silent version of her sister. When they first met, Tuuli wasted a lot of time trying to convert the abbot to atheism. Over the years she had given up and now just flirted rather outrageously with him.

Through his office window, the abbot heard them arrive. As usual, Tuuli was driving too fast on the unmade up lane, bouncing along in and out of potholes with Olga clinging grimly to the hand strap. They pulled up sharply in front of the monastery sending up clouds of dust from the sun-baked road surface. The abbot, waiting outside to greet them and based on previous experience, prudently retreated to avoid temporarily disappearing in a swirl of descending particles, not dissimilar to the aftermath of a volcanic eruption, which was rather how he always viewed the Finnish aunts' arrival .

'Tuuli, Olga, how lovely to see you both again.'

'Abbot, I swear you look younger every time I see you,' said Tuuli, kissing the abbot on both cheeks. Olga smiled nervously and followed suit.

'Your rooms are waiting. Here's Aarne. He'll take your luggage. We won't see you at the offices—unless, of course, you have had a change of heart since you were last with us,' said the abbot, eyes twinkling, 'but I hope you'll both join me for a nightcap before turning in.'

Tuuli bestowed upon Abbot Giacomo one of those smiles of hers that had turned so many men weak at the knees. The abbot, made of sterner stuff, said, 'I'll take that as a yes, Tuuli.' Aarne hastily hustled his aunts away to their rooms.

That evening, in his office, the abbot served the two women cloudberry vodka. He and the priest sipped a single malt. It was the first time their visit had coincided with the feast day so the abbot told the women about the events planned for the coming Sunday.

'Pétanque,' cried out Tuuli. 'I LOVE playing pétanque.'

The abbot froze, his hand holding his dram half way to his mouth. The priest tried hard to suppress a smile.

'Really? You play pétanque, Tuuli? I didn't know it was popular in Finland.'

It wasn't. It turned out that one of the relationships in Tuuli's colourful love life had included a torrid affair with a French torero from Tarascon. She had religiously attended bullfights in Nîmes, Arles and wherever else he was fighting in south west France, and when he wasn't, she had been taught to play pétanque.

A beatific smile slowly spread across the abbot's face. 'So you play quite well, Tuuli?'

'Well? WELL? I should think so. I must play on Sunday.'

'Indeed you must, Tuuli, indeed you must.'

The priest was really struggling now to suppress the overwhelming urge to burst out laughing. He had never seen the abbot so animated since the day he had been with him when a villager had delivered a parcel from the abbot's family chock-a-block full of hugely high percentage dark chocolate.

The women were tired after their journey, so having knocked back the vodka they took their leave.

'Strategy,' said the abbot to the priest, refilling their glasses. 'We must talk strategy.'

'Giacomo, it's just a game of pétanque—it's Amadeo's feast day, we all go to mass, we have lunch, drink and dance, lose the pétanque match, most of us attend Vespers then everybody goes home happy.'

'Écoute, o mon fils. We have the Buddhist monk. We have Tuuli. For once, we have a chance—oh, not of winning, no, but at least of not all being knocked out in the first round. We need a strategy. Do we put them in the same team? Or do we put them in separate teams? And in which case, who with? You and Ange-

Dominique are our best players, Louis-Marc is pretty good, Séamus and I are OK, just. Aarne, Matteo and Gianni, well . . .' The priest, realising that the abbot was serious, talked strategy.

The following day the abbot called an exceptional chapter meeting mid morning so as not to waste any time. He explained that they had been blessed with two exceptional pétanque players for the game on Sunday and that between now and then he would like them all—apart from the Ancients, of course—to use all available time, and if needs be, to make time available, to practise for the match.

So it came to pass that at different moments over the next few days various monks in varying combinations could be seen putting their heart and soul into playing pétanque under the olive trees, serenaded by the cicadas.

In the beginning there was just the thud of boules hitting the timber barriers. The following morning, however, the abbot heard the heavenly sound of steel on steel. Sadly, it was Matteo inadvertently knocking away one of his own boules. However, as he approached, the abbot noticed with pleasure that this second one had come to rest surprisingly close to the cochonnet.

Gradually the sound of steel on steel replaced the thud of boules hitting the barriers. Accuracy improved. Matteo, Gianni and Aarne listened carefully to instructions, concentrated, and quite often succeeded now in placing their boules—more or less —where they had been told to place them.

Tuuli gave invaluable help to everyone. The Buddhist monk pitched up to play when he had time between work sessions. The abbot was now rarely to be seen without a beaming smile on his face. As he saw his monks' progress, he could hardly contain his excitement.

Late afternoon on the Friday he and the priest, on their way down to the lake, walked past the pétanque terrain where Louis-Marc was playing Ange-Dominique, and Tuuli was giving a master class to Aarne, Matteo, Gianni and Séamus.

'Word has got around,' he said to the priest. 'Most of the visitors have delayed their departure so they can be here for the feast day.' Apparently even the imam, an influential liberal member of the Muslim community and the teacher for the session, had decided to stay on.

'Well, that'll add an international flavour to the proceedings,' said the priest. 'Do they want to play?'

'I'm not sure. If they do, we'll never have fielded so many teams,' chuckled the abbot. 'Mind you, there will be plenty of villagers to make up the numbers. They have grandmothers who play better than most of us.'

'What about Maddalena? Was she due to take people to the airport?'

'Yes, but I've told her about the change in plans so she's not arriving until Sunday morning now. I told her you were here but I didn't think to ask her—does she play pétanque?'

'I've no idea,' said the priest, 'but if she wants to play then we are,' he counted out loud, 'seven from the monastery—Luca never wants to play, does he?—me, Tuuli—Olga says she doesn't play—the Buddhist, Maddalena—that makes eleven. Plus another study group visitor and that will make four teams of three.'

'Hmm, we might need to revise our strategy,' said the abbot.

The priest, who found it really hard to treat the pétanque game with the same degree of seriousness as the abbot and had forgotten what their original strategy was, said, 'Yes, perhaps we should. What do you think, Giacomo?'

They about turned and as they walked back to the monastery the abbot, after some reflection, expounded his latest views on team formations until the bells started clanging, temporarily, as always, stunning into silence the cicadas.

The abbot ordained, as part of his strategy, that the normal monastic timetable should be resumed on Saturday morning. Brother Ange-Dominique took up his paint brushes again, Brother Aarne returned to his distillery, Brothers Matteo and Gianni returned to the workshop and repairs and renewals. The only exception was made for Brother Séamus who needed to practice his piping.

Pétanque practice resumed in the afternoon, Maddalena arrived, earlier than planned, the community continued a reading chosen by Séamus, *Travels Through France and Italy,* an educative and entertaining account by that curmudgeonly Scottish medic Tobias Smollett.

CHAPTER 15

Sunday dawned bright and clear and still and sunny. The monastery grounds soon became a hive of activity. Villagers started arriving in a variety of farm vehicles bringing large sacks of ice to cool drinks, and trestle tables and benches and chairs which they set up in the shade of the olive trees near the pétanque terrain.

The women and girls, dressed in pretty summer frocks and colourful cotton skirts and tops, drove up with food, wine, soft drinks, table cloths, glasses, cutlery, and started laying the tables. Children ran around in a joyous state of excitement, laughing, shouting, playing tag and football.

The bells rang out for mass. Everyone—believers and atheists alike—downed tools, ambled over to the church and filled up the pews. The mayor, as was his custom when he entered a church both before and after becoming an atheist, marched with his wife and family up the aisle and sat in the first pew on the right. Maddalena sat with Aarne's aunts. Pews filled up with families from the village and all the outlying hamlets.

Right at the back of the church, present out of courtesy for their hosts but wishing also to be able to leave early and discreetly, which they duly did, sat the Buddhist monk and the other remaining visitors—two Sikhs and two Hindus (one a rather lovely female, the abbot had noticed), a rabbi and the imam teacher of the group. The Russian Orthodox priest had been invited to join the monks.

At the beginning of each session, the abbot always told the teacher that everyone was welcome to attend the offices, and indeed mass, if they wished. During their stay at the monastery visitors of all creeds and none did make occasional appearances. The abbot had noticed that the Buddhists, in particular, often turned up in the early hours for vigils.

Chanting the entry hymn, the community processed through the cloister door into the abbey church—the monks wearing as usual their long wide-sleeved dark dove grey cowls, the priests robed in white vestments in celebration of Amadeo's feast day, the abbot wearing his mitre and carrying his crook. The novice Luca glancing surreptitiously to his left hoping to set eyes on the mayor's daughter, Espérite, met her steady gaze and smile. He blushed and quickly averted his eyes.

From the altar Abbot Giacomo turned to face the congregation. Some of his monks knew some of the villagers but as he looked at the faces looking at him, he was the only one who knew them all—elders, adults, teenagers, children, babies—he knew their names, he knew their hamlets. For decades he had baptised, confessed, married, and buried these villagers. These were not the normal duties for an abbot—but then this was not a normal community.

The religious education for first communions and confirmations was thankfully dealt with by priests in distant diocese churches in the town where the children were weekly boarders. Here in their remote valley the local parish priest had departed decades ago. When the monks of the Communità dello Spirito Santo had arrived, there was a stark choice. Either the adjective "God-forsaken" would be added to the description of the valley, or the monastery, that is, the abbot, would take on the role of providing minimal pastoral care.

Today it was standing room only in the abbey church. The abbot welcomed everybody, said a few words about Amadeo, thanked the villagers for their support and affection and started mass. The abbot had asked Tuuli to give the first reading and recite the psalm and its response; the mayor, in keeping with tradition, gave the second reading; with the abbot's blessing farmer Isnard's wife read the gospel. The abbot had chosen this auspicious Sunday for Luca to give the homily, based on that Sunday's gospel. It would be the first time. 'Keep it simple, Luca, and keep it short,' said the abbot and asked Aarne, as novice master, to supervise.

After the gospel reading, Luca made his way to the lectern and produced from the shelf below three A4 sheets of paper each of which appeared to be covered in writing on both sides. The abbot, who had eschewed the celebrant's chair up behind the altar and had sat down in the choir stalls, looked on in horror. He immediately turned a furious gaze onto Brother Aarne, who was sitting opposite and was looking even more horrified. What with the pétanque practice he had completely forgotten the abbot's instructions. The abbot slumped back into his seat.

It was not as bad as it seemed. Most of Luca's scribbling had been crossed out and each page only contained two or three legible paragraphs at most. He had spent an inordinate amount of time on this, his first homily, especially on the fish. He wanted it to stand out. He wanted it to be different. He wanted it to be remembered. He succeeded on all counts. He looked at the sea of faces and said, 'Mes chères soeurs, mes chers frères.' He was pleased with that opening. The others normally put it the other way round but he had put the sisters first. He repeated it, 'Mes chères soeurs, mes chers frères.'

He looked down at the first A4 sheet, cast his eye over it, turned it over and skimmed through the other side, put it to the bottom and did the same with the next sheet. Panic quickly set in when he realised that he had not thought to number his sheets. The silence was rattling his nerves. Espérite was giving him an encouraging smile which only made matters worse.

He plunged in and started reading out a paragraph from a sheet that if he had thought to number each side would have been marked 4. Bereft of an introduction, it caused a few furrowed brows but the second paragraph from the same page followed on logically. Then he turned the page over and read out the three paragraphs on page 3, which did not. The abbot closed his eyes, Aarne had his head in his hands, the Ancients, sitting in pairs like double bookends at the end of one stall, were fast asleep.

Having finished both sides of that sheet Luca placed it with now trembling hands under the other two, stared wildly at the sheet now at the top, turned it over, turned it back again, and put it, too, to the bottom. He opened his mouth to continue reading from what was now the top sheet, realised it was upside down, put it the right way up, and launched into what in an ideal paginated world would have been page 1.

'He could have read it out upside down for all the sense this is making,' muttered the priest. This was too much for Brother Ange-Dominique who had been studying with great concentration the upper reaches of the abbey church. His shoulders began to shake. The abbot gave a glacial abbatial glare in his direction. If BAD got a fit of the giggles he would set off the others. But with a superhuman effort the artist monk managed to control himself while Luca staggered from one non sequitur to another.

The abbot flashed another furious look towards his master of novices. *Dio mio*, thought the abbot, *he's only got one.* To be fair —but the abbot was not in the mood to be fair—he realised that the pétanque practice had completely turned their monastic routine upside down which was presumably why Aarne had forgotten about Luca and his first homily.

The congregation, to their credit, made a sterling effort to keep up. They had realised that the novice had not thought to number his pages. Yet brows continued to furrow. What they had not realised was that Luca had mistakenly based his homily not on the gospel they had just heard, but on the following Sunday's gospel.

The villagers—some regular church goers, others not—split up into different categories. There were those who listened attentively to the gospel and drifted off during the homily; and those who did the opposite. There were those who paid scant attention to either, and then there were those—rare birds, these —who listened to both. On this occasion everyone fell into this latter group. The villagers always paid attention when one of their own read the gospel. Luca had told Espérite that he was giving his first homily so naturally the whole village knew and, sadly, gave him their undivided attention.

Among the congregation, neighbours nudged each other and quiet whispered murmurings circulated around the church.

'But they're in the desert . . . surely there are no sword fish in the desert.'

'What have loaves and fishes got to do with anything? The gospel was Jesus talking about sending the Holy Spirit, wasn't it?'

'I thought she said it was the gospel according to St John. Why does he keep talking about Luke?'

'Sea bass in the Sea of Galilee—I don't think so. It's a fresh water lake, isn't it?'

'I can't make head nor tail of this, can you?'

The abbot was due to give the homily the following Sunday. He had glanced quickly at the relevant gospel that morning. In all fairness—but the abbot was not in the mood to be fair—he could see what had happened. This year there were, exceptionally, five Sundays in June. He guessed that Luca had looked at the dates and just assumed that today's date was far too early to be the third Sunday, and so had plumped for the following one.

As Luca lurched on, the abbot thought, *This has to be stopped.*

Again, he caught Aarne's eye and with his extended right hand, palm facing downwards, made a couple of short, sharp, vicious horizontal slicing movements through the air. Brother Aarne rose quickly to his feet, walked over to the lectern, whispered a few words to Luca who, in mid sentence, suddenly said, 'Amen,' and stopped talking. He replaced his three sheets of paper on the shelf under the lectern and remained standing looking out at the sea of faces and feeling more than a little sick.

For a moment there was complete silence in the abbey

church. Then everyone burst into a warm sympathetic round of applause.

The rest of the service passed off without incident. There was never a collection at mass whether it was at the monastery or in the village church. The abbot felt that the villagers were more than generous enough with their time and produce. Occasionally someone left a sum of money in their will, always welcome. And there was a wonderful windfall when a group of youngsters drove to Italy for a friend's wedding, stopped off at the Casino de Paris in the Principality of Monaco on their way home, and had extraordinary success at the roulette table. Not only did they recuperate the entire expenditure of the trip (including the wedding present), they had also presented the abbot with an envelope stuffed with one hundred euro notes.

They were soon on the home stretch. The abbot pronounced the final words of the mass, 'Allez dans la paix du Christ,' followed by the words everybody had been waiting for which signalled the beginning of the festivities, 'Bonne fête, tout le monde!'

Brother Louis-Marc, cantor for the mass, sang the first line of their hymn to Amadeo (words: Brother Ange-Dominique, music: Brother Gianni). The congregation then joined in, voices young and old, tuneful and less so, in a rousing rendition sung *con brio* and a bit more *affrettando* than it should have been because everyone was now keen to get back outside for the aperitif.

One of the tables had been set up as the bar. Corks popped and glasses were filled with chilled local white or rosé wine, pastis was poured over ice which cracked as water was added, there were jugs of homemade lemonade, apple juice and cider. Platters of Corsican charcuterie - sliced coppa and lonzu and prisuttu – and bowls of small black olives and squares of toasted wholemeal bread spread with tapenade were handed round by youngsters happy to help out. One of the village lads started playing the accordion, drowning out the chattering cicadas but not the chattering villagers. Children ran riot, there was laughter, more popping of corks.

The religious visitors who had been standing awkwardly a little removed from the action, were quickly welcomed and gathered into the heart of the proceedings by the villagers who, although vaguely aware that the monastery was involved in some sort of ecumenical work, did not really comprehend why these people were here and cared even less.

The abbot, the traumas of Luca's homily behind him, looked around, sipping his white wine, a felicitous assemblage, when well chilled, of clairette, ugni blanc and chardonnay, and smiled with contentment. The mayor, who had been making eyes at Tuuli until his wife caught *his* eye, was now talking animatedly to the imam and Brother Ange-Dominique.

The normally reserved farmer Isnard and Brother Aarne had engaged with one of the now smiling Sikhs. The other one was listening attentively to a group of youngsters who had recently studied Sikhs in their religious education class and were visibly thrilled to have not one but two real live examples in front of them and were now busy trying to recall the five Ks. The smaller children were delighting the Ancients with their antics.

Tuuli's lipstick and nail varnish matching the colour of her thick upswept auburn hair made a stunning contrast with the saffron robes of the Buddhist monk with whom she appeared to be deep in conversation—in what language the abbot had no idea. He wondered what she looked like with her masses of auburn hair let down, immediately dismissed such a thought from his mind, but instinctively searched out young Luca and Espérite. He found them both, nowhere near each other, he, recovered from the trauma of his homily, talking to a couple of boys from the village, she playing with some of the younger children.

The other visitors, too, had been gathered up into the wonderful web of friendship weaved by monks and villagers. Now the Russian Orthodox priest was playing football with Brother Matteo, the rabbi and various youngsters. The male Hindu was chatting to the doctor and Brother Gianni. The female Hindu— she really was a beautiful woman, thought the abbot, resplendent in her kingfisher blue silk sari bordered with a band of canary yellow which matched her short-sleeved silk blouse—was listening with great attention to Brother Séamus explaining how his bagpipes worked.

Watching her reminded the abbot of a beautiful photograph he had seen in the newspaper of dozens and dozens of differently coloured saris, vibrant pinks, mauves, greens and yellows, which had just been washed in an Indian river—it might have been the Ganges—and were now laid out to dry in the sun. He had memorized the accompanying quotation from the French philosopher Denis Diderot: "When writing about women, we must dip our pens in the rainbow and dry the ink with the dust of butterfly wings." The abbot did not know what else Diderot said in his Essay on Women but he loved that bit.

The abbot felt a warm glow of satisfaction as he surveyed the scene. He wasn't at all sure they all fully understood each other in spite of the best efforts of interpreters cum chauffeurs who had remained behind at the monastery. Somehow it didn't seem to matter. *This is how it should be*, he thought, *regardless of what we believe or don't believe, this is how it should be.*

As the abbot surveyed the scene, it changed continuously, rather like a kaleidoscope, he thought, as groups broke up and reformed elsewhere, apart from the Ancients who had put down roots in the shade of a large olive tree and had now been joined by village elders. As he walked over to refill his glass, he overheard snippets of conversation here and there.

'How's the knee, Aarne?' said the doctor. 'I hope you remember to bandage it up when you're lifting those cases.'

'Talking about swordfish,' said the priest—to peals of laughter —'You've got a really simple recipe for that, haven't you, Maddalena?'

'Yes, *pesce spada alla siciliana*. And you can eat it hot or cold.'

'What's the recipe?' asked the mayor's wife.

'You chop up a small onion, celery stalk and garlic and soften them in a couple of tablespoons of olive oil with a bay leaf. Then add three tomatoes, peeled and chopped, a little sugar and cook, stirring for a minute; pour in about three hundred milli-litres of dry white wine, season and simmer for five minutes; put in a couple of slices of skinned swordfish and poach for less than ten minutes, turning the slices over once, et voilà.'

'This bit here is wrong, isn't it, Brother Ange-Dominique? I keep trying but I just can't get the perspective right,' said one of the village girls, showing the monk a drawing of the village church in her sketch book.

'Agathe has been broody for ages now,' said a farmer's wife from one of the hamlets to Brother Matteo. 'Well,' said the monk, racking his brain to remember the names and ages of her daughters, and taking a punt. 'Well, early thirties, I suppose it's natural.'

'Agathe is my hen, Brother.'

'Let me know the next time you're here at the weekend, Mad-dalena, and we'll go out and shoot some rabbits,' said farmer Isnard. Oh good, thought the abbot. He had been unaware that she shot but hoped the invitation would extend to other small game and water fowl when the hunting season opened.

'What on earth happened there, Brother Aarne? You've only got one novice,' laughed the mayor.

'I know, I know,' said Aarne, 'mea culpa. I was so busy practis-ing for—' He suddenly stopped as he realised he was talking to the person who headed up the village pétanque team.

'Excellent reading, Mayor, as usual,' said Brother Séamus com-ing to the rescue.

'Thank you, Séamus, thank you—always a pleasure.'

These snippets all contributed to the abbot's sense of well-being. God was in his heaven, all was well with the world. The abbot was a happy man. The priest, too, seeing the religious vis-itors mingling, smiling, laughing, exchanging with monks and villagers and more importantly with each other, thought, *This makes it all worthwhile. Now, how do we make this happen all over the world?*

Daily existence was always tense in the regions he travelled to—where these visitors came from—but recently the number of bomb attacks, assassinations, wanton destruction of ancient monuments and places of worship just because they were not your own monuments or places of worship had increased. He sometimes had moments of deep despair when he wondered what he was doing there, one step forward, two or three steps back, what was the point of it all?

He looked over at the imam, now chatting and laughing with Tuuli and the Russian Orthodox priest, at the male Hindu smiling and waving his arms in the air to emphasise a point to the Sikhs and Brother Gianni. This microcosm of what it could, what it should be like—that was the point of it all. He smiled to himself as he made tracks towards the bar to replenish his glass. On his way, he, too, overhead snippets of conversation.

'I've been meaning to ask you, Rabbi. Those dietary laws of yours—about what you can and cannot eat, food preparation, separate kitchens—just how immutable are they?' said the abbot. The priest smiled.

'Brother Louis-Marc says the Holy Spirit is female. I *love* that idea,' said a young village girl. The priest's smile disappeared. Maddalena certainly seemed to spend a lot of time in the kitchen garden.

Suddenly, what everyone—apart from the religious visitors for whom Amadeo's feast day was a first—had been waiting for happened. The accordionist stopped playing and over the general chatter came the unmistakeable skirl of the bagpipes playing "Scotland the Brave." The faces of the visitors were a sight to behold. As indeed was Brother Séamus as he appeared, to enthusiastic cheering, in full Highland dress, his kilt in Ancient MacNeil tartan—black and light blue and green squares, yellow and off white stripes—swinging from side to side as he piped the assembly to the picnic tables.

It was an extraordinary sight and one the monks and villagers never tired of beholding. Even those who no longer prayed, prayed that Brother Séamus would continue to have enough puff for many years to come. The astonished visitors—the Sikhs were particularly interested in Séamus's sgian dubh tucked into his sock—gathered round the monk to examine his bagpipes.

Soon all benches and chairs were occupied and tables were laden with plenty of platters prepared by the villagers, the monks, and the visitors' cooks who had kindly prepared ethnic culinary contributions for the event—there was catering for carnivores, omnivores, vegetarians and vegans. The abbot said grace and under the shade of the olive grove the feast day lunch began.

As wine stocks went down, noise levels rose. The abbot tried with little success to keep an eye on the alcohol consumption of his key players. He had no worries about the Buddhist, of course, but he noticed that Tuuli and her sister, who were sitting on different tables, both had beside them a plain glass litre bottle of colourless liquid. A generous interpretation would have been that it was cool, pure, local spring water. The small shot glasses suggested that a more realistic interpretation was that it was fiery high strength beloved-nephew-distilled vodka. Was this a wise way for one of his two top players to prepare for the pétanque match, he wondered?

It would have taken a braver man than the abbot to tackle Tuuli. He stopped fretting, tried to remember the strategy, and poured himself another glass of the rather good rosé, a pleasing blend of grenache noir, syrah, cinsault and a smattering of counoise.

In due course, cheeseboards carved out of olive wood by Matteo arrived bearing round creamy raw goat's milk cheeses, wrapped up in brown chestnut leaves and tied with raffia, and various other hard and soft cheeses made from local cow and ewe milk. More large, round, freshly baked *miches* appeared and the menfolk cut off hunks with their wooden-handled, carbon steel bladed folding knives—the endless supply of bread on these occasions always reminded the abbot of the Feeding of the Five Thousand, which in turn reminded him of Luca's homily. Now he chuckled. He would ask Luca, under Aarne's supervision, to give the homily next Sunday, minus the more imaginative piscatorial passages.

More corks were removed from more bottles of red wine. People started moving around now, changing places and tables to talk to others. As the abbot got up to stretch his legs he overhead the mayor's wife talking to Brother Gianni. 'I gather you made those peppers, Brother, they were really delicious. What's the recipe?'

'Oh, it couldn't be easier,' replied the monk. The abbot smiled.

As he started to stroll over to join the priest, Louis-Marc and Maddalena—who was looking lovely, he thought, with her brown skin and wavy black hair offset by a belted linen short-sleeved dress of emerald green which just covered her knees—he was approached by the rabbi.

'I thought only a priest could read the gospel, Père Abbé.'

'I don't think Jesus ever said anything about that,' replied the abbot, 'not least because they were written well after his crucifixion.'

'Heretic,' smiled the rabbi.

'I think we all have a bit of the heretic in us, don't we?' laughed the abbot, and continued on his way to join the others.

'So I think I may have lost most of the crop this year,' Louis-Marc was saying. 'Oh, that's a shame,' said the priest.

There was an almost, but not quite, imperceptible something in his tone that went unnoticed by Louis-Marc and indeed would not have been picked up by anyone who did not know the priest well. The abbot and Maddalena did know the priest well. Both turned sharply to look at him.

The abbot suddenly remembered his novice Luca and looked around until he found him standing a little way off, talking to Espérite. There was no doubt they made a handsome couple, thought the abbot. What was to be done? It had been the boy's decision to come to the monastery to see how he got on with monastic life, and his decision, later, to formalise the arrangement by becoming a novice. The abbot had no doubt about Luca's genuine love of the Lord, and the boy had adapted well to their monastic way of life—and yet . . .

His thoughts drifted back. He had been in his late twenties when he gradually realised he had a vocation to become a monk. Absurdly after all this time, he felt pinpricks of tears in his eyes as he recalled that bitter-sweet moment in his life when he gave up Livia the young woman he loved for a God he loved more. The vow of poverty had provided a great sense of liberation. Just like his monks today, he had always been obedient to his abbot in the big things. And just like his monks today, possibly less so in the little things.

The constant battle was, is, and ever would be the vow of chastity. He had likened it to giving up smoking. They started young in his day. He began trying to give up in his late teens—a few weeks, then a few months, extending the period each time but never quite managing to kick the tobacco habit completely. His best effort had been thirteen months then something had happened, a disastrous love affair from memory, and he had started smoking again. He finally kicked the habit at the same time he took the monastic one, in his early thirties.

He discovered that monastic hours—possibly partially designed with this in mind—made remaining chaste comparatively easy. By the time his head hit the pillow at night he was out like a light. However, comparatively was the operative word. His aim, of course, was to subdue, control, and overcome his sexual desire. In the meantime, while he was endeavouring to achieve this—and he certainly did endeavour—it seemed to him that there were times when it made more sense to take matters in hand in time honoured tradition to relieve sexual tension so that he could get back to thinking about God.

The abbot's reminiscences were interrupted by farmer Isnard, who was standing with the doctor by a table with several bottles on it, beckoning him over to taste some of his experimental wines. He vinified them from ancient local varieties—mollard, espanenc—mixed with modern carignan, mourvèdre, merlot in varying percentages, and with varying degrees of success.

'I added a bit of syrah to this one,' said Isnard, pouring a deep purple wine into the abbot's glass. The three men raised their glasses to the light to study the wine's colour, twirled the liquid around in the glass, solemnly sniffed in the aromas, took a mouthful of the wine, swirled it around the palate, sucked in air, swirled the liquid around a bit more, and swallowed it. 'Now try this one, Père Abbé, same percentages but with three years in bottle. I'll bring you up a few bottles for mass.'

Cheese was replaced with cherry clafoutis, apricot tarts, thirst-quenching slices of bright red water melon and sweet scented slices of orange Cavaillon ones, bowls of fragrant strawberries which had been tossed in a little sugar and red wine vinegar.

The aroma of coffee made from freshly ground beans heralded the beginning of the end of the meal. The abbot, aided by Aarne, Gianni and Matteo and hissing out of the side of his mouth, 'Don't give any to Tuuli,' circulated with bottles of colourless kick-like-a-mule marc which Aarne distilled from the wine lees brought to the distillery by the villagers each autumn after grapes had been pressed.

Although the abbot did say grace at the beginning of the lunch, he had never yet managed to say grace at the end of it. This year was no exception. Everybody had dispersed—some clearing things away, others dancing to a valse musette played by the accordionist, pétanque players getting their boules and plenty of spares out of car boots and weaving their way to the pétanque terrain. The Ancients were fast asleep.

While the priest handed out the sets of boules from the wooden box, the mayor stood by the blackboard, chalk in hand, to note down the teams. The visitors had laughingly refused to play but the abbot needed one more person to make up four teams of three and used all his persuasive powers—which were considerable—to convince the lovely Hindu to play.

The monastery players gathered expectantly around the abbot, who had completely forgotten his carefully-worked out strategy, and so now turned to the priest, who had never really known it.

'Right,' said the abbot. 'I'll play with you, Tuuli, and you, ma fille,' he said, smiling at the female Hindu, and ushered his little team over to the mayor.

The priest thought quickly, realised that even with Tuuli playing the abbot's chances of success were slim, and so chose Brother Ange-Dominique and the Buddhist, and left the others to sort themselves out. As each monastery team paired up with a village team, names were chalked up on the board and the teams walked off to start playing.

Soon all four games were under way and the air was alive with the thud of boules falling onto sun-baked ground, the different sound of boules hitting the timber boundaries, the clink of steel on steel, cries of approbation or despair as boules did, or did not, reach their target.

The visitors, who had only a tenuous grasp of the rules primarily because nobody had explained them, moved around the terrain watching different games, remained silent when play was in progress, then clapped or cheered every time a player knocked someone else's boule out of position, regardless of which team it was.

At the end of each game a small retractable tape measure was produced, where necessary, to decide distances before totting up points. Results were reported to the mayor's wife who chalked them up on the board. Winning teams played in the quarter-finals; losing teams played each other.

For the first time since the inauguration of Amadeo's feast day and the pétanque match two of the monastery teams made it through the first round.

The abbot's team struggled but Tuuli—in spite of, or possibly because of, the vodka consumption—was on top form and the happily relaxed abbot played remarkably well, for the abbot. The Hindu, her shining black hair centrally parted and tied back at the nape of her neck, had been watching how everyone played. Now, she disappeared briefly behind the wide trunk of an ancient olive tree and returned having rolled up her petticoat and rewound her sari so that it hung looser and at calf-length so that she, too, could drop down onto the balls of her feet to point.

She followed the instructions given to her by Tuuli and the abbot and, once she got her eye in, succeeded in placing her boules with ever-increasing accuracy to the encouraging cries of 'Brava, brava!' from the abbot. She also quickly picked up the pétanque players' habit of clinking together the two boules held in her hands. At the end of each game, the abbot showing great chivalry used his magnet to pick up and return their boules to his two team mates.

Having proudly announced their win to the mayor's wife and delighted to have achieved his wish of getting a team through to the second round, the abbot walked back to watch the priest's team play.

As he looked around him at Aarne's atheist aunts, the rabbi and imam, the Sikhs, the Hindu, the Russian Orthodox priest and the Buddhist monk, all laughing, chatting, mingling with monks and villagers, the abbot thought, *This is the answer, a globally ongoing open to all-comers pétanque competition. This is the way forward.*

After a nervous start, the priest's team stormed to victory. Brother Ange-Dominique, his tiny wooden cross tucked inside his shirt, and, as usual, carefully wiping sand and gravel off his boules after each game with the cloth hanging out from his jean pocket, had practised assiduously over the past few days. He could not hope in such a short time to regain the form of his youth but he was poised and concentrated and played well. The Buddhist monk was on fire.

It had quickly become apparent to all concerned that the monastic miracle was due to the presence of Tuuli and the Buddhist monk and there were raucous good-humoured comments about the legality of using 'overseas players.'

As the competition progressed, losing teams played each other in the Petite Finale. The original drawing of teams fortuitously meant that the two winning monastic teams were not playing each other but were matched against two village teams.

The others, who had heard the good tidings, wandered over to watch the semi-finals, apart from the straw-hatted Ancients who were now wide awake and had paired up with four elderly village ladies to play belote, seated around two card tables which the young folk had set up for them under the shade of the olive trees.

The visitors, who thanks to explanations furnished by other onlookers, had got the hang of pétanque and now knew their shooters from their pointers, looked on with mounting excitement. The abbot forgot all about Luca which was just as well because if he had looked around, his novice and Espérite were nowhere to be seen.

The abbot's team, after a long and closely fought game with some impressive shooting from Tuuli and pointing from the Hindu, lost. The priest's team, with good accurate play from him and Ange-Dominique and some spectacular shooting from the Buddhist, won.

The final, against the mayor's team, turned out to be a nail-biter which had monastery supporters saying a little prayer to all their gods, except, of course, for the atheists. The score got to 11-12. The mayor's team required just one more point to win. They had played all their boules in this round and had no less than three point-scorers scattered around the cochonnet. Two, to the naked eye, were equidistant, about ten centimetres either side of the cochonnet; the third, the closest and the mayor's boule as it happened, was trickily placed just in front of it.

One point for the priest's team would bring them equal and they would have to play another round and Vespers would be delayed, thought the abbot. Two points for the priest's team would give them the thirteen they needed for victory. That meant scattering all three opposing boules, to be absolutely sure of victory.

The priest, Ange-Dominique and the Buddhist monk walked over to examine the lie of the land, and after a brief discussion, Ange-Dominique returned to stand in the circle. Throughout the afternoon, the Buddhist had, much to the abbot's approbation, religiously extended both the priest's and Ange-Dominique's half circle into a full one. His face a picture of concentration, Ange-Dominique launched his last boule which covered most of the distance in the air then came down, and rolled merrily on its way to come to a halt perfectly placed between the left hand opposing boule and the cochonnet. Cries of approbation—that would be one point, provided they could now scatter the other two.

The three of them walked over again to have another look. By this late stage, the visitors had all really entered into the spirit of the game and along with the other spectators were also discussing the situation and indicating to each other where they thought the priest should be aiming for.

After a brief exchange with the Buddhist and Ange-Dominique, the priest came back to the circle, tipped back the straw hat he had borrowed to keep his hair from flopping over his face, hitched up his chinos, squatted down on his haunches, balancing on the balls of his feet. The buzz of conversation ceased as, slightly bending his left arm behind his back and with a languid flick of his wrist the priest launched his boule into the air. It came down with a thump half a metre or so before the opposing team's right hand boule, rolled into it nudging it away and out of the points.

The visitors were by now well versed in the principles of pétanque point scoring. They knew there were no points for coming second. As things stood, if the Buddhist monk could not dislodge the mayor's boule, it would remain closest to the cochonnet and would give the mayor's team the single point it needed for victory.

Everything now depended on the Buddhist. Much to the onlookers' delight, he had been shooting like a star all afternoon, including some spectacular carreaux sur place, the hardest shot of all. Twice, his boule had hit and perfectly replaced his opponent's boule sending the latter skittering off well away from the target. This was precisely the shot now required to clutch victory from the jaws of defeat.

Both teams walked over to examine the state of play. The Buddhist returned to the circle and carried out the ritual that everyone was now familiar with. He stood motionless in the circle, his saffron robe moving gently in a whisper of wind, sandaled feet together, passing his boule from palm to palm, eyes half-closed concentrating on his target, blanking everything out. Then he opened his eyes. All talk and movement ceased. The only sound now was the singing of the cicadas in the lazy, hazy afternoon heat.

The boule flew out of the Buddhist's thin and bony and brown hand. All eyes followed its trajectory, heard the crack of steel on steel as it made contact with the mayor's boule at the perfect angle, rolling it out of the way and taking its place.

A great cheer went up from everybody. The silence was now filled with shouts of laughter, congratulations, more jokes about the number of overseas players allowed per side. Backs were slapped, cheeks were kissed. The winning team shook hands and embraced each other and the opposition, the abbot embraced his team, the mayor his, then they embraced each other, the Sikhs embraced the Hindus, the iman embraced the rabbi and the Russian Orthodox priest. Everybody embraced the Buddhist monk who was named Man of the Match. The abbot, positively radiating peace on earth and goodwill to all men, was, that June afternoon, the happiest of men.

The bell rang—so the abbot knew where Luca was—and most of the gathering wended their way to the abbey church. Afterwards, everything was packed up and loaded back into pickups and cars. In no time at all, peace and tranquillity returned to the monastery. Apart from the odd cork that would be found in the olive grove over the following weeks, you would never have known there had been so many people and so much gaiety and laughter that Sunday on Amadeo's feast day.

As the mayor and his wife drove off he suddenly jammed on the brakes and reversed back to the main monastery gate at a speed fuelled by the afternoon's alcohol consumption, sending up a swirling cloud of dust. In the excitement of the feast day celebrations he had forgotten to deliver the monastery mail—a handful of letters that had accumulated at their house over the past few days.

Next to the main door a large and ancient niche in the stonework, which presumably housed a statue in days of yore, had been converted by Gianni and Matteo, by the addition of hinges and a wooden door, into a general post box. Most village folk driving up with post or other deliveries were more than happy to park, walk into the monastery and shoot the breeze with one of the monks. Those in a hurry could park right alongside the post box, open the door and make their delivery, if it was small enough, through the car window.

Thus the abbot, or whoever thought to check the post box, could find along with any letters a bowl of large and porcelain-white duck eggs, an envelope from the doctor with the results of a blood test, a pot of paint for the workshop, a prescription for one of the Ancients, a couple of litres of the local red wine, sweet pea seedlings for Louis-Marc.

The system had come seriously unstuck only once when, after a late autumn Sunday morning shoot in the vineyards, one of the hunters had despatched his son up to the monastery to deliver, sadly without specifying where, a couple of brace of red partridge. The boy stuffed them into the post box, carefully closed the door (which was always left open when a delivery had been made) to stop the game birds from falling out. There they remained for the best part of a week during one of the hottest October spells in the region since records began.

Now the mayor reversed level with the post box, leant out of his window, put in the post, left the door open, and shot forward, sending up another cloud of dust into the early evening azure blue and still cloudless sky. But other clouds were gathering on the horizon—storm clouds, these. One of the envelopes, addressed to the abbot, was postmarked Rome.

CHAPTER 16

Normal service resumed the following day. The visitors left early for the airport, Maddalena taking the imam, rabbi and Russian Orthodox priest. The journey to the monastery had passed in silence. The return journey was rather like a day trip to the seaside, thought Maddalena, except nobody said, 'Are we there yet?' The holy men never stopped talking—about their exchanges with the villagers and monks, about the pétanque match, about the spectacular shooting of the Buddhist monk. The priest left later that morning.

No longer could the clink and chink of boules be heard between offices. The only noticeable signs of Amadeo's feast day were a certain sense of euphoria which could be felt floating through the cloisters, and the almost constant grinding of coffee beans from the espresso machine.

The abbot, having taken the last packet out of the pantry and added coffee beans to the shopping list in the kitchen, was on his way to fill up the espresso machine when he saw Tuuli, trailed by her ever-silent but always smiling sister Olga, walking towards him.

'Père Abbé, bonjour. What a wonderful day that was. We did enjoy ourselves, didn't we Olga?' Olga opened her mouth to speak but once again did not get the chance. 'You know that we leave for Finland in a couple of days—there is a matter we wish to discuss with you. Would you have time later today?'

'Come in now,' said the abbot. 'Coffee?' he said pointing to the machine. 'No? Then please—go and sit down in my study while I fill up the machine.'

Tuuli's wide skirt swished as the two women walked away —Olga did not wear clothes that swished—and the abbot wondered whether Tuuli's upswept auburn hair was kept up by a series of combs, or whether you just had to remove that large one for it all to come tumbling down.

The abbot emptied the coffee beans into the machine and stood looking at it wistfully for a moment. Earlier in the year he had given up espressos for Lent. It had not been a happy time, either for him or for the rest of the community. The previous year his ambitious and commendable efforts to give up both dark chocolate and whisky—forty days seemed such a long time, even if you were allowed to indulge every Sunday—had proved beyond him. He had settled on giving up chocolate for the first half, and single malts for the second, a Lenten respite much appreciated by his liver.

Now he picked up a small cup, hesitated, put it down again. He had already knocked back three heart-starting ristrettos that morning. The caffeine was making his heart race. With great reluctance he turned away and walked along to his office. He closed the door, sat down behind his desk and waited for Tuuli—he knew it wouldn't be Olga—to speak.

'We are as you know, Père Abbé, atheists.' *Oh dear God, please, not a theological discussion this morning*, thought the abbot, rather wishing now that he had made himself the fourth espresso.

'We do not believe there is a god,' continued Tuuli, 'you and our dear nephew Aarne, however, do.'

'Well,' said the abbot, 'in a philosophical sense—and I know you are interested in philosophy, Tuuli—the question is: Does God exist? None of us have any proof one way or the other. You, as a thinking atheist, must answer, "I don't know, but I don't believe he does." Our answer to the same question is, "We don't know, but we believe he does."'

Tuuli nodded her head in agreement. 'Quite. We are extremely fond of our nephew Aarne. We have other nephews and nieces but we do not love them as much.' *At least she's honest*, thought the abbot. 'We have no children of our own. We have accumulated through judicious investments and less judicious but lucrative—let us call them liaisons—quite a lot of money.' The abbot thought the liaisons were more on Tuuli's side than Olga's. 'We give some of it to the nephews and nieces in Finland, of course. But we would like to give quite a lot of it to Aarne. That is to say, we would like to give it to the monastery. One hundred thousand euros.'

The abbot's jaw dropped. He looked at the women in astonishment.

'As a first instalment. For tax reasons, you understand.'

'Of course. Why render unto Caesar what you don't have to render.'

'Quite.'

'Well, thank you Tuuli, Olga—that is really most generous of you. Aarne knows?'

'He does. If you will give me the monastery's bank account details before we leave, we will make the first transfer when we get home.'

'Here they are,' said the abbot, opening a desk drawer, whipping out the cheque book and carefully removing the relevant slip from the back of it. 'This is most unexpected, Tuuli. Most generous of you,' he repeated, 'particularly given our divergence of opinion on the existence of God.'

'And the rest,' came Tuuli's tart response.

The abbot laughed and rose from his seat to see the women out. They both remained seated. The abbot sat down again.

'There is just the matter of the sauna,' said Tuuli.

'Ah,' said the abbot.

'Aarne tells us he has drawn up plans for a sauna. As I am sure you know, saunas are very much part of traditional Finnish life. They are places for physical and mental cleansing, dimly lit, just the smell of fresh birch and natural tar, bonding places. Many people say you should behave in a sauna as you would in a church. Plus you have the advantage of the lake. The perfect plunge pool. We would like to give Aarne something he really wants.

'We understand that your Rules of Saint Barnaby—'

'Benedict,' corrected the abbot.

'—say he cannot receive personal gifts. So we would like to gift a sauna to the monastery—to be used by you, the community, and by your guests. We think, don't we Olga, that it will be a great asset for the monastery. To be paid for out of the first instalment.'

The abbot looked at Tuuli, then at Olga, who immediately lowered her eyes. He rested his elbows on the desk, interlinked his fingers and rested his chin on them. He lowered his eyes, glanced across at Gandhi. He had to confess he had always rather liked the idea of a sauna but financially it had been absolutely out of the question. Now it wasn't.

He looked across the desk at Olga, then at Tuuli, and smiled. 'It will be up and running for your next visit, Mesdames.' He opened the drawer where he kept the chocolate, took out a tablet of Peruvian 72%, removed it from its wrapper, snapped it in half—he felt the sums involved merited a whole bar not just a couple of squares—and handed one silver-wrapped half each to Tuuli and Olga.

Later that day he asked Aarne to come to his office. When his distiller monk walked in the abbot asked him to sit down. He opened up a drawer and removed the pile of plans Aarne had supplied him with over the years. He opened the top folder, spread out the most recent plan on his desk and said, 'This one, don't you think? Down by the lake. Near the birch grove—I think that would be appropriate, don't you?' His monk grinned, popped the plans back in the folder, picked it up and left the office.

On the kitchen front, Maddalena and Brother Gianni were making gazpacho for the first time. She didn't know why it was the first time—she loved this cold soup—but there it was. In Gianni's notebook, she wrote down from memory the recipe she used, which was for five people which had always struck her as a curious number, and doubled the quantities. Then they picked up the chestnut trug and walked over to collect a dozen ripe tomatoes, two red and two yellow peppers, and a large bunch of Genovese basil from Louis-Marc.

Back in the kitchen, Maddalena peeled four small onions and a couple of cloves of garlic, while Gianni squeezed the juice of five lemons into a small jug.

'We may need more,' said Maddalena. 'We'll taste it and see.' They removed pips from peppers, peeled a couple of cucumbers, roughly chopped everything up.

'Now we put all the vegetables into the blender—we'll probably have to do this in two goes, and make sure the onion and garlic get well puréed. If it looks too thick we'll add a little water.'

They did have to do it in two goes. Gianni poured the first batch into a very large bowl. 'Now we'll blend this second batch and add the olive oil, about 200ml, the red wine vinegar, 180ml give or take, lemon juice, basil, salt, pepper and a little chilli powder – although I often don't. See what you think.'

Gianni poured the second batch into the bowl and carefully mixed it all together. They both dipped in their spoons to taste it. Gianni grinned. 'Now into the fridge for a good hour—you can add ice cubes but I don't bother,' said Maddalena. 'If you want it smooth, you can push it through a sieve before chilling. I don't bother with that, either.'

Two days later the atheist aunts left the monastery. Beforehand, Tuuli and the abbot walked down to the lake and he showed her where the sauna would be sited. On their way back to the car they talked and laughed about the pétanque match. Then Tuuli said, 'I don't know— eternal life, reincarnation, nirvana. Do you really believe in all that? When you're dead, you're dead.'

'But what a waste,' said the abbot. 'If this wonderful creation that is the human being just, well, dies, decomposes, disintegrates—what a waste. What's the point of that?'

Aarne had put baggage in the boot, kissed his aunts, thanked them again for their generosity. Tuuli said, 'We've seen the site. At the lake. By the birch trees. Excellent.'

She and Olga kissed the abbot on both cheeks and they climbed into the car, Aarne holding open the passenger door for Olga, the abbot the driver's door for Tuuli. Once settled in the driving seat she opened the window and said to the abbot with one of her provocative smiles, 'Eternal life – I don't know, Père Abbé, but if it makes you happy . . .'

'I hope it won't be for a long time yet, Tuuli, but when we've both left this world I shall look forward to continuing our discussion.'

Tuuli laughed. 'Me, too, Père Abbé,' and she drove off, waving. Within a few seconds there was a screech of brakes as Tuuli realised the implication of the abbot's parting words. She looked in the driving mirror to see Abbot Giacomo and their nephew smiling broadly as they waved them farewell.

CHAPTER 17

It was July. It was hot. The community was spared the unbearable heat of lower altitudes. The temperatures here were a few degrees cooler and there was often a bit of a breeze. Nevertheless, it was hot. Daily monastic life continued much as before, except everyone moved more slowly and siestas were extended.

Maddalena was worried about her aunt in Sicily—her favourite aunt—who had been unwell over the winter. She had spent Christmas and New Year with her and tried to travel south when she could in between her own translation work and her chauffeuring duties for the monastery. Perhaps because of her aunt's failing health, she found she was thinking more about her parents—her mother who had died when she was so young, and her father Corrado, a fisherman all his life, who had died at sea.

She was in the monastery kitchen with Brother Gianni showing him how to prepare one of her favourite Sicilian dishes, caponata. 'This you can make in large quantities, Gianni, and keep it in a large jar, or ideally that clay pot in the pantry. Then you have a ready-made antipasto or you can serve it to accompany cold fish or meat for supper on your day off, for example.'

He was frying in olive oil the cubed aubergines which had been salted, rinsed and dried. When they were brown and tender he drained them onto some kitchen paper. 'Now fry the sliced onions and then add the chopped tomatoes, salt and pepper. And we'll simmer that for a quarter of an hour.'

Meantime, he cut the celery sticks into pieces while Maddalena pitted the green olives. She told him to bring a small pan of water to the boil. 'We need to blanch them and the capers, just throw them into the boiling water and as soon as it comes back to the boil drain them into a sieve. Then add them to the tomato sauce with the wine vinegar and sugar.'

While she was spooning out the capers she found herself transported back to another July morning—much hotter than this one—when her parents had taken her and her cousins to the Valley of the Temples near Agrigento. She, the youngest of the party, had not been much interested in the temples. They were far too high up for her. But she remembered vividly the wild caper bushes which clambered and climbed along, around, and among the old stones. It's funny how certain sights, sounds, smells resurrect old long-forgotten memories from the subconscious—Maddalena's madeleine de Proust moment. She smiled to herself. She could remember that day as clearly as if it was yesterday; here in the monastery kitchen she could feel the heat of that Sicilian summer on her skin.

Gianni's voice asking what to do next shook her out of her reverie. 'We'll reduce that a bit, let it simmer for another fifteen minutes. Stir it now and then, Gianni. Then we'll mix it with the aubergines and leave it to stand for half an hour or so.'

Gianni made a pot of coffee and they sat outside in the sunshine. 'I can't thank you enough, Maddalena. I was a bit nervous to start with—what with no pasta—but I'm really enjoying making these dishes, learning about the ingredients, how to prepare them, what I can do with them.'

'It's a form of prayer, I suppose, isn't it? You're cooking for God, Gianni.'

The young man smiled. 'And Louis-Marc is gardening for God, Ange-Dominique is painting for God.'

'And Aarne is distilling for God—that doesn't sound quite right does it?' said Maddalena, and they both burst out laughing.

'Mind you, I can remember a time when I don't know what we would have done without Aarne. It was shortly after I arrived here, things were pretty desperate,' said the monk. 'We had to stop sending money to the other monasteries, we barely had enough to keep things going here. We didn't starve, the villagers wouldn't let us starve, but it was pretty grim.'

'What about Ange-Dominique?'

'He was here, painting, but they hadn't created the network, there were no commissions, no sales. He was just painting small icons.' Easily transportable in times of need, thought Maddalena.

'The abbot said that Aarne saved the day with his vodka. I think it must have been those crazy aunts of his. Anyway, we suddenly started receiving orders—he'd just started producing the cloudberry one. They weren't particularly large orders, but they were regular and because we are paid before the goods leave the monastery it provided us with a much needed income. So yes, Aarne is distilling for God,' he laughed.

They went back into the kitchen, tasted their caponata which was delicious and would become even more so as the flavours married and mingled in the large pot in the pantry.

The dog days of August arrived. Everyone and everything moved ever slower—even water seemed to flow more slowly out of taps. Siestas were extended. Cicadas were stunned into somnolent silence.

Maddalena continued her work with SOS Amitié when she could. The summer months were particularly difficult because many listeners were away on holiday. Most of the callers, however, were not.

She listened to callers whose lives have been ruined by addition to alcohol, gambling, drugs. She listened to an old man, about to be evicted from his home, who intended to set fire to it with the petrol and matches on his kitchen table.

She listened to a young woman who was beaten by her husband. Did she want to leave? Yes, she wanted to leave with her children but had nowhere to go. Maddalena gave her a telephone number. Would she ring it?

She listened to people who had been sexually abused when they were children by fathers, brothers, uncles, grandfathers, family friends. Some, with years of therapy, had just about managed to come to terms with what they had experienced. Others, still traumatised decades later, talked of ruined lives, the inability to have happy relationships, the sense of guilt, shame, incomprehension. 'My mother knew what was happening? Why didn't she say anything?'

She listened to a paedophile who knew he risked a prison sentence but said he had the permission of the child's father. She listened to two callers who as adolescents had been molested by priests. She knew there were many, many others. The media continued to be rife with shocking revelations of sexual abuse within the Roman Catholic church.

She listened to lonely people—old, young, middle-aged. Sometimes they telephoned to talk about things that they could no longer say to their partner who was sleeping in the bedroom next door. Sometimes Maddalena was the only person they had spoken to in days. Often family was present, but not as present as the caller, often elderly, would like. Sometimes they understood that their children had busy lives and couldn't always call or visit so they rang the association for a chat. Sometimes they didn't understand and railed against their offspring, 'After all I've done for them over the years, the sacrifices I made . . .' Sometimes Maddalena wasn't surprised that the children didn't call.

She listened to callers who were bipolar, schizophrenic, depressed, suicidal. They knew that listeners could not help them with their pathology, but their psychiatrists would suggest that they call when things got bad, usually, but not always, during the evening or late at night—which was often when she listened to insomniacs, callers suffering from panic attacks, and terrible solitude. She listened to a man who liked to wear calf length boots with two centimetre high heels on Tuesday evenings up until midnight, and all day on Saturdays.

One day, in the afternoon, she listened to a deep rich voice that sounded familiar. In the background, birdsong, singing cicadas, a bell ringing. A voice that talked to her about his kitchen garden, the life choice he had made—single, no family—which he didn't regret except sometimes he felt a painful emptiness in his life . . .

After a short conversation the man thanked her and hung up. Maddalena put the telephone on pause and her head in her hands. The voice sounded just like Brother Louis-Marc's. Surely he wasn't still calling the association. Or had she made a terrible mistake?

The mystery was resolved a few weeks later. She was working one afternoon in the kitchen garden with Louis-Marc when the abbot arrived to say that his brother had been on the telephone. 'He's left you various messages on your mobile, apparently, but you haven't responded. He just wanted to check you were OK. It was very odd—it sounded just like you—asking to speak to yourself,' laughed the abbot.

As the abbot walked away, Maddalena said, 'Your brother, does he have a family?'

'No, he has chosen to lead a similar life to mine—without the praying. In fact he lives a more solitary life than I do—I have my fellow monks. He doesn't seem to have anybody. He spends his life pottering around in his kitchen garden. I think the solitude is beginning to weigh on him now, with the passing of the years.'

The monk stopped digging and leant on his spade. 'The last time we spoke he told me he had discovered the existence of an association where apparently he can ring any time of day or night. Someone will answer and he has a little chat with them. Sometimes it is a man who answers but mostly it is a woman. He prefers the women.

'The first time he called he was a bit nervous, he told me, but he spoke to a really nice lady. He said it was just lovely to hear a female voice, to have a little talk about this and that. He said he felt wonderful afterwards. So now I think he rings occasionally when he's feeling a bit lonely. It's marvellous, isn't it? Volunteers giving up their time like that.'

'Yes,' said Maddalena, 'isn't it?' She looked at the monk—face tanned, eyes twinkling, battered straw hat protecting his head from the sun. She started to chuckle to herself as she thought back to their first meeting. Soon she had an uncontrollable fit of the giggles. He gave her a surprised look. He had no idea what had amused her but her giggling was so infectious, he started laughing, too.

The abbot, who was enjoying the sunshine and had paused to answer a call on his mobile telephone, heard the laughter and turned around to look at his monk and Maddalena. By now, they were both shaking with merriment, tears streaming down their cheeks.

He looked at the couple and he thought of Livia. When he saw how happy Louis-Marc was in the company of this woman Maddalena, he remembered those carefree loving moments he had shared with the woman he had loved. He felt inside him a fleeting but painful stab of—of what? Jealousy? Surely not.

Perhaps he should have a word with his monk. Perhaps he should suggest that Louis-Marc spent a little less time with Maddalena. *Wretched woman*, he thought. They took three vows when they became monks. Louis-Marc had never been particularly obedient. The abbot sincerely hoped that his vow of chastity would not be put to the test. He consoled himself with the fact that at least Louis-Marc was poor. He walked back to his office and opened up his computer to have a quick look at *Avvenire*, the Italian Catholic newspaper.

He read the headlines. A senior cardinal in the Curia had been accused by dozens of victims of sexual abuse. This on top of the recent announcement of another cardinal accused of paedophilia. The abbot felt sick. His old arthritic hands started to tremble with anger. How could they betray the Christ in this way? Then he thought, *But he has always been betrayed, hasn't he? He was betrayed right from the beginning by Judas Iscariot.*

He started skimming the article for the name of the cardinal. Could this shocking betrayal also be their salvation? He found the name but it wasn't the one he wanted to see. He sat for a few moments staring at his laptop screen.

He opened his desk drawer and took out a bar of 72% Dark Ghana. As he bit into the rich dark chocolate square he made up his mind. He recalled Louis-Marc's brief flirtation with Facebook. He would let things be. Maddalena had simply provided him with the friendship he had been looking for. As for Luca and Espérite, well, he was extremely useful around the monastery and, frankly, it wouldn't be the same if he were to leave. There was nothing that required comment about the friendship between Giovanni—the abbot was the only person to occasionally call him by his full name—and Matteo.

No, he would let things be. Let's have some affection, laughter and happiness among the horror. He thought back to the two of them laughing their heads off in the kitchen garden (what private joke were they sharing that had made them so happy?) and felt, just for an instant, a pang of loneliness.

Somehow, as was so often the case, one square of chocolate never seemed to be enough so he snapped off a second. As he sat letting it melt in his mouth he made up his mind that the next time the priest came to the monastery he would tell him about the letters and why he had gone to Rome.

The next time the priest came to the monastery was for a funeral.

CHAPTER 18

Nobody was sure, not even the doctor, if it was the fall that caused it, but one August night, when the only sound was the singular hoot of the Scops owl and the blue-black sky shimmered with twinkling stars, one of the Ancients died.

One morning he had fallen off his seat during Vigils. One minute he was there singing psalms, the next there was the awful sound of human skull hitting limestone slab, and where he had been sitting was now an empty space. The psalmody continued without interruption.

Quietly Matteo and Gianni left their seats and walked across to where the inert body of the monk lay on the old, cold stone. He opened his eyes, they gently raised him to his feet, and accompanied him slowly out of the church, into the cloister and along to his ground floor room.

'I thought he was dead,' said the abbot when he rang the doctor, 'but he seems all right now. Can you come up this morning?' The doctor duly arrived, checked out and patched up the Ancient who was back in church for mass with a large dressing on his cheek. The doctor or the local nurse called in regularly over the next few days to check on him and change his dressing. All seemed well. Then one night he died.

The monks laid the Ancient in a simple pine coffin, which had been ready for years, and placed him in the abbey church where he remained overnight. Matteo, Gianni and Aarne dug the grave in the little cemetery in which the Ancient had spent so much time above ground, and where his physical body would now spend forever below it.

They said a funeral mass the following morning. Aarne, Ange-Dominique, Gianni and Matteo hoisted the coffin onto their shoulders and the Ancient was piped to the cemetery by Brother Séamus playing, at the Ancient's earlier request, "Westering Home".

When they arrived at the grave, the pall bearers lowered the coffin onto the two wooden slats which lay across the gaping hole and fed two leather straps through the woven handles and underneath the coffin. Matteo was pleased with these biodegradable handles—two along each length of the coffin, and one each at either end—and particularly proud of the eco-friendly wooden pegs he had made for closing the coffin lid.

Once the leather straps were in place, the four monks—Aarne standing front left opposite Ange-Dominque—seized one end each and raised the coffin a few inches so that Louis-Marc and Luca could remove the two slats. It was at that moment that Aarne's weak left knee, which he had forgotten yet again to strap up, gave way. Suddenly letting go of his end of the leather strap, he lurched down to his left and so did the coffin, gently nose-diving into the grave until it came to rest wedged into the freshly dug earth a couple of feet down, the back end sticking up in the air at a rakish angle.

The Communità dello Spirito Santo stood in silence looking down at the coffin then at the abbot who in turn looked, raising his eyebrows questioningly, at Brother Matteo who left the cemetery and hurried back to his workshop. Everybody apart from the abbot was trying hard to keep a straight face. Louis-Marc caught Ange-Dominique's eye and had to turn away. Luca suddenly seemed to be taking enormous interest in something on the ground by his foot. The abbot thanked God that the other Ancients had decided, perhaps understandably, not to attend the burial.

Brother Gianni stood gazing down at the coffin with his hand over his mouth. Then he looked across at Aarne who had hobbled over to the nearby bench and was massaging his knee. Gianni, who was standing next to the abbot, touched his arm and indicated Aarne. The abbot nodded and Gianni, too, left the cemetery.

Brother Séamus thought it might help if he played something in this unforeseen interval and began piping "Amazing Grace." The abbot indicated with his hand for Séamus to stop playing. The elderly monk was already so red in the face from his earlier piping that he looked as if he could keel over at any moment. The abbot felt they were having enough trouble burying one monk, let alone two.

As Séamus put down his pipes, a mobile telephone started ringing. Furious, the abbot looked round at his monks to find the culprit. They all had mobile phones but because much of their waking hours were spent either on the way to church, in church or just coming out of church, their phones, nestling deep down in their habit pockets, were invariably in silent mode. There was, however, no sign of panic and frantic delving into deep pockets. His monks were all staring at the coffin.

The abbot bit his lip as he, too, stared down at the coffin. The phone stopped ringing and a terrible silence fell on the small assembly until thankfully the cicadas started singing again. And the phone started ringing again. Brother Ange-Dominique's shoulders were quivering; Aarne, head bowed to hide his face, was busy massaging his weak knee; everyone was desperately, trying with varying degrees of success, to mask their mirth and keep faces composed as befitted the solemnity of the occasion.

The abbot closed his eyes. They had buried the Ancient with his mobile telephone buried deep in his pocket. It had been in his pocket because today was the Ancient's birthday. The abbot had remembered this—he had a note of all their birthdays—but it had slipped his mind what with the Ancient dying. Now his family were ringing to wish him a happy birthday.

All four Ancients had asked for simple pay-as-you-go phones so that they could receive messages and calls from relatives at Christmas, Easter and on their birthdays. Each Ancient kept his phone in a drawer in a little bedside table, battery flat, no credit, until a few days before each event when he would take it out, charge the battery, and ask one of the younger monks to top it up. He would then drop it down into one of the deep pockets of his robe so he wouldn't forget to have it with him when the day—Christ's birthday, Easter, his birthday—arrived. He would then wait for the calls.

The abbot looked down at Matteo's bio-degradable wooden pegs which had been knocked flush into the coffin lid. There was no question of opening up the coffin to remove the phone. The telephone had stopped ringing. Suddenly the abbot delved into his own pocket, removed his muted smart phone and saw two missed calls from Italian numbers he did not know. If the Ancient did not answer his calls, relatives would worry, and ring the abbot.

Brother Matteo returned with a grappling hook. He walked round the grave surveying from all angles the slewed coffin. The monks had more or less regained their composure. However when the phone started ringing again the look of astonishment on Matteo's face, who was hearing the mobile for the first time, gave them all—apart from the abbot—another fit of the giggles.

Matteo stood at the head of the grave and slowly lowered down the grappling hook trying to secure it through the woven handle. The coffin was a prototype. The Ancients, until now, had showed no signs of shuffling off this mortal coil so this was its first utilisation. Matteo quickly realised that he would need to create a handle with more space between it and the coffin in the, admittedly unlikely, event of a recurrence of the current situation.

As Matteo swayed gently trying to latch the hook onto the handle, the monks standing behind him started swaying with him. Brother Gianni returned with anti-inflammatory gel, knee support, pain killers and a small bottle of water for Brother Aarne.

Meanwhile the abbot, who was looking at his mobile phone and wondering why the monastery possessed a grappling hook, decided to answer the next call that came in. He saw that the priest had texted him to say that there had been an accident on the motorway and that he would be delayed.

The priest had telephoned the abbot the night before. He had just returned from another gruelling Middle Eastern trip—more bomb explosions, kidnappings, assassinations. He was exhausted but he was fond of the Ancients and told Giacomo that he would leave early to drive up to the monastery. As he sat in the traffic jam, he started fuming.

It didn't happen often, but every now and then, usually when he was physically shattered, he started to resent what he considered to be the cushy life led by the monks, cloistered away in their monastery, physically untroubled by terrorist traumas and religious hatred which he, the priest, encountered continuously in his travels. *They live in a silent world of contemplation while I spend my life talking, listening, exchanging,* he thought, drumming his fingers on the steering wheel.

Now here he was stuck on the motorway when he could have been reading poetry with a cold beer, listening to Diana Krall, catching up on his sleep.

He knew he was only thinking this way because he was dog-tired. The city-centre suicide bombers—screams, blood, people running, terrible destruction—had perhaps rattled him more than he realised. He learned later that miraculously only the two bombers had died in the attack.

Just a few minutes beforehand he had popped a card to Maddalena into a post box. It bore an Iranian New Year stamp he had bought in January and forgot to use depicting two turquoise-breasted, yellow-throated birds, one small, one large, perched on a branch, a lovely stamp. The post box was in the immediate vicinity of the attack and had probably been destroyed in the explosion. That had really put him in a bad mood.

And spending all that time in church—what was all that about? What was the point of monks? They should get out more, and see what it was like in the real world.

By the time he arrived at the monastery he would rather have been anywhere other than where he was. He parked, knowing that mass would probably be over, and walked towards the cemetery where he could see the monks gathered together. He rubbed his eyes, yawned, and wondered yet again why he had not simply, sensibly, stayed put to recuperate from his journey. Why on earth was he here?

He opened the small gate and walked over to the grave. In a glance he took in the scene—the unusual position of the Ancient's coffin, Matteo fishing with his grappling hook, Brother Aarne sitting on a bench with his dove grey robe hitched up, one loose trouser leg, it looked like his pyjama bottoms, rolled up, strapping up his knee, the abbot talking into his mobile phone at the graveside.

'Pronto, pronto. I'm so sorry, my child, but your great-uncle – ah, great-great uncle—I'm afraid he has died . . . just two days ago . . . no, no, he wasn't sick, he died during the night, it was very peaceful . . .' At this point, Matteo succeeded in hooking the coffin handle, gave a short sharp upward tug dislodging the edge of the coffin from the earth. It fell to the bottom of the grave with a bone-shattering crash which, in spite of the fact that the occupant was already dead, made everyone wince. Those standing too close to the grave, like the abbot, partially disappeared in a cloud of dust.

The abbot clamped his phone as close as he could to his ear. 'What noise? Oh, that? That was nothing, nothing,' he said into his phone. 'I called the contact number I had to advise the family, but the line was disconnected. Oh, I see, I'm sorry to hear that. I tried the other number but it just kept ringing so I . . . oh, I see, yes, he seems to have outlived everybody. The burial? This morning, we're trying to, we're burying him this morning.'

The Ancient's phone started ringing again. *Dear God,* thought the abbot, *how many relatives does he have?* 'Listen, figlia mia, I have to go now. I wonder, does he have, did he have any other relatives who might ring him today? Ah. That many. I wonder, could you possibly contact them and let them know . . . Well, the ones for whom you have numbers, grazie, grazie. I'm so sorry, I must go now. God bless you, my daughter, God bless you. We will keep you in our prayers . . . yes, and your great-great uncle, of course. We will miss him. Ciao, ciao, ciao.'

The priest took all this in, looked around at the monks, at the contorted faces, the shaking shoulders, the tears rolling down Ange-Dominique's cheeks. All anger and resentment disappeared. He ran his left hand through his hair, pinched the bridge of his nose with his right, and as the abbot intoned, 'Dust to dust, ashes to ashes—' he, too, soon had tears trickling down his face.

Luca held the small bowl of holy water, the abbot dipped the sprig of boxwood into it, made the sign of the cross over the coffin and stepped back to let the other monks file, and Aarne hobble, past, repeating the gesture, with Luca bringing up the rear. Louis-Marc shovelled a spadeful of earth onto the now silent coffin. Gianni and Matteo picked up the other spades and the monks started filling in the grave.

That afternoon, the priest recounted his latest harrowing trip to the abbot as they walked down to the lake. On their return, as they walked past the cemetery, they paused and thought they heard the muffled sound of the Ancient's mobile phone. It might have been their imagination. In any case, they reasoned, the Ancient's mobile phone battery would soon—like his own—run out.

At day's end, the priest would have gladly headed straight for his bed. But he knew Giacomo would appreciate his company over a dram after the traumatic events of the morning. He went for a stroll to stretch his legs for a few minutes then walked back into the monastery and along the cloister to the abbot's office. He saw the light under the door, knocked and entered.

The abbot was standing by the open cabinet surveying all the bottles. Two whisky glasses stood on his desk next to a small blue jug filled with spring water. The priest walked over and put his hand on Giacomo's shoulder. The abbot turned to smile at the priest. 'Grazie, figlio mio, I know you would rather be in bed. What'll it be?'

The priest paused before replying then said, 'I think—after the events of this morning—we should start on the top shelf and work our way down.'

The abbot chuckled. 'You may be right. What a fiasco.' He pulled down an almost empty bottle of single malt, took it over to his desk and poured them both out two stiff drams, finishing the bottle. They both added spring water, a good dash for the priest, considerably less for the abbot. 'Careful, Giacomo, don't drown it.'

They raised their glasses to the Ancient and then to their lips. The priest felt the fire of the spirit fill his palate. As he swallowed the amber liquid, its consoling warmth worked its way down his throat. He leant back in his chair and closed his eyes. He took another sip and was pervaded by a sense of well-being and that, although he knew only too well it was not the case, all was well with the world.

The abbot looked across at the peaceful expression on the exhausted younger man's face, and decided this was not the time to tell him about the Roman storm clouds. In any case, he consoled himself, while the current incumbent remained head of the Roman Catholic church—he was old, yes, but he appeared to be in reasonable health—there was no immediate cause for concern.

CHAPTER 19

It took a little while for everyone to get used to seeing three Ancients where there used to be four. But the gentle rhythm of monastic life continued untroubled and the bells continued to call the monks to prayer. Maddalena continued her chauffeuring duties, the priest continued his travels. The violence in the countries he travelled to also continued. One of the study sessions had to be cancelled at the last minute because the teacher, a liberal scholar in an illiberal country, was assassinated a few days before she was due to travel to the monastery.

Brother Ange-Dominique was at last working again on a copy of a painting by Francisco de Zurbarán, *Agnus Dei,* which had been commissioned by a private buyer through their New York agent Mannie Morgenstern. The abbot had no trouble, of course, with the *Dei* bit but he was getting a little fed up with the *Agnus.* His monk had borrowed another one from farmer Isnard and it bleated a lot probably because it missed its mother, and also because its four legs were tied together.

As soon as Ange-Dominique started painting visitors would collar the abbot, 'Père Abbé, Père Abbé, there's a lamb somewhere in the monastery grounds.' Yes, he said, he knew that and he explained what their artist monk was painting. He repeated this so many times over the next few weeks that it got to the stage that when the abbot saw a Hindu or a rabbi rushing towards him, he would pretend he hadn't seen them and duck through a door or up a staircase. Eventually he asked Luca to put up explanatory notices in the visitors' cloister, study rooms and anywhere else he could find a space.

On one of the priest's visits, as the two of them were walking past the cemetery on their way down to the lake, the lamb bleated. The priest, unaware of Ange-Dominique's current model, said, 'Oh, you've got a lamb in the monastery grounds, Giacomo. Saves cutting the grass, I suppose.'

'Don't you start,' replied the abbot, and he explained the trials of the past weeks.

'It's in the Prado. I saw it once when I was in Madrid. Is it almost finished?'

'I think so, looked like it the last time I popped in. There's a young lad from one of the kitchens who often comes over to have a look to see how it's coming along. It's rather gratifying to see the interest he takes in the painting.'

'Young Muslim, is he?'

'Yes, he is, as it happens. How did you know that?' The abbot stopped in his tracks. Oh no. Surely not?'

The priest smiled. 'I think his visits may be due more to a culinary interest than one in Spanish baroque painters. Ah, the sauna. No expense spared I see.'

Brother Aarne and the abbot had agreed it was best to wait until the heat of summer was over before erecting the sauna. It had been ordered as soon as the money from his aunts had been transferred and duly arrived in the autumn. He, Gianni and Matteo prepared the chosen ground near the birch trees and the lake, and had erected it with help from Ange-Dominique and Louis-Marc.

Cedar exterior, Nordic white spruce inside, abachi pre-built benches, not one but two spacious changing rooms (one for the visitors, one for the monks) both with shower and lavatory. They had also rigged up a simple outside shower on the lakeside. On the outside of the sauna building hung a wooden plaque that Matteo had made engraved with a Finnish saying and its translation (the abbot would have preferred just the original Finnish):

'Jos ei viina, terva tai sauna auta, tauti on kuolemaksi.'

If booze, tar, or the sauna won't help, the illness is fatal.

The two men went in, the abbot gave the priest a guided tour, turned on the kiuas, then, while the stones heated up, they set off round the lake. The priest gave the abbot the latest news from their small monastic communities in Pakistan and Iran. They talked about the increasing religious and political tensions there and in the other areas he had visited.

When they got back, they went inside, stripped off, hanging clothes on hooks, showered, didn't bother with towels and entered the sauna. The abbot ladled water onto the stones, steam hissed up and the two men sat down on the benches. For a while they remained silent while the steam opened and cleansed clogged pores.

'Are the guests making much use of it?'

'Oh yes,' said the abbot, 'indeed they are.'

The priest turned to look at him, waiting for the explanation required by the abbot's tone of voice. It was shortly forthcoming. The abbot had recently walked down to the lake at a quiet time of day to have a sauna. Aarne had explained to them all how it worked and had produced a little instruction booklet. The abbot expected to be alone—the visitors were in their study groups, the monks were working—and he was not disappointed.

He had been happily sitting naked, eyes closed in meditation in a far corner of the sauna when the door opened and in walked one of the study groups, all wearing towels apart for the Sikh who was also wearing his turban.

They were as delighted to see the abbot as he was horrified to see them, immediately removed their towels, presumably to make the abbot feel at home, and sat themselves down on the benches. Everybody was completely naked apart from the Sikh who was also wearing his cotton underwear.

'Oh, Giacomo,' laughed the priest, imagining the scene. 'I would give anything to have been there.'

'What could I do? I got up to leave but they wouldn't hear of it. So we sat there sweating and thrashing out the finer points of the four Vedas of Hinduism. Did you know that the Rig Veda, the oldest, was composed around 1500BC? They are the primary texts of Hinduism and had a vast influence on Buddhism, Jainism and Sikhism. Did you know that? No? You should join one of the study groups, figlio mio.'

The priest got up to ladle more water on the stones. The abbot started gently whipping himself with a bundle of fresh birch twigs. 'It's called a vihta, Aarne says, good for the circulation.' Clouds of steam sizzled and hissed up into the small room.

'But I shall tell you something, my son,' continued the abbot, 'as I looked around, each of us—apart from the Sikh who must have felt rather overdressed for the occasion—each of us as naked as the day we were born, some circumcised, some not— I thought that in spite of our different beliefs, underneath all our outward religious signs, our crosses, headwear, robes, paraphernalia, we're all exactly the same, we're all just ordinary men, ordinary human beings. It's a great leveller, the sauna, I've decided.

'And as I looked around, I also thought, "What makes us so certain that we are right and they are wrong? That ours is the one true faith?"'

'Oh, dear,' said the priest, 'I think I'll go and have a shower. Be right back.' He reappeared a few minutes later and sat down again on the bench. 'Having a bit of an existential moment, are you, Giacomo?'

'Don't tell me you never have doubts,' said the abbot.

'All the time. I've always rather liked the idea of reincarnation, myself. What I can never come to terms with is the idea that there is nothing after death. Seems such a waste, doesn't it? For man to have evolved into the amazing thinking creature he is today to then die and disintegrate into nothing . . . don't see the point of that.'

'Here,' said the abbot handing the vihta to the priest. 'You have a go. Does the world of good. We must drink lots of water. The Finns cook sausages in tin foil over the stove, apparently, and drink beer and cider. But I don't think I want to encourage that. It's like a meeting place, the sauna, for purifying body and mind.'

'I think I'll stick with the Nazarene,' said the priest, continuing his own train of thought while he whipped himself with the birch twigs.

'Aarne says up until a few decades ago women would give birth in saunas and when someone died the body would be given a final wash in one. We could have done that with the Ancient if he hadn't died before it arrived.'

'"If we don't believe in Christ's resurrection after death then our faith is in vain,"' said Saint Paul. The question is, do we choose to believe in life after death because we don't much care for the alternative? Or do we truly believe? Do we have faith? And what about those of us who are baptised at birth into the Roman Catholic church whether we want to be or not because our parents decide for us?'

'Apparently Finnish embassies have a sauna. There's even one in the Finnish parliament in Helsinki. I'm going for a shower,' said the abbot. 'You should arrange to be here the next time the Hindus are talking about reincarnation.'

'Shouldn't we be plunging into the lake, Giacomo?'

The abbot gave the priest a horrified look. 'Are you mad?' Then he grinned and said, 'All right, let's go.'

The two men left the sauna, grabbing a couple of towels which they left on the lakeside bench, and without giving themselves the chance to change their minds plunged into the lake. The cold water made the blood rush through their bodies. They clambered out of the water, invigorated, and dried off with the towels.

They dressed and as they walked back towards the monastery, the abbot had a noticeable bounce in his step. They both agreed later over a nightcap that the sauna was both a physically and mentally cleansing experience. The abbot, who always slept well, slept even better. The priest climbed into his bed and immediately fell into a deep, solid, recuperative sleep of unremembered dreams and untroubled by Luca's early morning reveille.

CHAPTER 20

Autumn turned to winter. The abbot celebrated Angel's mass on Christmas Eve in the village church, packed to the rafters as usual. At dawn, Matteo celebrated the Shepherd's mass in Amadeo's chapel by the lake. He was not alone. Several farmers, including Isnard, headed over the hills and down to the lake. The King's mass on Christmas day was celebrated by Louis-Marc in the monastery.

Winter turned to spring. Maddalena continued to teach Gianni simple tasty dishes using the produce Louis-Marc grew, the priest continued to think she spent too much time in the kitchen garden, Aarne distilled and despatched with her help, Ange-Dominique painted while she posed.

The abbot read with a profound sense of sadness the annual list of over five hundred homeless people, young and old, who had died in the streets of France over the past twelve months. It was produced by the association Les Morts de la Rue. The names were published in *La Croix*. He felt helpless yet he knew that their little community could not be all things to all men. They had their work to do and, in spite of often great difficulties, they did it. All they could do was pray that others would continue to do their own work to reduce that terrible number towards zero.

Maddalena realised she needed to spend more time on her translations. She was getting behind with her work, clients were chasing her, and she needed the money. After Easter, she had a word with the abbot. They consulted the timetable and found a period when her chauffeuring services were not required, and if they were, he would send Aarne or Louis-Marc, he assured her.

She decided to head off to another little island she had never visited before. She travelled by train and bus to a small coastal port and took the boat across to the island where she had rented a little studio with balcony. Her hosts were charming, the sun shone most of the time, the mistral blew now and then, there were few people at that time of year.

It was perfect. She quickly got into a rhythm that suited her. Her balcony and the large terrace below her room received the sun all day. She worked mornings and evenings, starting early after a breakfast on her balcony of eggs fried or scrambled or poached. She had long ago acquired the habit of eating a good breakfast and lunch, and dining simply in the evenings.

Mid-morning she took a break to walk outside and down the steps onto the terrace. Here she made herself an espresso, did a few stretching exercises—her lower back started to ached if she sat for too long—gazed out over the trees, listening to birds chirruping and bees busy buzzing around plants and shrubs, particularly the long shiny dark green leaved pervasively perfumed pittosporum.

She continued work until the chapel bell up on the hillside chimed midday. No escaping the bells, she thought, although she quickly realised that the bell only seemed to ring at midday and at seven in the evening. She walked a few minutes down the hill past bushes of blood red roses and tall irises to a general store to shop for her meals, or up it to the tiny village where there was another store, a couple of bars and restaurants, and a bakery.

The car-free island was a beautiful example of insular Mediterranean vegetation. Everywhere grew succulents of all shapes and sizes. She strolled past gardens of gigantic agaves and aloes, yuccas and cacti. Yellow spurge, Hyères island lavender, large orange-yellow petalled wallflowers provided splurges of colour.

She lunched simply in the sunshine on her balcony. She cooked some long grain basmati rice using the method an Iranian friend had taught her, boiling it for ten minutes or so, with a couple of bay leaves, till the water was gone, then covering the pan with a dish cloth and lid, turning off the heat and leaving it for another ten minutes or so. The top grains would be almost standing up on end, and at the bottom of the pan the rice would have browned a little and needed to be gently scraped off.

Her friend always said you should cook rice as and when you want it and not keep it as leftovers. She ignored his advice and put some aside to cool for the following day. In what remained she warmed up a couple of whole tinned sardines. Then a raw chicory salad dressed with virgin olive oil and fresh lemon juice with a little Auvergne blue cheese, Greek yoghurt with apple, a glass of wine. On other days she lunched on the rest of the rice with fillets of mackerel or chunks of tuna, cooked pasta, kept it simple.

In the afternoons, she would set off to walk along narrow paths through woodland, down and around the coastline. She returned in time to spend an hour or so in the sun, lying on a chaise longue on the terrace, watching tiny lizards darting here and there. Everywhere, released now and then by the warmth of the sunshine, the intoxicating scent of the tiny white pittosporum flowers would waft through the air.

She walked up to the tiny village to sit outside one of the bars in the late afternoon sun with a glass of crisp white wine from the Var listening to the chat of the villagers. Then back home to work during the evening. If she felt peckish she had a spoonful or two of yoghurt. With no street lighting on the island, at night the only lights to be seen came from other houses nestled among the vegetation. The only sounds to be heard were the high short hoot of a Scops owl, sometimes joined by the nocturnal song of a couple of nightingales.

The island had an interesting history. It seemed that many centuries ago both Cistercian and Benedictine monks had settled here at different times. Now around ninety percent of the one thousand hectare island belonged to the military and was fenced off. The remaining land bit was a private naturist domain open to the public, created by two brothers, both doctors, in 1931. There were over two hundred homes on this end of the island, many visible on the hillside from the boat as she arrived into the little port.

The islanders had judiciously decided to halt any further development and had created in the northern part of their domain a twenty hectare natural reserve criss-crossed with rustic nature trails.

The terrain was hilly and by the end of the third day she could feel the effect on her calf muscles. She returned to the mainland with her work up to date and the beginnings of another year's all-over tan.

Then her aunt died.

In true Legionnaire fashion, the priest and the monastic community knew little of Maddalena's background. The abbot knew that she had an elderly aunt she was very fond. She had once left at very short notice to visit this relative whose state of health was giving cause for concern. As it coincided with arrivals and departures at the monastery, the abbot had informed the community at chapter and Brothers Louis-Marc and Aarne had immediately volunteered to replace her.

Maddalena's aunt had recovered on that occasion. Now, a cousin had telephoned to say her aunt was dying and was asking for Maddalena. She flew to Catania and spent the last days of her aunt's life at her bedside in the family home.

As soon as Maddalena arrived, her aunt, still conscious at this point, asked her niece to open the bedside drawer and take out the letter which had had been lying there for decades. 'Your father gave this to me just before he,' she paused, 'drowned.' On the envelope was written one word "Lena." *At last he will explain to me why he went to sea that day when all the other fishermen stayed on shore at their nets*, she thought.

The aunt, who knew the contents of the letter, said, 'Only read it after I've gone, Lena.' The priest came and a few hours later, her beloved aunt, Maddalena's last remaining contact with her parents' generation, slipped into unconsciousness and peacefully passed away.

Over the next few days Maddalena often fingered the white sealed envelope but she did not open it. She looked at her name written in now fading black ink. She did not recognise the handwriting. She had been too young. She cried a little but the worst was the pain deep inside her, a constant dull ache.

They buried her aunt alongside her parents in the sailors' cemetery. She had thought of opening the letter when she got home but then realised that she must open it here in Sicily in the dusty sun baked fishing village where she was born and grew up. It had been written here, this letter, whatever it said, and had remained here all these years, untouched, in her aunt's bedside drawer.

The day before her departure she walked down to the tiny harbour, and sitting down along the jetty as she used to do as a child with legs dangling above the water, sun sparkling on the Ionian Sea, Etna in the distance, she finally opened the letter. She dearly hoped it would explain what she had come over the years to believe was her father's suicide. Why had he done it? Why had he deserted her? Why had he left her an orphan?

The letter was not from her father. It had been written by her mother a few days before her own death. The writing was shaky but legible. Her mother talked about the future she and her father wanted for their daughter, the plans they had for Maddalena to leave Sicily—which would always be her home—but to leave like she, her mother, had done to live life elsewhere.

Her father had been born and spent all his life in Sicily. Her mother had left Sicily but had stayed in Italy. She wanted more for her daughter. She wanted her to visit other countries, meet other people, learn other languages, experience other cultures. When she knew she was dying and would not be able to make this happen herself she had talked to her husband Corrado and to her sister, the keeper of the letter, and had asked them to ensure that it did happen.

After her father Corrado drowned it was Maddalena's aunt who had ensured her sister's wishes were carried out. The little girl had moved away, had grown up in France with loving, caring relatives, had lived and loved in other countries, in other languages, absorbing other cultures and cuisines. She looked up from the letter and out across the water. She thought, *Grazie, Mamma, grazie mille.*

Then she read the last paragraph.

The following day she left her cousins—tearful embraces and hugs and promises to ring, write, and return soon. She was always sad when she left Sicily but this time she felt a deep and painful emotion at leaving after burying her aunt, the last tangible link with her mother. There remained friends and cousins —and she would return to her fishing village to see them—but their memories of Maddalena's parents were as indistinctly distant as her own.

As she sat in the plane looking out of the porthole waiting to take off, the hostess announced with a certain pride in her voice that they were in a brand new airplane and that this was only its second flight. Maddalena's neighbour turned towards her and said, 'I'm not quite sure how that's supposed to make me feel.' For the first time since she had arrived in Sicily, Maddalena laughed.

During the flight back to France she removed the letter from her handbag and read it again, as if she thought that last paragraph was a figment of her imagination and would now say something different. As she folded the letter and put it back in the envelope, its contents and the tension of the past few days overwhelmed her. Tears—silent, unstoppable—coursed down her cheeks. The stewardess, instead of asking if Maddalena wanted anything to eat or drink, gave her a small pack of tissues.

By the time she got home, she felt emotionally exhausted. She didn't unpack but sat on the sofa with a large glass of Côte-du-Rhône, opened before she flew to Catania but still perfectly drinkable. It got dark. She didn't turn on the lights. She was hungry. She didn't eat. She just sat staring into space, the letter on her lap. She read it again. She poured herself another glass of wine.

The only person she wanted to talk to was the priest. But he was away on his travels and, although it had never been mentioned, it was an unwritten rule that they never contacted each other when he was away. Never here when you need him, that man, she thought, as she finished the bottle. Mind you, she would have been rather incoherent if he had been.

When Maddalena finally got up the following morning after a terrible night's sleep she felt ghastly and it was almost midday. She showered, dressed, walked down to one of the fish restaurants at the port and on a kill or cure basis ordered a glass of champagne and a seafood platter. When she got home, she slept for a couple of hours, and then telephoned the abbot to tell him that her aunt had died, that she was back in France and would drive up to the monastery the following day.

The abbot sensed the sadness and a certain strain in her voice. He was ready with some dark 60% with crystallised ginger when Maddalena arrived late afternoon. She sat silently in his office eating the chocolate, gazing into space. She looks exhausted, thought the abbot, waiting patiently for her to speak. At last Maddalena turned to look at him and smiled.

She started talking, slowly, in a firm voice to begin with but which soon seemed to be on the verge of breaking with emotion. The abbot knew nothing about her past. She told him in a halting voice about her parents dying, and how she had always felt that her father Corrado had committed suicide by deliberately going to sea that day.

'I had no proof but learned later of his all-encompassing love for my mother. I came to assume that he simply could not bear life without her. My aunt gave me a letter before she died—a letter that my father Corrado had given to her shortly before he drowned. I thought it would explain why he had abandoned me.'

The abbot remained silent, waiting.

Maddalena paused. 'It wasn't from him. It was from my mother. She wrote it just before her death and gave it to my father. He was only to give it to me at the end of his life—which came much sooner than anyone had anticipated. I believe he knew he was not going to return from that fishing trip—that's why he gave it to my aunt.

'In it she says that when she returned to her home village she was almost certain she was already pregnant with me, which was confirmed very shortly afterwards. She told my father, Corrado, the man I thought until now was my father. He had always loved her. He said they would get married, that he would be the father of the child. The timing raised eyebrows, but you know in tiny villages like ours folk close ranks—the villagers kept their counsel.'

Maddalena stopped talking, swallowing hard to regain her composure. The abbot said, 'He *was* your father, figlia mia, he held you as a baby, he looked after you, he picked you up when you fell over, he loved you. And you have known no other. He may not be your biological father, but in every other aspect—I would say the most important aspects—he was your father. You must never forget that.'

They sat in silence. The bell rang for the evening office. The abbot made no move to get up. It was Maddalena who rose from her chair. 'May we talk again later, Padre Abate?'

'Certo, figlia mia. Come to my office after Compline.'

When Maddalena returned to the abbot's office he opened the wall cabinet, pulled down a bottle and poured out two drams. He did not ask her if she liked whisky. He knew she drank vodka and just assumed, correctly as it happened, that she drank whisky, too.

They both added a drop of water to their glasses. Maddalena removed her mother's letter from her handbag and placed the envelope on the abbot's desk.

She said, 'They said it was an accident, when my father drowned at sea. He, who had been a fisherman all his working life, who had taken me out to sea as a small child just like my grandfather had taken him out.

'Nobody knew those waters better than my father did. And yet he went out one morning when the weather had kept all the other boats in harbour. My father went out to sea and didn't return and a few days before he gave this letter to my aunt.' Tears rolled down her cheeks.

She sipped her whisky gazing into space. The abbot sipped his and remained silent trying not to look at the distraught woman until she had regained her composure.

'They found his body washed up further along the coast. They said it was a terrible accident, the weather, already bad, got worse. And nobody talked about it anymore. Not in front of me.' Maddalena turned to look at the abbot. 'I was too young to know or to think any different then. I was sent away to France. I started a new life. But over the years when I was much older, I started having this little nagging thought that he had deliberately set sail that morning with the intention of not returning alive. He had loved my mother so much, she had died, and his suffering was so great that he could no longer face the world without her.'

She paused to blow her nose, took another sip of whisky and continued, 'I wondered how he could have deserted me? Was his love for Mamma so all-encompassing that he could no longer bear living without her, not even for my sake? Did I remind him too much of her? Was it painful for him every time he looked at me? All these thoughts have gone through my mind over the years. I would mention it now and then to my aunt but she could or would not add anything new. "It was a terrible accident, Lena, your father loved you e basta," she would say.'

'And now this,' she touched the letter. 'He could not have loved me as much as he loved Mamma. I was not his child. So when life without her became unbearable for him, he committed suicide. That's what I now believe.'

The abbot remained silent for a few more minutes, nursing his whisky. He said, 'You will never know what happened that day, Maddalena. Maybe your surmise is correct. Maybe it's not. But I repeat, for those first few years of your life he was your Papa and you were his daughter. He loved your mother, I am certain he loved you.' Does the letter tell her who her biological father is, he wondered. Does she want to trace him?

Maddalena seemed to read his thoughts. 'Mamma tells me who my father is, someone she loved very deeply but he—' Her voiced tailed off and again the tears came.

'Do you want to find him?'

She sighed and bowed her head. 'Find him?' She picked up the envelope, removed the letter and looked at the abbot. 'My mother's name, her maiden name, was Livia Di Pietro."

The abbot felt the blood drain from his face. With trembling hands he picked up the letter and looked at the handwriting. Familiar handwriting. Livia's handwriting. Livia, Livia, Livia. He did not read the letter. He stood up rather shakily, supporting himself with his hands on the desk, and walked round to Maddalena, took both her hands in his and helped her to her feet.

The priest had arrived back earlier than planned because the last person he was to meet on this trip had been badly injured in a terrorist attack. He had telephoned the abbot who had told him that Maddalena's aunt had died and that she was driving to the monastery the following day. The priest, who imagined she would be very upset, said he would get a good night's sleep, deal with various things that had piled up during his absence, and then he, too, would drive up. It would, he hoped, be a nice surprise for her.

As he drove, he chuckled to himself as he always did when he thought about the SOS Amitié case of mistaken identity. Maddalena had told him how she had found out. It explained why she had spent so much time with Louis-Marc in his kitchen garden. How silly he'd been. *You'd almost think I was jealous,* he smiled to himself.

It was late when he arrived at the monastery. He parked the car, opened the main monastery door and walked inside. He could see light shining under the abbot's door, so he knocked and, as was his custom, entered immediately.

He had hoped Maddalena would be happily surprised by his visit. It was, however, he who was unhappily surprised to find her enfolded in the abbot's arms. She was crying, the abbot looked as if he was about to, the priest was speechless.

The abbot who had been stroking Maddalena's hair looked up slowly and slowly smiled at the priest. 'Buona sera, figlio mio.' He appeared to think no explanation was necessary.

The priest, jaw gaping, heart thumping abnormally loudly, remained as motionless as a statue chiselled out of a marble slab, and suddenly felt just as cold. He tried to speak but no words came out. He wasn't even sure what those words would have been if he could have found his voice.

It was Maddalena who, raising her head from the abbot's chest and looking at the priest, realised how incongruous the situation must appear, broke out laughing and thus broke the ice. She looked at the abbot and raised a silent question with raised eyebrows. He smiled at her and said to the priest, 'My son, I have just found out, now, this minute, that Maddalena is my daughter. Whisky?'

He brought over a third glass, served the priest whose mouth was still half open in astonishment, turned to replace the bottle in the cupboard, changed his mind and put it down on the desk.

The priest raised his glass, looked at Maddalena then the abbot—could he see a likeness? Or was it just his imagination? —and spoke for the first time, 'I simply don't know what to say. You will explain, I know, but—' Slowly shaking his head in amazement he raised his glass. 'Let's drink to—' He paused searching for the right toast. 'Let's drink to—fathers and daughters.' The other two raised their glasses. 'To fathers and daughters.'

They sat down and in a shaky voice, Maddalena started to explain to the priest the contents of her mother's letter. While she was talking, the abbot said, 'May I, Maddalena?' and, when she nodded, he picked up the letter, walked over and sat down in the chair by the small birch wood table. He looked at the familiar handwriting in black ink.

His thoughts travelled back almost half a century, back to when he was a young man in love. How many times had he opened his mailbox hoping to find a letter or card from Livia?

Their studies had taken them to different cities, family holidays to different resorts. No mobile phones or emails in those days so they had written regularly to each other when they were apart.

Now against the gentle background hum of Lena, his daughter, talking quietly to the priest, he started to read Livia's letter to their daughter. Their daughter—tears welled up in his old eyes—their daughter, the fruit of those last bitter-sweet days together.

He skimmed through to the final paragraph. He could hear Livia's voice in his head as he read, "I returned to Sicily because the man I loved and thought I was going to marry had told me that he believed he now had a vocation, a calling, to dedicate his life to God. The feeling had been growing, I had noticed nothing, he had waited until he was absolutely sure. It was the saddest time of my life. For him, too. He loved me but now he loved God more. He told me over a weekend on the coast. I think I knew that night that I had conceived a child. We returned home on the Sunday evening and I never saw him again. I will be dead when you read this, and as I intend to live to a ripe old age, he will probably be dead, too. His name was Giacomo Ravasi. He was going to enter a monastery in Liguria. Corrado is your papa, the man who brought you up, who gave you his name, who learned to love you. The man I loved and who gave you life is Giacomo."

The abbot, eyes moist with tears again, felt a hand, his daughter's hand, on his shoulder. She couldn't yet bring herself to call him Papa. 'I think,' she said, kissing gently the top of his head, 'I think we should go to bed. You are tired. We are all tired. It has been a long, long day.'

Outside, the priest rinsed out the glasses under the cloister tap. He was surprised to see that his hands were shaking slightly. The abbot turned off the light, put his hands on Maddalena's shoulders, gazed into her face and kissed her gently on each cheek. Then he turned towards the priest who embraced the old man with great affection and warmth, patting him gently on the back. They each walked away to their separate rooms and their separate dreams.

The priest immediately fell into a deep much needed sleep. He did not recall his dreams and awoke refreshed the following morning. Maddalena, who had known the abbot was her real father for several days now and had had to keep that knowledge to herself, felt such a profound sense of relief that she, too, slipped quickly into an unconsciousness of unremembered dreams. She was woken by Luca ringing the bell. After a brief hesitation, she scrambled out of bed, into some clothes and headed in the moonlight to the church.

The abbot had a terrible night. Sleep came fitfully and each time he awoke, his recalled with vivid clarity his Livia-filled dreams, a chaotic kaleidoscope of muddled memories, some so intensely real that when he opened his eyes he was distraught not to find her lying beside him. Now of course he could see the similarity, the eyes, the hair, certain mannerisms. Now he realised why long-ago Livia had occasionally drifted into his mind when he had seen Maddalena talking and laughing with Louis-Marc. He was awake when the bell rang out in the dark to start their day.

As he walked into the church from the cloister he saw his daughter, Lena, kneeling in the front pew. She looked up and smiled at her father, a smile of such radiance and warmth and love that the abbot thought his heart would break. He smiled back. After the office, he walked over to her. 'Have some breakfast, Maddalena—Lena, that's what your mother called you, isn't it—then we'll go for a walk.'

They walked down to the lake, wrapped up to keep warm in the cool early morning air. The abbot put his arm around his daughter's shoulder. They walked and they talked and they cried. 'I think your mamma's letter explains things very well. She was always very good at getting straight to the point. We loved each other. We were so happy together. I could not imagine a life without Livia. And then, slowly, over a period of time, I don't know, months, perhaps a year, I started to, something inside me seemed to be . . .' He paused.

'That Holy Spirit up to her tricks again, she gets everywhere,' said Maddalena, with a little laugh. 'It was she who brought me back into the fold. I'll tell you about it one day.'

'She's female?'

'Of course, papa.' The word sounded strange to her but she wanted so much to get used to saying it. The abbot had immediately started calling her Lena, the diminutive Livia had used for their daughter.

'They forgot to mention that in the seminary.'

'Well, they would, wouldn't they?'

They sat on the bench by the lake. The abbot fished in his pocket for some 70% Dominican Republic.

'I loved your mother.'

'But you loved God more.'

'Yes. I did not really have any choice. Slowly but surely I just knew deep inside me that my future was no longer to live the rest of my life with your mother. For me it was the happiest and the most painful of times.'

'And for mamma just the most painful of times.'

'Yes. Except that you were conceived out of our love.'

The abbot sat bolt upright. 'Am I a grandfather?'

'Twice over.'

'But you, your husband?'

'Divorced.'

The abbot sighed. 'I'm sorry.'

Maddalena shrugged her shoulders. 'We have lots to talk about.'

Dawn was breaking as they walked slowly back to the monastery. 'Will you tell the community?'

'I'll tell them at chapter tonight.' He chuckled to himself.

'They'll be surprised.'

'Surprised? They'll be flabbergasted. They always seem to know what's going on here before I tell them. Not this time.'

Indeed they were and the abbot relished every moment. At chapter, he said he had just one announcement to make, made it, bestowed a beaming smile on his little community, rose

221

from his seat and headed off to church, leaving his monks open-mouthed and speechless.

The small pragmatic Communità dello Spirito Santo had become so self-contained over the decades and so used to bending like an ear of wheat in the wind that they simply absorbed this new situation. The hard of hearing Ancients had failed to grasp the substance of the abbot's announcement. The others, in quiet conversations over the following couple of days, agreed it didn't change anything at all, and that life would be simpler if they didn't bother trying to explain to the Ancients.

Life continued much as before except that father and daughter spent time together because they had much to say to each other. Louis-Marc, who missed her company, would see them walking together around the kitchen garden, through the orchard and the olive grove. If they looked out of their respective windows Aarne and Ange-Dominique, who missed his model, would see them strolling through the monastery garden deep in conversation.

The Ancients sitting, when the sun permitted, in the cemetery would see the couple walk past talking, laughing. Within a week, one of them, feeling under the weather, was confined to his room. When Brother Gianni popped in to check on him, the others shuffled into the room and they expressed their concern about the abbot who suddenly seemed to be spending a lot of time with Maddalena.

Gianni explained in a clear voice what had happened. There fell on the little room a terrible silence. Gianni feared the worst although he wasn't quite sure what the worst could or would be. The Ancients looked at each other with slightly puzzled expressions as they tried to take in the information.

Then, speaking for all three although no words had been exchanged, one of them said, 'Grazie, Gianni. Va bene così.' Gianni, when he recounted the incident to the others, said he wasn't at all sure the Ancients had fully comprehended the situation. Nevertheless from then on the three of them would wave cheerfully to the abbot and his daughter when they passed by.

Maddalena sensed, correctly, that the abbot, still coming to terms with having a daughter, was in no rush to meet his grand-children. She told him briefly about them—where they were living, who with, their work—and left it at that.

They could not suddenly love each other, but they were united by the love they had both had for Livia. Perhaps in time, mused the abbot, the mutual respect and affection they had for each other would transform itself into something stronger.

Meantime, he wanted to know everything about her and listened with great attention, and the occasional sigh, as she recounted in suitably general terms her somewhat turbulent life to date. 'Well, I'm glad she blew into your life, the Holy Spirit,' he would say at various junctures.

The priest was worried that Maddalena might move into the monastery permanently. If she did, he would miss their times together in the town by the sea. When he tentatively enquired —they were rubbing garlic over croutons, dolloping on a spoonful of rouille and floating them in a tasty and concentrated and aromatic richly rust-coloured fish soup down by the port —she assured him that she had no intention of doing any such thing. She would miss their moments together like this, she added, sprinkling parmesan over her croutons and picking up her spoon.

CHAPTER 21

Time passed. The monastery finances were in good shape. Brother Ange-Dominique was painting, Aarne was distilling, Louis-Marc was gardening. The air was filled with the hammerings of Matteo and Gianni as they continued their work transforming various rooms and outbuildings for the guests.

The atheist aunts, who continued their money transfers, visited the monastery, were thrilled with the sauna where they spent much time with Aarne when he was free. The abbot kindly but firmly refused their invitation to join them. 'We'll wear towels,' said Tuuli, with a beguiling smile. But he could not be persuaded. He had to confess that the sauna had proved such a success that he was toying with the idea that everyone should give it up next Lent.

Maddalena continued to help Gianni prepare simple dishes. His notebook was now full of easy recipes which did not require pasta. Stocks in the larder had been substantially reduced.

When the peas were tender and small and sweet she showed him how to make risi e bisi, a Venetian minestra. 'We're going to fry the pancetta and chopped onion in butter and olive oil, add the peas, cover with a little chicken stock and cook for five minutes of so, not long, the peas are so tender. Then we'll add the rest of the stock, bring to the boil, throw in the risotto rice, season and cook gently, stirring now and then, till the rice is tender. And finally we'll add the rest of the butter, finely chopped parsley and parmesan. Taste it, you'll see, it's delicious, Gianni. They'll love it.' And they did.

When tomatoes were red and their flesh juicy and scented

they prepared Lebanese taboulé. Together they chopped up the tomatoes Louis-Marc had left on the kitchen table, and put them in a large bowl. They chopped up white onions, a pile of flat leaf parsley, some mint and added that to the bowl, then lemon juice, olive oil, fine sea salt and freshly ground pepper. They mixed everything gently together and tasted a teaspoonful. By lunchtime the flavours had mingled and married. Gianni served it as a refreshing first course.

When you couldn't move in the kitchen garden for courgettes, Gianni with Maddalena's help made zucchini ripiene. He trimmed the ends, cooked and drained them then cut them lengthways. 'Now, remove some of the pulp and put them on the baking tray,' instructed Maddalena as she oiled it. 'We need a well flavoured filling. We'll finely mince what we've got here —some cold veal, ham—that's it. We could put it in the blender but I prefer to do it by hand.

'Then add these chopped tomatoes, some tomato paste, parmesan, breadcrumbs, a couple of eggs—we might need a third.' As she spoke, Maddalena grated some nutmeg over the mixture and added flat leaf parsley and marjoram. 'Sprinkle in some sea salt, add pepper and give it another good mix.' They filled their courgette boats, brushed the tops with oil and baked them in the oven for half an hour or so.

Village life, too, continued as it had in this valley for generations. The abbot baptised and married villagers. Brother Matteo was now quite a proficient piper thanks to Séamus's tuition and one or the other was often invited to pipe at these important events in village life.

When the slow, continuous, mournful toll of the village church bell was heard at the monastery—one higher chime, one lower one—the abbot buried villagers. He knew by the slight variations whether it was a man or woman who had died. He had never heard the bell toll for a child.

Ange-Dominique, given his pre-monastic experience in the field, would be called on when occasional explosive work was needed at the quarry or elsewhere.

The villagers, in return, were ever generous in their support of the monastic community. The abbot would return from a burial with a hare; in season whoever was on kitchen duty would find a brace of mallard, partridge, snipe or woodcock hanging over the kitchen door, or from a long rusty nail in the wall.

The priest's work continued to produce results. Senior representatives of various faiths and none made their own way to the monastery or were collected by Maddalena.

The abbot continued to ensure his monks attended the study groups. Indeed he sometimes wondered if he would end up being the only christian left in the monastery. He could have sworn he had seen Brother Giovanni performing puja to a bushy basil plant in the kitchen following a session on Hinduism. One summer afternoon, walking through the kitchen garden towards the orchard, he spied Brother Louis-Marc sitting in the half Lotus position under a fruit tree, eyes closed, deep in meditation.

Just a few weeks earlier Luca the novice had sat in on a session on Jainism. He had been so taken with their concern for all form of life that he had decided that he, too, would wear over his mouth a mukhavastrika, a piece of cloth, so that there was no chance of him digesting even the tiniest flying insect.

Luca headed off to the kitchen where he knew there was always a metre or so of muslin. Small squares or rectangles were regularly cut off this large piece to wrap up a bouquet garni, except when Louis-Marc was pulling leeks when they would use the wide outer dark green leaves to enclose the herbs. The muslin or leek-leaf parcel was then tied up with string and popped into whatever dish or sauce required it.

Luca cut himself off a large piece of muslin and a long piece of string, anticipating, correctly, that he might not succeed on his first mask-making attempt. He eventually created himself a rather curious-looking but nevertheless effective mask to cover his mouth which he attached around his ears with two pieces of string which dangled down the side of his young face.

He had also learned that certain Jain monks swept the ground in front of them with a peacock feather duster to avoid injuring any life forms. Due to a dearth of peacocks in the valley he decided to forgo this particular practice and just paid particular attention to where he put his feet. He was mortified when one morning he had looked up from the ground because the abbot had called him and thus inadvertently stepped on a thin line of ants marching across the cloister paving stones.

For the next two or three weeks—until the incident with the Ancient and the fly—with the exception of mealtimes, he spent all his waking hours—and presumably his sleeping hours, although the abbot had never enquired—wearing his muslin mask so that no insect would lose its life by being accidentally swallowed by the novice.

Anything out of the ordinary—and seeing Luca in church and walking around the monastery with muslin mask over his mouth and eyes glued to the ground was out of the ordinary—unsettled the Ancients. Matteo and Gianni explained about the Jains adding that they thought Luca would probably get fed up in due course.

One morning when the abbot was in his office—most doors around the cloister were open in an attempt to create a breeze in the suffocating summer heat—he heard from the opposite side a noise that sounded like a rolled up newspaper being thwacked on a hard surface.

The abbot, walking over to his door, saw across the herb garden and through his open door, one of the Ancients shuffling around his room clutching a tightly rolled up copy of what had to be *La Croix* given that it was the only newspaper they received. Every now and then the Ancient thwacked something—presumably a fly—paused, slowly turned his arthritic neck around, up, down, waited, shuffled slowly out of the abbot's view. *Thwack!* The Ancient reappeared, stood stock still, cocked his ear, raised his head, and tracked the fly in a battle that he could never hope to win.

At this point the abbot, who had been tormented at night

by a mosquito in his cell until he had succeeded in thwacking it with an old newspaper, far removed from the reproving eyes of Luca, at this point he saw the muslin-masked novice enter the cloister from the monastery garden. As the young man walked around the cloister a *thwack* rang out. Luca froze. He approached the open door to the Ancient's room, heard the fly buzzing around the room, and watched the Ancient watching the fly, his rolled up newspaper grasped tightly in his gnarled right hand.

The abbot leant against the door frame to see what would happen next. What happened next was that Luca gently remonstrated with the Ancient explaining that it was wrong to kill any living creature and that that was why he, Luca, wore his muslin mask so that nothing, not even the tiniest insect, could inadvertently disappear down his throat.

The Ancient listened to the novice then continued his losing battle to flatten the fly. Luca moved towards him to remove the newspaper from the old man's hand. The Ancient, who had been driven mad by the fly all morning and was in no mood for the finer points of Jainism, raised his newspaper and with it repeatedly thwacked the young novice on the shoulder.

Luca, beaten, backed out of the room. On the threshold he made a final attempt to reason with the Ancient who in turn made a final ferocious onslaught on the young novice, brandishing his newspaper. That evening at supper Luca appeared minus his muslin mask.

Now the abbot gazed at Brother Louis-Marc meditating in the orchard, a beatific smile on his garden-tanned face. The abbot couldn't help wishing that, rather than reaching for nirvana, his monk would reach for the greengages which had taken on their most appetisingly green-gold hue which meant they were absolutely ripe for picking.

The abbot was particularly fond of greengages. He also liked the small yellow Mirabelle plums, and he was quite keen on the larger deep purple quetsch plums. He and Maddalena were going to make a couple of greengage tarts. They enjoyed cooking together and when she was at the monastery they always planned to spend a morning or afternoon in the kitchen depending on the abbot's schedule.

When there was a good harvest, the kitchen would be pervaded with the delicious fragrance of various types of stoned plums being gently cooked in a drop of water and sometimes a little honey. These would then be cooled and put into jars and enjoyed by the monks at breakfast, or perhaps, with yoghurt or crème fraîche, as a pudding.

They had had a bumper crop of raspberries this year and the abbot had spent much time prising out the seeds from between his teeth. He was now preparing to peel off from his palate bits of plum skin.

His real madeleine de Proust moment, however, which in an instant took him back decades to his childhood, came later when the apples ripened, and he would inhale the kitchen aroma of apples stewing gently with cinnamon sticks or vanilla pods.

Everybody was by now well used to the fact that Maddalena was the abbot's daughter. It made little difference to their lives. There were only two noticeable changes. She was there more often than she had been and when they were together they did not hide the signs of their affection. She would link her arm in his when they went walking. He would bend to kiss the top of her head when he found her sitting on a bench.

The priest had never mentioned Rome again to the abbot, and the abbot, while the present incumbent of the Chair of Rome showed no signs of vacating it any time soon, had seen no necessity to mention Rome to the priest. The priest had however been dancing.

When in town, he often walked in the evening along the sea front to one of the beach restaurants where they played music, either a small live band or a DJ. One balmy evening he was attracted by the sound of Cuban salsa being played and stopped off for a beer to watch the dancers twirling and swirling under the stars just below him.

The almost full moon hung languorously over the bay shedding a silvery path of light over the water. Sitting at a small table he closed his eyes and let himself be carried away by the music, the rhythmic pattern being tapped out by the clave. When he opened his eyes he saw Maddalena dancing with a man, around his age, he guessed.

She was smiling, her eyes almost out-sparkling the stars above. He watched, mesmerised. She was wearing a short-sleeved dress he had never seen before. It was made in some thin material—a rich scarlet—that rippled and flowed to the movements of her body as her partner guided her to the music. There was a brief break as the music ended but before she had a chance to regain her table someone else came over and asked her to dance.

And so it went on for almost an hour. The priest finally saw where she was sitting when the music stopped and, exhausted, she made her way back to a table she was sharing with a couple around her own age. The priest watched as she cooled herself down with her fan, laughing and chatting to the couple. He did not dance the salsa. But he had spent many an evening in his teens dancing the paso doble, le slow, of course, and le rock at village balls and fêtes. The DJ now put on some rock and roll. The tiny dance floor filled up again with couples of all ages rocking to the raunchy rhythm.

He would ask her to dance. No, he wouldn't. Priests don't dance. He got up to make his way to her table. Another man beat him to it. He sat down again. He watched her as she rocked and rolled effortlessly to the beat, smiling, her eyes rarely leaving her partner's as he guided her through various steps. The priest watched as her partner moved from basic steps to more advanced ones and noticed that she followed with ease.

The DJ had kicked off with something gentle and as "I Ain't Got Nobody" came to an end the priest got to his feet and walked purposefully down the couple of steps to the dance floor. Maddalena saw him and with a delighted cry walked over and kissed him on both cheeks. The DJ upped the tempo, the priest offered Maddalena his hand and they started dancing to "Crazy Little Thing Called Love." And "Rock Around The Clock". And "Hound Dog." And "At The Hop."

By the time the salsa came back on they were both exhilarated and exhausted. She asked him to join her table, he thanked her but refused, said goodnight, paid for his beer and walked home beneath the stars, humming, and with a happy heart.

He departed later that week on his travels once again, in buoyant and carefree mood.

One afternoon as the abbot sat at work in his office his telephone rang. It was the priest. He was in Afghanistan at Kabul airport. The abbot could hear all the usual airport background noise. 'I'm on my way back, Giacomo.'

'How's it gone?'

'Good, good. I'm pretty tired but it's gone OK. Lots to tell you.'

'Come up when you've got over the jet lag. You can tell me all about it in the sauna,' he laughed.

'I'll look forwa—'

There was a huge deafening explosion and the line went dead.

For a few moments, the abbot sat immobile, holding the receiver, looking at it as if he expected to hear the priest's voice calling his name. He felt sick. With shaking hands he replaced the phone and sat transfixed, not knowing what to do. He opened up his laptop and looked for news. Nothing. Then it started coming through. "Reports of a bomb explosion at Kabul International airport . . ." "Dozens of people have been killed and many more wounded . . ." "Suspected suicide bombers . . ."

The abbot's old eyes filled up with tears as he sat at his desk watching his screen. The bell rang for Vespers. Afterwards, he quickly checked online before supper. The situation still seemed confused. At chapter he told the community what had happened. They all knew how fond the abbot was of the priest. It broke their hearts to hear his voice quavering with emotion as he told them he would contact their other monasteries. He would let them know that the priest had been at the airport. 'They will make enquiries. They will find out if he is all right.'

Later, the abbot called Maddalena. She had heard the news but did not know where the priest was and so had not been unduly concerned. As soon as she heard the abbot's voice she knew something had happened. As her father recounted the priest's final call she felt the colour drain from her face. A tight ball of fear formed in the pit of her stomach.

CHAPTER 22

The long wait began. The priest's incognito existence, discreetly slipping shadowlike in and out of these troubled countries had served him well in his work. Now, it worked against him. Nobody knew who he was, nobody knew his name. Had he died in the explosion? Was he among the wounded? Nobody could find out.

There was talk of people being kidnapped. Apparently the suicide bombing could have served as a distraction to spirit away certain people. The situation was and remained confused. The abbot had to rely on the members of their daughter communities who in turn had to rely on their shadowy network of contacts in Afghanistan and the surrounding countries. 'Until we have proof that he is dead, he is alive,' said the abbot. And that was what kept everyone going.

The community's work continued. Study sessions already planned took place. Other men and women in other places took up where the priest had left off. It had always been planned that way. The work had to go on. And the Communità dello Spirito Santo waited.

'It's really strange,' Maddalena said to the abbot one day when they were down by the lake. 'Life goes on, I go to the airport to pick up people, I take them back. And yet it is as if time has stopped. It stopped when you heard his voice for the last time.' Their eyes would become moist with unshed tears.

The priest's disappearance had brought the old man and his daughter closer together. They had both loved Livia. And although neither could say that they loved each other—yet—in their different ways they both loved the priest. 'Until we have proof that he is dead, he is alive,' said the abbot, repeating his mantra.

Out of this tragedy, however, was born great beauty. Maddalena had been posing for Brother Ange-Dominique when the priest went missing. On her next visit to the monastery shortly after the bomb explosion everyone noticed the dark circles beneath dark eyes in her pale, strained, thinner face. When she walked into the atelier, Ange-Dominique took one look at her, removed from his easel the oil painting he had been working on and replaced it with a virgin canvas.

That morning he started on the first of what would become a series of works known as the Sicilian Madonnas. As the series progressed, the monk sent photos to Mannie Morgenstern. Within a short space of time the art dealer had buyers for every piece the monk could produce.

They were sublime uncluttered drawings, initially in Indian ink, of the Madonna at the Crucifixion. Some were Pietàs. Luca posed—just a brief outline, because the central figure was the mother, not the son—as the crucified Christ lying across his mother's lap.

Two memories remained with the young novice all his life. One was the scent and taste of the small wild strawberries they had been eating in the woodland the first time he kissed Espérite. The other was the salty taste on his lips of a tear as Maddalena cradled his head in her arms in Ange-Dominique's atelier.

Other works were depictions of the Messiah's mother at the foot of the cross looking up at her crucified son. Again, the whole focus was on her, her face tormented with suffering and suffused with an ineffable sadness, the Christ on cross just a hinted outline in the background.

Maddalena sat, lost in her thoughts. Ange-Dominique sketched, drew, painted, catching the changing moods and emotions reflected in the woman's face. Sometimes the abbot would stand silently behind his monk watching him work, watching him transfer his daughter's sadness, despair, exhaustion—she often slept badly since the priest's disappearance—onto virgin paper.

Each time they heard on the news that a body, bodies, had been found in the region—beheaded, shot—Maddalena and the abbot felt sick with fear. Then he would receive a call. It wasn't the priest. 'One day it will be,' she said to the abbot. 'One day it will be.' But although their people on the ground still could not trace him, they somehow succeeded in confirming that when corpses were discovered his was not among them.

Seasons changed. Delicate, scented February violets on mossy woodland banks were replaced by pale yellow bursts of primroses which in turn were replaced by tiny, perfumed wild strawberries.

The waiting continued and the community's work continued to show small but solid results. Every now and then, the abbot would read or hear about a slight softening in what had been previously entrenched positions in those dangerous, edgy parts of the world unflaggingly criss-crossed for almost a decade by the priest.

The abbot had no concrete way of knowing whether it was the direct or indirect result of their work. But often when these miniscule conciliatory movements were discussed in the media, names were mentioned that were familiar to the abbot. Names of people who had passed through the monastery.

They never made the headlines, these discreet, thoughtful visitors. They rarely appeared in photos, but he would occasionally find their names buried somewhere in the body of the newspaper article. Sometimes they were just buried. But if the priest, too, had been killed, at least his work would not have been in vain.

Another letter arrived from Rome. The abbot read the contents then sat for a long time at his desk, thinking. He had never got round to telling the priest about this sword of Damocles hanging over their heads. Now he could not tell him. But it had become too much to keep to himself—he decided he would tell his daughter when she returned to the monastery.

Maddalena was spending a few days in her apartment by the sea. She tried so hard to continue as before. She had translation work which, immediately following the priest's disappearance, she completed with heavy heart. Now, with time—it always took time, didn't it, she thought to herself—now she found consolation in the linguistic challenges of her work.

Everywhere she went seemed to remind her of the priest. She shed a couple of tears into her seafood platter; at the beach restaurants waiters wondered quietly to each other what had happened to her companion. Then one evening the DJ at the salsa bar noticed that she had started dancing again.

During the first few weeks after his disappearance she ate little. She had no interest in cooking. She recalled the words of an old French flame, 'You can only cook well if you are happy.' She was not happy. One morning the scent of the Genovese basil in the market propelled her into making some pesto.

As she pounded a couple of crushed garlic cloves and the pine nuts with a little salt in her pink granite mortar, her thoughts strayed back over her life and loves. She added the chopped up basil leaves, pounding them against the sides of the mortar. The whole thing was quicker in the little blender but she always found it therapeutic to use the pestle and mortar.

In the fridge she had both grated pecorino sardo and parmesan. She added equal quantities of each, mixing everything together well as she thought about her childhood in Sicily, about her children, about the men she had loved, left or lost. Finally, she gradually beat in the olive oil. Sometimes she added a spoonful of fromage frais or prescinsoa, a creamy acid ricotta, but she hadn't thought to buy any.

If she had been thinking more clearly, she would have put the water for the trenette on to boil while she was making the pesto and would have already poured herself a glass of dry white wine. She now did both of those things, popping a cover on the pan to speed things up. As she waited for the water to boil, images of the two men who had serendipitously come into her life—her father and the priest—flowed into her mind. One would remain in her life until death separated them. Death had perhaps already separated her from the other.

She had enough pesto for at least another two meals—well, at least one, she was very partial to pesto. It would keep with a thin layer of oil on top. Perhaps she would have it with gnocchi. She poured herself another glass of muscat.

When she next drove up to the monastery, arriving early one afternoon, she was surprised to see her father pacing back and forth in front of the church, apparently waiting for her.

'Ciao! No siesta?'

'Ciao, Lena. No. I was waiting for you.'

For a moment, she thought there was news about the priest. The abbot, looking at her face which so openly reflected her hopes, her fears, said, 'No, Lena, still no news about him. But I have something else I would like to talk to you about. I should have told him months ago but somehow I never did. It never seemed to be the right time, and now—'

His daughter looked concerned. 'Cosa c'è, Papa?'

'Go and drop your things off. I'll walk across to see Louis-Marc. Come over when you're ready.'

He watched the woman who was his daughter walk quickly back to the car to get her things. Up until now what had joined them together was their shared love for Livia: filial love for the one, romantic love for the other. The rising wind—the mistral was due—ruffled Maddalena's shiny dark hair and her colourful cotton skirt. He wondered if he was learning to love his daughter.

'Happy to walk down to the lake, Lena?' By now, they were both used to him calling her by the same diminutive used by her mother and all her family in Sicily. It had been considerably harder for the abbot to get used to being called Papa. But he was getting there.

'What's happened?' she said quietly, trying hard to hide her anxiety.

For a while the abbot remained silent, deep in thought, as they walked past the cemetery and down towards the lake.

'A few years ago I received an anonymous letter from Rome.'

'From the Vatican?'

'It was from someone in the Vatican but he had posted it in the city. You know our history here, Lena. You know that since the beginning, since Amadeo founded our community in Liguria, we have operated—how shall I put it—we have operated under the Vatican radar.

'Over the decades popes have come and gone, vaguely aware of our existence but happy or at least prepared to leave us alone. The Vatican has no contact with us. And we have no contact with the Vatican. Perfect. True, we have had to finance our community and its work ourselves, which has not always been easy. But we have managed, and recently, in no small part thanks to you, Lena, inspiring our artist.' The abbot smiled.

The mistral was gaining strength. When they reached the lake little waves were skimming across the ruffled water. They sat down on the bench. 'Not too cold?'

'No,' replied Maddalena. They both wore jackets and scarves against the rising wind. She waited for the abbot to continue. He would, at his own pace.

'The first letter warned me that we had a dangerous enemy in the Vatican, a powerful man within the Curia, one of just a handful of senior cardinals who knew about our work. His name is Cardinal Malerba. He works for the Congregation for the Doctrine of the Faith—which some regard as a modern day Inquisition—and as far as he is concerned there is only one faith: ours. This man's burning ambition is to see our monastery—this one and our daughter communities—closed down for good.'

'But this cardinal, he's not in a position to do that, is he?'

'Not yet, he isn't. My anonymous correspondent was flashing a warning light. "Be careful, be even more discreet, be aware that you have a powerful enemy, you are no longer flying under the radar." He has continued to write occasionally, always posted from Rome not the Vatican, to apprise me of anything new—and the new things were always more and more worrying.'

They sat in silence, both gazing out over the lake. The water was getting choppier as the mistral got into its stride. Maddalena zipped up her blue gilet and wrapped her long blue and white woollen scarf twice around her neck. She turned to see if the abbot, too, was protected from the rising wind.

'One day he wrote asking me to go to Rome. You'd have thought he might have telephoned. But he has never, ever telephoned. That's odd, isn't it? I drove down, staying with family and friends. They were very generous on the return trip. Crates of fruit and vegetables, cases of wine, bags of flour for my bread.'

'Chocolate?'

The abbot laughed. 'Certo! We met in the city, in Trastevere. This man—on our side, so's to speak—he is also a cardinal. I don't know his name, I'm not sure I would recognise him if I saw him again. He assured me that, although we didn't officially exist, the pontiff believed absolutely in the importance of our work.'

'Well, that's good news, surely,' said Maddalena.

'Yes, of course, as far as it goes. But this Cardinal Malerba is a very dangerous man. He keeps records—names, places. I don't know where he gets his information from. Our Vatican friend could not enlighten me. We must be even more vigilant, Lena. We have our network. This man, it appears, has his.

'The pope is very old and very tired. Cardinal Malerba is neither. He becomes more powerful almost daily.' The abbot paused and hugged himself. 'Let's walk some more, around the lake to the chapel,' he said. As they set off along the narrow path, he delved into his pocket and produced a bar of Equator 74%, snapped off a couple of squares and handed one to Maddalena.

'Could this Cardinal Malerba get elected at the next conclave?'

'Our friend says no. Malerba is a kingmaker not a king. He prefers to remain in the shadows pulling strings from the wings. But he has the ear of a man who is gaining support and who could be a very likely candidate in the next papal election.' He mentioned a name. It meant nothing to Maddalena who had never been the slightest bit interested in the carryings-on of the Curia or the Council of Cardinals or of anything else to do with the running of the Roman Catholic church.

'Our friend says that if that man becomes the next pope, Malerba will have no trouble in convincing him to close us down. All our work, over a hundred and fifty years of building bridges, talking to each other, listening to each other—wiped out, gone. In a puff of smoke.' The abbot gave a rueful smile.

Maddalena said, 'The pope may well be very old and very tired but I'm sure he's got a good few years left in him. After all, they don't retire, do they?'

The abbot laughed, then he said, 'We may have a powerful enemy in the Vatican, but at least we know that we also have a highly-placed friend there, too.'

'What about him, the letter writer? Is he a likely candidate whenever the next election takes place?'

'He says no. He, too, prefers to remain in the background.'

The affair was out of their hands, it always had been, there was nothing they could do. Nevertheless, after speaking to Maddalena, the abbot felt a weight lifted from his shoulders.

He should have spoken about this long ago to the priest. He had always put if off. Now he had been able to share the burden with his daughter. For the time being, there was no need to speak to the community. There was no papal conclave in the offing.

They had reached the chapel and went inside to shelter from the wind. They both stood silently for a few moments looking up at the linden wood Christ, in agony upon his cross. Then, heads bowed against the wind, they headed back round the lake and up to the monastery.

In between trips to and from airports and railway stations, Maddalena made her way to the atelier. Brother Ange-Dominique continued his sketches, drawings, paintings of his Sicilian Madonna. But as the months passed, the strain and the pain which had been etched into her face gradually disappeared. The dark smudges were still there beneath her eyes but the monk realised that he had lost his tragic model. He returned to work on other commissions.

Everything he had produced in the series had been snapped up by Mannie's clients. As with all his work, each Madonna left the atelier with the monk's signature in a corner—three small ears of wheat, waving oh, so gently in the wind. The money rolled in—and rolled out again, much of it to the daughter monasteries who continued tirelessly in their discreet search for news of the priest's whereabouts.

Life in the monastery continued, as it always had and always would. Luca rang the early bell, the monks rose from their beds in darkness and made their way to church. During the day, Aarne distilled, Louis-Marc gardened, Matteo and Gianni worked on the buildings and kept an eye on the Ancients, the abbot coordinated the study sessions with the other communities, Maddalena drove back and forth to airports, they all shared kitchen duties. Gianni and now Luca were both producing good simple and tasty dishes.

Their day ended back in church for Compline, the haunting chant of the "Salve Regina", and the abbot's nightly blessing of his monks—and Maddalena if she was present—with a branch of boxwood dipped in holy water, before they all retired for the night.

Village life continued as it always had and always would. The abbot, Matteo, Aarne or Louis-Marc celebrated Sunday mass in the village church. Tinkling jingles and deeper jangles told farmers where their goats and cows were; cocks crowed, hens cackled and large freshly-laid brown eggs would appear on the table in the monastery kitchen; when they stopped cackling, boiling fowl arrived, plucked and ready for the pot; wild trout would be dropped off by fishermen, making a detour on their way back from hillside streams and lakes.

There were moments of sadness—illnesses, funerals, young folk moving away; and moments of great joy—weddings, baptisms, and the arrival of the cooking chocolate from the abbot's great-niece in Italy.

The first to know was the postman, who dropped the parcel off with the mayor's wife for onward delivery to the abbot.

Every now and then the abbot invited a small group of villagers to join the community for lunch. For dessert he usually made his chocolate mousse. It was sinfully delicious and everyone had asked for the recipe. The mayor's wife rang round. By the time the postman had finished his rounds, he brought back to the mayor's wife for onward delivery to the monastery, all the items the womenfolk thought might be missing from the monastic kitchen: a dozen eggs, 250g of caster sugar and 300ml of whipping cream.

Maddalena had never tasted the abbot's chocolate mousse so he proposed that they make it together. While he chopped up the chocolate, put it in a good sized bowl and stood it in a bain-marie to melt, she laid out on a tray the shallow bowls they would serve it in and separated the eggs—'we need a dozen whites in a large bowl, and eight yolks in another—we'll make mayonnaise or something with the rest,' he said. He removed the chocolate from the heat once it had melted. Maddalena took down the large egg whisk and started whisking the whites, raising the whisk in the air as the whites started to solidify. The abbot smiled, 'Quicker with an electric whisk—which we don't have—but never as light.

'Now, when they are half risen start adding the sugar, a little at a time and keep whisking to a very firm snow—perfect.' He stirred the egg yolks into the melted chocolate, followed by 100ml of the cream, then with a spatula delicately folded in the beaten egg whites. 'As soon as it is homogenous we'll divide it up into the bowls and put the tray in the fridge. Don't overfill them, Lena, we want to be able to lick the bowl clean.'

'What happens to the rest of the whipped cream?'

'I usually don't have the time, but sometimes just before serving I use that to make a cappuccino topping: two tablespoons of instant coffee dissolved in four tablespoons of water, whip the remaining cream into a runny foam, add the coffee, top the mousses with the foam, and sprinkle with a little unsweetened cocoa powder.'

As they were clearing up, Gianni and Matteo walked in. 'Too

late,' said the abbot. He held up the bowl for inspection. You would never have known that he and his daughter had been making chocolate mousse—except for the smudge of chocolate around her mouth and on the tip of his nose.

Life went on. But one thing had changed. The bell no longer rang out across the fields from the little Romanesque village church announcing a weekday mass. Farmers no longer trundled their tractors up to the church. They no longer enjoyed together their aperitif afterwards in the late morning sunshine—because the priest no longer walked down to the village.

CHAPTER 23

It was a late summer evening, when the abbot had briefly popped back into his office before retiring for the night, that his land line rang. It was the abbot of their daughter community in Pakistan. They had found the priest—alive. He would be on a plane back to France in a couple of days.

'What happened?'

'He was injured in the blast, quite badly concussed, I think, he can't remember much. Apparently there were people there, bad people, who had overheard him talking on his mobile in French —to you—just before the bombs went off. They thought he may be someone very important. They whisked him away, took him up into the hills. They planned to hold him hostage and exchange him in return for some members of their group who had been arrested.'

Abbot Giacomo said, 'But he's worthless to them, nobody knows his name far less who he is, what he does. Nobody knows about our work. That's the whole point, isn't it? Nobody over there in their right mind—mind you, a lot of them aren't, of course—nobody would give anything in exchange for him. He has no value at all to them.'

'Precisely. That's what they eventually realised. So they have let him go.'

The abbot, moist-eyed, thanked his colleague and slowly walked up the stone steps to bed. Maddalena was in Sicily with her family. He would not tell her. It would be a surprise. He climbed into bed. For the first time since the priest had disappeared, not even the owl woke him from a deep untroubled recuperative sleep.

Two days later the priest returned to the monastery. As soon as he heard the car, the abbot hurried outside. The priest was tired, thinner and browner, but appeared none the worse for his experience. The two men remained some time in a silent close embrace. Both had tears in their eyes.

The abbot had given the community the news at chapter the day after the telephone call. He looked round at the smiling faces and became aware of a tremendous sense of relief. He thought, 'I have been so distressed by this affair—perhaps I never realised how much the others were suffering, too.'

'We have plenty of time to talk,' said the abbot. 'Go and see the others, will you?' The priest walked over to the distillery to see Aarne, who poured them both out a shot of cloudberry, to the atelier to see Ange-Dominique, who would have offered the priest a joint if he had smoked them. He followed the hammering and sawing to find Matteo and Gianni, and the sound of the bagpipes to greet Séamus. He found Louis-Marc among his vegetables and the Ancients in the cemetery with Luca the novice. It was an emotional experience for everyone.

The following day the priest slept in. When he eventually awoke mid morning he told the abbot he would celebrate mass in the village and would be back by lunchtime. The abbot thought, *I don't think you will, figlio mio,* but remained silent. He just smiled and nodded.

The priest walked down to the village and rang the church bell. Isnard, the mayor, the doctor, farmers from outlying hamlets, wives, old women and men—they all dropped what they were doing when they heard the bell ringing out loud and clear.

'It's not Sunday, is it?' they said to each other. 'The only time the bell used to ring during the week was when the priest was here...'

Villagers started making their way on foot towards the church. The first to arrive was the owner of the café in the square opposite the church. The young teacher left the schoolhouse with her kindergarten class. The doctor left his surgery with his patients, bandaged, hobbling on crutches, arms in slings. Farmers left their fields and arrived in trucks and tractors. On their way they stopped colleagues heading in the opposite direction taking sheep and cattle to market who about turned and headed back to the village church. In a short time there were more farm vehicles in the square than you would see at the Salon d'Agriculture in Paris. Cows lowed, sheep baaed, hens cackled (it seemed as if every single one in the entire valley had just laid an egg to celebrate the priest's return), cockerels crowed.

The priest, in his vestments, stood waiting on the church steps. They were not given to overt displays of emotions, these villagers, but they threw their arms around him—the men hugged him and kissed him on both cheeks, eyes moist in weather-beaten faces. The women hugged him and kissed him on both cheeks, tears streaming down their cheeks.

Everyone filed into the church. The priest celebrated mass. In the past, after the gospel, his "homily" had always just been a simple couple of sentences, relevant to the gospel—food for thought. He was well aware that they needed to get back to farming and household chores.

When the moment came, he looked out at the sea of happy, smiling faces. All he could manage, in a voice trembling with emotion, were the words, 'It is . . . so very good to see you all again.' The priest ran the back of his index finger under an eye. In the congregation noses were blown, handbags and jacket pockets were rifled for handkerchiefs, damp cheeks were dabbed dry.

When the mass was ended, with one accord they all filed out of church and piled onto the café terrace. Glasses, bottles of pastis, jugs of homemade cider, apple juice and lemonade, carafes of water, buckets of ice, bottles of chilled local rosé miraculously appeared on chequered tablecloths, together with little white china bowls of black olives and slices of saucisson on olive wood platters.

Noise levels rose, everyone talking to the priest at once, touching his arm, slapping him on the back, shaking his hand, wiping away tears. The abbot had told them shortly after the event about his disappearance. Now, these normally reserved men and women did not ask the priest what had happened. He was back, that was all that mattered. He would tell them in due course where he had been.

Women disappeared and returned with bread, terrines, pâtés, cold chickens, salad leaves, the café owner supplied plates and cutlery. Everyone sat down to an impromptu lunch to celebrate the priest's return. He did not get back to the monastery until mid afternoon.

Over the following days, the abbot and the priest spent afternoons talking and walking in the hills or talking and sweating in the sauna down by the lake, and the evenings after Compline talking and drinking malt whisky in the abbot's office.

'Just like the good old days, Giacomo,' said the priest. He briefly told the abbot what had happened. 'It very quickly all became rather monotonous, same routine day after day after day.'

'Rather like here.'

The priest laughed. 'Not quite, Giacomo. Once they had realised that I was completely worthless to them as a hostage, they wanted to know what I was doing in Afghanistan. We got quite a dialogue going. I started by asking what they were doing, about their beliefs and aspirations. It was a bit tricky to begin with, not least because of the language, but a couple of them spoke some English. We managed. Then I talked about our work. I wasn't quite sure how they would take it. But I had no shortage of time to explain the thinking and aims of the Community's work.'

'And how did that go down?' asked the abbot, remembering only too well the disconcertingly intense gaze that could suddenly shine out from those gold-flecked hazel eyes opposite him.

'You can ask them yourself, Giacomo. Two curious senior members of the group should be arriving next month.'

The Afghans had then decided to pass him on to another mili-

tant Muslim group in Pakistan. A long trek through the mountains, different faces, different food, same monotonous daily
routine, more time for talking.

'Don't tell me,' said the abbot, 'let me guess. They're coming
next month, too.'

The priest smiled. 'That would be too much to hope for, Giacomo. No, they hope to come in the spring.'

The abbot now told the priest about the anonymous letters,
about the inquisitorial Cardinal Malerba and about his visit to
Rome. It was disturbing news but the priest agreed that there
was no immediate cause for concern. The pope looked as if he
still had a few more years in him. 'Thank goodness it's a job for
life,' he said.

He had still not told Maddalena about the priest's return. She
had flown back from Sicily to her apartment and was due in a
couple of days to collect visitors from the airport to drive them
up to the monastery. Ange-Dominique was anxious to have his
model back to put the final touches to his own stunning version
of Gauguin's La Orana Maria. It depicted Mary holding the Christ
child as per the original but covered up the bare breasts of the
two female worshippers.

Maddalena arrived. The abbot came out to greet her and the
visitors. She made her way to the atelier, popping in to the distillery to say hello to Aarne who, like the others, was privy to
the abbot's planned surprise, and greeted her as usual.

The priest had left much earlier, with floppy hat and picnic,
for a long walk in the hills, happy to again be breathing in warm,
heady scents of crushed-underfoot thyme, wild thyme, lemon
thyme. It was a still day and the late summer heat hung heavy
over the hills. A couple of buzzards circled lazily above. In the
distance, clinking cowbells and jangling goatbells.

Once in the atelier, Maddalena took up her position and
Ange-Dominique his brushes. After lunch everyone went off for
a siesta except Ange-Dominique and Maddalena who went back
to work.

It was late afternoon when the priest walked back round the

lake, up the slope and let himself into the monastery garden through the door in the wall opposite the cemetery. The door to Ange-Dominique's atelier was wide open in an attempt to create some movement of air. Sheltered most of the day from direct sunlight, it now received shafts of warm bright light which fell onto Maddalena's face, illuminating it, bathing it in a rich glow. Ange-Dominique loved that light on her face. He stood back from his easel to look at her and his painting.

Maddalena, looking out through the door into the monastery garden, directly into the shaft of light, saw the indistinct outline of a figure in the hazy heat walking towards her. She could not make out who it was. She assumed it was the abbot. As the figure approached the door and finally blocked out the sunlight she saw it was the priest. He smiled at her. She stared at him, mouth half open. Tears welled up—she had shed so many tears since his disappearance—she got up and walked slowly towards him.

'You're back.'

'Yes. Miss me?'

'Not really.'

He put his arms around her and kissed her gently on both cheeks, his lips remaining a fraction of a second too long on her skin. He moved her gently away so he could look at her face. Then she broke down and sobbed. Brother Ange-Dominique, realising that their session was over for the day, went off to clean his paint brushes and smoke a joint down by the lake.

The following day, Brother Ange-Dominique began painting a radiant Maddalena. He called this series the Corsican Madonna. This Madonna smiled, sometimes laughed, always had shining eyes that sparkled like dew on a cobweb caught in the morning sunlight. Sometimes he painted the Madonna holding the Christ Child. Sometimes they were both laughing, sometimes both smiled at each other. Sometimes one was smiling while the other laughed. They were joyful works of art. As before BAD sent photographs to their New York agent. It became as successful as the Sicilian series. Mannie Morgenstern was seriously thinking of retiring on the commissions. The monastery finances had never been healthier.

The monks would pass by to watch work in progress. The most regular visitors were the abbot and the priest. He was soon back to his previous physical form and would head off on his travels again. Meantime, visitors continued to arrive for study sessions, including his former captors from Afghanistan who managed to make a rather perilous journey to get there. It seemed rather odd, thought the priest, welcoming them to the monastery and introducing them to the abbot.

He spent time with Maddalena when she was there. They walked, they talked. The two of them had strolled down to the sauna one afternoon. They had just settled themselves onto the benches, wrapped in their towels, and were talking about the Grand Inquisitor, the malevolent Cardinal Malerba.

The sauna door opened and in walked the abbot. 'Oh, I didn't realise you two were in here,' he said. *Yes, you did*, thought the priest and Maddalena, separately.

'We were just talking about our cardinal enemy,' said his daughter.

'Well, even when the pope does die, there's absolutely no guarantee that Malerba's man will get elected. You know, every time I come in here, I give thanks to dear Tuuli. It really is the best place in the world to unwind, cleanse mind and body. We spent a lot of time in here, didn't we, Lena, while you were away,' he said, looking over at the priest who could still not quite get used to Giacomo calling her Lena.

The priest left on his travels. Brother Ange-Dominique finished his Gauguin, Aarne's aunts visited for a week. Nobody died. The monastery finances were in good shape. Autumn arrived—always a lovely time of year in these parts. The air was sharp and crisp, hillsides were covered in russet-coloured bracken, the woodlands were glorious shades of golds and burnished copper.

Louis-Marc collected walnuts and hazelnuts. Maddalena went out shooting with the mayor, Isnard and the others. The crack of shotguns pierced the early morning and evening air. The kitchen was alive with dead rabbits, partridges, snipe and woodcock. By now Gianni knew how to pluck, skin, gut and clean—and Louis-Marc and Maddalena welcomed the extra pair of hands.

When she and the priest were both in the town by the sea at the same time they went to the occasional opera or concert, shared the occasional meal, talked and smiled and laughed. Various waiters in various venues did not know what had happened to him, of course, but they had seen the younger man and older woman together and they had seen her on her own. They were glad he was back.

Both the priest and Maddalena were at the monastery for Christmas that year and stayed on till the New Year. Snow fell, not enough to cause severe access problems, just enough to lay an entrancing magical carpet of white on the ground and a silvery dusting over the trees. The community celebrated the three Christmas masses.

The first day of the New Year dawned and even the priest made it to Vigils, crunching his way through the cold night air. He knew Maddalena was already in church. He could see her footsteps in the snow.

On February 2nd, Maddalena and Gianni made a pile of pancakes for La Chandeleur, Candlemas, the celebration of the presentation of Christ at the Temple. Nine days later, in Rome, the pope, in Latin, quietly announced to a small gathering of cardinals his intention to retire from the papacy.

CHAPTER 24

March 2013

Maddalena and the abbot gazed in amazement at his computer screen and the grey smoke spiralling into the Roman sky. In the space of minutes the sound of sirens could be heard, emergency vehicles arrived, people were rushing here and there, the commentator got very excited. Gradually bits of information came out—a small explosion in a cardinal's private office... fire now under control ... nobody hurt ... the cardinal was in conclave ... part of the Congregation for the Doctrine of the Faith... room gutted ... contents destroyed ...

The abbot and Maddalena sat transfixed to the screen. The abbot opened his drawer. This seemed like a two-bar chocolate moment. He extracted an already opened bar of organic Bolivian 75% and an unopened one of fair-trade organic Haiti and Peruvian Andes cocoa with caramel slivers and a touch of salt. He snapped off two squares of each, snapped those in two and gave his daughter a square of each chocolate, his eyes not leaving the computer screen.

The grey smoke continued to rise up into the sky, decreasing in intensity as the fire brigade got to grips with what appeared to be just a small fire. There were no signs of any flames, just the smoke.

No white or black smoke emerged from the Sistine Chapel chimney.

The rolling news titles rolled on, faulty wiring was mentioned, various people who had been in the vicinity of the office at the time of the explosion, secretarial staff, prelates, a visiting monk, had been quickly eliminated from enquiries.

The abbot opened another drawer, drew out a file, opened it and ran his finger down to the name and telephone number he was looking for. He dialled, put the call on speaker. He waited.

Ange-Dominique's mother, supposedly on her death bed, had made a recovery of Biblical rapidity and answered the telephone. The abbot introduced himself.

'Oh, Père Abbé, this is a surprise. Is he all right? He was on the telephone just the other week, wanting information for another of his projects.'

The abbot struggled to find a reason for his call but was saved, temporarily at least, by Madame Zigliara who, for somebody who had been at death's door, was remarkably chatty.

'You know we had an ancestor, a priest with the Dominicans, who was a cardinal back in the 19th century. He was born in Bonifacio. But much more recently the island has produced another cardinal, he is the son of a friend of mine in a neighbouring village, we were all thrilled, of course. My friend has been to see him in the Vatican, he has his own office, he's pretty high up in the Curia, I think. Very senior. We're all very proud.

'Ange-Dominique wanted to know what information I could find out about the new cardinal. I gave him my friend's number. I think he was going to call her. A project about Corsican cardinals, I think he said.'

The abbot paused with his second square of chocolate halfway to his mouth and exchanged glances with Maddalena.

'You know Cardinal Fesch, Napoleon's uncle, was from Ajaccio,' continued Madame Zigliara. 'That's how Ange-Dominique got started with the painting—copying works of art in the Fesch collection.

'I can't thank you enough, Père Abbé, for having faith in Ange-Dominique and welcoming him into your community. After, you know, his difficult period. The nationalists have started blowing up second homes again. I'm just so relieved that he's not involved in all that anymore.' The abbot looked at the chaotic scenes in Saint Peter's Square.

'He is all right?' she repeated.

'Er, yes, yes, he's fine.' He assumed his monk was fine although he had absolutely no idea whether he was or not.

'So why are you calling, Père Abbé?'

The abbot, flummoxed, searched desperately for a reason. Maddalena scribbled something on a piece of paper and pushed it over the desk.

'Charcuterie,' the abbot read the word out loud. The penny dropped. He gave his daughter a relieved smile. 'That's why I'm calling. I've been meaning to thank you for your really excellent Corsican charcuterie. We all enjoy it so much. The, er, lonzu,' he continued, reading as Maddalena wrote, 'the coppa. Delicious. Excellent. You are so kind.

'And I must say the figatelli you send, your son cooks them to perfection over a wood fire, we ate them the other day with lentils—it's a really delicious winter dish.'

'Or with chestnut flour polenta, have you tried that? I sent him some flour,' said Madame Zigliara.

'Yes, yes, thank you, you have been very generous with the chestnut flour. A couple of weeks ago one of the brothers made some polenta with it to accompany a really excellent daube of wild boar.'

'That's sounds nice—how did he make it?'

Maddalena, who feared her father was moving off message, now wrote on the paper in underlined capitals WHAT'S HIS NAME???? and pushed it under the abbot's nose.

'What's whose name?' said the abbot.

'I beg your pardon, Père Abbé?'

'No, no, Madame Zigliara, I was just talking to myself. Yes, you mentioned he is working on a project about Corsican cardinals. He never mentioned it, I expect he wanted to surprise me. I don't follow these things. I must have missed it in the newspaper. What is the name of your friend's son?'

'Malerba. Cardinal Malerba. Maybe he'll be the next pope.' *God forbid*, thought the abbot. 'Au revoir, Père Abbé. Thank you so much for calling. Please give my love to Ange-Dominique.'

'Of course, Madame, I will have lots to say to him when I next see him. God bless you, my daughter,' and he ended the call.

'So,' said the abbot to Maddalena, 'even if the wrong cardinal gets elected pope, it would appear that any records of our activities have been completely destroyed.'

Just after seven in the evening in the refectory—the community should have been listening to Gino Paoli, one of the abbot's favourite singers but instead, under the circumstances, were listening to events in Rome—the radio presenter excitedly described the appearance of white smoke coiling out of the Sistine Chapel chimney and drifting skyward above the Vatican. Shortly afterwards the Cardinal Protodeacon appeared on the balcony and announced to the huge expectant crowds massed into Saint Peter's Square, and to millions of faithful and not so faithful watching and listening around the world, 'Annuntio vobis gaudium magnum: habemus papam.'

Everyone in the refectory froze. Soup spoons, glasses of water, slices of baguettes remained poised in the air. Apart from the radio, there was silence in the room. No one coughed, no one scraped chair on floor, no clinking of cutlery. It seemed for a second as if everyone had stopped breathing. Some eyes were fixed on the radio. Other eyes remained lowered fixed on the soup, Gianni's excellent broad bean stew—fried pancetta and onion slices, sliced potatoes, broad beans, cut up artichoke hearts, no pasta, seasoned and gently simmered in a little water to cover— as the name of the cardinal who had been elected the new pope was announced.

CHAPTER 25

The priest telephoned the abbot. 'Ciao, Giacomo, well, that's a huge relief, isn't it? On both counts. Would I be right in assuming Ange-Dominique has been away from the monastery for a couple of days?'

'Yes, it is and yes, you would. To visit his dying mother who was very chatty on the phone when I rang earlier having just seen the news about the explosion.'

'Ah. It sounds as if he might just have got away with it though.'

'I don't want to talk about it, figlio mio. I really, really don't want to talk about it,' said the abbot.

The priest laughed and changed the subject. 'If it makes you feel any better, I'm already in Marseille. He's due to arrive mid morning tomorrow by a rather circuitous route—scheduled flights. This is really important, Giacomo. If we can pull this off ... I'm still worried something may go wrong.'

'I don't suppose you thought to bring a—'

'—cool box for some fish? Yes I did, and extra money to pay for them. What would you like?'

'Sea bass would be good. Get a couple the same size and ask him to scale and gut them but keep the liver and any roe,' said the abbot. 'Bit of salt inside and out, rub them over with olive oil and we'll simply bake them in foil—it's such a good fish. Maybe some sardines. Perhaps a piece of swordfish. I'll leave it up to you.'

In the chapter house that evening the sense of relief was palpable. Faces were wreathed in gentle smiles. Once they were all seated the Ancients dropped off to sleep quicker than usual, possibly exhausted by the tension.

'Well,' said the abbot, looking round at his smiling monks, 'that's a relief.'

Luca coughed and said, 'Père Abbé, who *is* the new Pope?'

The abbot narrowed his eyes and stared at the novice. He opened his mouth, closed it, shifted in his seat and turned an enquiring look onto his small community.

'He's not black,' said Brother Séamus who prayed that he would see a black African pope in his lifetime and had lost interest as soon as he saw the shortlist was all white.

'An Italian I think. His name ends in an i or an o.' said Louis-Marc.

'No, South America,' said Brother Aarne. 'I think he's from South America. Brazil, Colombia...'

'He's a Franciscan,' added Matteo, 'I'm sure I heard Franciscan mentioned. I think.'

'I don't think so, Matteo, I think he's a Jesuit,' said Gianni. At this news there was a communal and therefore audible sucking in of air through teeth.

'So to resume,' said the abbot, 'he's not black, he may have a name ending in i or o, be Italian or South American, from Brazil or Colombia, a Franciscan or a Jesuit— Let's hope he shows as little interest in the Communità dello Spirito Santo as we appear to show in him.'

He closed the chapter. They walked over to the church for Compline. By nine all lights were out and the monastery lay in darkness beneath a midnight blue star-studded sky. Maddalena was asleep as soon as her head hit the pillow. In Marseille, the priest while enormously relieved about the election result, was nevertheless nervous about the following day. He did not sleep well.

The abbot stood by his window and gazed out towards the dim outline of distant snow-capped hills. Somewhere, his old friend the owl hooted. The gentlest of breezes rustled through tree branches bearing new spring leaves. Renewal. He recalled his daughter's words, 'She's female, you know, the Holy Spirit.'

He smiled to himself. Holy Spirit, World Spirit, female or no, what does it matter? Just as long as she continues to waft into our lives.

He left his shutters open, knelt down briefly at his prie-dieu, then climbed into bed. The moon shone through into his cell bathing his white hair and his old face with its soft light, rather like a halo. There was a hint of a smile on his lips. In repose, signs of age—the lines, the wrinkles—somehow seemed less pronounced. Abbot Giacomo fell fast asleep.

CHAPTER 26

The following morning in Marseille the priest walked down La Canebière to the Vieux-Port. He strolled through the fish market past gleaming, glistening displays of mackerel, red mullet and tuna, slithery squid and octopus, swordfish and sea bream. He bought what the abbot had requested and added on impulse some red mullet.

They did not get much fresh fish up in the hills—local wild trout, the occasional wild Scottish salmon courtesy of Séamus's family—so the priest understood why the abbot had taken advantage of his trip to Marseille. Giacomo was going to bake the sea bass but the priest wondered whether the abbot had given any thought to who was going to cook the rest of the fish and how.

Ange-Dominique, whose return from Rome must be imminent, would find himself on kitchen duty whether the Muse was upon him or not, figured the priest. That took care of the sardines. BAD would get going the barbecue that Matteo had built in the monastery garden. He'd throw on a bundle of dried vine cuttings, supplied by the villagers when they pruned their vines over winter, followed by the sardines. The priest could almost smell the delicious aroma. His mouth began to water. On another impulse, he bought a bagful of dark blue-black mussels. They'd put them round the edges of the barbecue and they would open up while the sardines were cooking.

Matteo had the receipe for a simple Ligurian dish with olives, only possible on the rare occasion half a dozen or so red mullet made an appearance in the monastery kitchen.

From memory, you cleaned and scaled the fish, put them in an oven dish with olive oil, white wine, salt, stoned black olives, chopped garlic and a lemon cut in half. You covered the dish in foil, baked it in the oven for twenty minutes or so, then sprinkled the cooked dish with chopped flat leaf parsley. Couldn't be easier, thought the priest. He had made it once for himself, eaten one red mullet hot, and the other one cold the following day.

That left the swordfish. Maddalena had an easy Sicilian recipe for that. Or perhaps Matteo would use his Calabrian one which was equally simple and delicious—slices oven baked with olives, capers, chopped tomatoes, basil and sprinkled with olive oil and breadcrumbs.

It looked like they'd be eating fish for the next week. Perhaps the swordfish would join Séamus's salmon in the freezer, he thought.

The priest realised that it did not seem right to meet his guest carrying a large cool box. He asked one of the fishmongers to keep it for him then he made his way to the Ombrière. He did not need its shade—it was early March—so he stayed on the edge, in the sun. The mistral, which had been blowing hard for the past couple of days, had dropped. It was a glorious early spring day.

The priest was not sure how long it would take his visitor to travel from the airport at Marignane into the city, so he was prepared for a wait. He had made a rough calculation and he was not far out.

As he walked around under the Ombrière he saw the man he was waiting for. He had only met him a couple of times but every time the Middle Eastern prince appeared on television or in the press, his cousin—the man now walking towards him—was there, discreet, in the shadows, but always present.

He was dressed in casual, expensive Western clothes—no robes, no headdress—but the priest instantly recognised the dark black hair, the carefully trimmed beard, the strong aquiline nose, and the shining deep brown eyes set in a dark-skinned face.

The priest caught his eye. The man, returning his smile, walked swiftly towards the priest. With his hand outstretched in welcome, he was, again, momentarily mesmerised by the shining intensity in the priest's gold-flecked hazel eyes.

He showed no signs of nervousness although God knows—his God, the priest's God, the God of the Jews—he had every reason to be. Although he had travelled alone on scheduled flights, the risk he was taking was enormous.

In the melting pot that is Marseille, there was nothing at all unusual about the two men standing chatting under the Ombrière. 'Norman Foster,' said the priest as the prince raised his eyes to examine the structure. 'Inaugurated earlier this month — Marseille is European Capital of Culture this year.'

The prince's French was reasonable but his English was fluent so they quickly switched to that language. 'Yes,' replied the prince. 'He's building Masdar City for our neighbours, the Abu Dhabi government—desert community, aiming to be carbon neutral, zero waste—should be finished next year.'

The priest explained that he had to collect some fish.

'Fish,' said the prince, not a question, a statement.

'Yes, for the abbot. He asked me to get some fish since I was here near the market.'

'Yes, of course,' said the prince, as if that was a perfectly understandable request.

'It's just over there,' said the priest.

As the men strolled over to the fish stalls, the priest's telephone rang.

'Ciao, Giacomo. OK, will do. He's here, he's arrived safely. See you later.'

When they reached the fishmonger, the priest asked him for a large piece of red tuna, paid, and reclaimed his now rather heavy cool box.

'May I have a look at the fish,' said the prince. The priest opened up the cool box and the prince looked down at its gleaming contents and nodded slowly. 'Fish,' he repeated.

Although he had been looking around the busy port he had heard every word of the short conversation between the priest and the abbot. As they started to walk away from the Vieux Port, he paused in his tracks and turned to look at the priest. His warm smile had disappeared like a desert mirage. The priest put down his cool box. The prince balanced his designer hand luggage on top of it and said, 'I am a Sunni Muslim prince. I have flown half way around the world to arrive here—I sincerely hope unnoticed—to spend time in a Roman Catholic monastery. And yet your abbot calls you not to enquire whether I have arrived safely—*you* volunteered that information—no, he calls to add tuna to his fish order.'

The priest half opened his mouth to reply, realised denial was pointless, gave a helpless little shrug, and remained silent. *This is not a good start*, he thought.

'A question of priorities,' continued the prince. His face broke into a wide smile. 'I am looking forward to meeting Abbot Giacomo. I think we will get on just famously. I have a rather good recipe for tuna steaks—cover them in a mixture of crushed black peppercorns and coriander seeds, wrap them in foil, then sear each side for a minute or so in a very hot pan.'

The priest was about to ask where a Middle Eastern prince had come across a recipe like that, thought better of it, and said, simply but sincerely, 'Sounds delicious.' He cocked his head on one side and added, 'Could work well with swordfish, too.'

As they talked, the two men headed off to the car park and the long drive up to the Communità dello Spirito Santo, the prince carrying his expensive, embossed, dark brown leather hand luggage, the priest his blue and white fish-filled cool box.

And the work goes on, thought the priest, *our work goes on*. Talking. Always be talking. Into his head popped a quotation from the New Testament—Luke, was it? Or maybe Matthew? "Follow me, and I will make you fishers of men." He smiled to himself. Giacomo would be happy with the day's catch.

ACKNOWLEDGEMENTS

My thanks to my sister, two sisters-in-law and my oldest friend who took the time to read my story. I am grateful for their comments and suggestions.

The recipes come from a variety of sources. I am particularly grateful to Claudia Roden and her much-thumbed copy of *The Food of Italy*, and to the late Michel Roux for his chocolate mousse recipe.

ABOUT THE AUTHOR

Blanche Pagliardini

lives in southern France. This is her first novel.

Printed in Great Britain
by Amazon